PROXY

PROXY

Medical Kidnap Files #3

P.D. WORKMAN

ISBN: 9781988390444 (IS Hardcover)

ISBN: 9781988390437 (IS Paperback)

ISBN: 9781988390390 (KDP Paperback)

ISBN: 9781988390406 (Kindle)

ISBN: 9781988390413 (ePub)

ALSO BY P.D. WORKMAN

YOUNG ADULT FICTION:

Medical Kidnap Files:

Mito

EDS

Proxy

Toxo

Pain (Coming soon)

Between the Cracks:

Ruby

June and Justin

Michelle

Chloe

Ronnie

June, Into the Light

Tamara's Teardrops:

Tattooed Teardrops

Two Teardrops

Tortured Teardrops

Vanishing Teardrops

Breaking the Pattern:

Deviation

Diversion

By-Pass

Stand Alone YA novels

Stand Alone

Don't Forget Steven

Those Who Believe

Cynthia has a Secret

Questing for a Dream

Once Brothers

Intersexion

Making Her Mark

Endless Change

Gem, Himself, Alone

MYSTERY/SUSPENSE:

Reg Rawlins, Psychic Detective

What the Cat Knew

A Psychic with Catitude

A Catastrophic Theft

Night of Nine Tails

Telepathy of Gardens

Delusions of the Past

Fairy Blade Unmade

Web of Nightmares

A Whisker's Breadth

AND MORE AT PDWORKMAN.COM

To those who have been hurt, in hopes of healing.

CHAPTER ONE

Leva aimed her phone at Seth as he stood proudly in front of the roller coaster. There were smiles all around, children who were excited at being in the theme park, the dream of every kid in America.

But none were like Seth's. None of the other kids had worked as hard as Seth had to get there. He had fought through his illness, through countless hospital stays, never wavering from his wish to visit Disneyland. His face was pale, his spiky dark-blond hair damp with sweat, and his lanky teenage body too thin, but he had made it there. He'd made it to his goal. And, as he had insisted, not in a wheelchair but under his own power, though she noticed that he was leaning against the signpost for support.

He was her brave boy. Strong in heart, if weak in body.

"I can't believe we're here," Seth said, for about the hundredth time that day. But this time it wasn't just 'here' in Disneyland, it was 'here' in front of the roller coaster he had always wanted to ride. Successfully raising the money to get to the park had been exciting. Entering the grounds had been thrilling. But standing in front of *his* roller coaster was the pinnacle of joy for Seth. "We're finally here!"

"Yes," Leva agreed. "Give me a big smile."

He smiled and gave a thumbs-up. Leva took a couple of shots and then lowered her phone.

"Well, are you ready to actually go on it?" she asked. Roller coasters weren't her thing, and Seth had never been on one. She was still waiting to see if he would go through with it.

Seth looked up and watched the roller coaster go through its loop-the-loop, passengers screaming wildly and waving their arms. He swallowed.

"I have to go on it," he asserted.

"You don't have to. It's up to you. We don't have to go on every ride, you know."

"I know… but I have to go on the roller coaster."

"Only if you want to."

He nodded. His face was sweating and Leva wondered whether it were because he was scared, because of the heat, or because he was sick.

"Are you feeling all right, baby?"

"I'm not a baby," Seth growled.

That, at least, was a normal response for when he was well. When he was sick, he didn't argue about not being her baby. He wanted to be held and nurtured just like any helpless child.

"I'm fourteen," Seth reminded her. "You can't call me a baby." His eyes shot around at passersby to make sure that no one had heard her.

"Sorry," Leva apologized. "You're right. I should be more careful when we're out in public."

He nodded. "Let's get in line."

Leva led him over to the disabled entrance. Seth opened his mouth to argue. He didn't want to look different. He didn't want people looking at him and wondering what was wrong with him that he had access to the disabled line. But when he looked over at the regular line-up and how far back it stretched, his lips pressed together, and he didn't protest. Walking around the park and standing in line was exhausting. If he wanted to be able to continue to live the dream, he had to stick to the short lines.

Leva flashed her pass at the ride attendants to confirm that they were qualified to be in the disabled line. A pretty blond girl who didn't seem like she could be much older than Seth leaned over and opened the gate for them, giving Seth a brilliant smile.

"Come right this way," she offered. "We'll put you on the next car that comes in."

They watched another train rush through the curves of the roller coaster, screams washing over them. They could see the LCD screens displaying everyone's photos as they went through the last curve. Open mouths, flying hair, shrieks of delight.

Seth leaned against the wall; one hand pressed to his stomach. The young woman who had let them in grabbed a wheelchair from a nearby corral.

"Here, sit down. Are you okay?"

Seth tried to wave off the wheelchair, then collapsed into it with a sigh. "Just tired."

"Okay. You sit there until I have a space for you. Give me or Derek a shout if we can get you anything else. Okay?" Her voice was bright and encouraging. No pity here. It was the happiest place on earth. Everyone got the same smiles. Everyone was on equal footing, healthy kids and terminal alike.

Leva moved closer to Seth to rub his shoulders and analyze just how tired he was. She had hoped to be able to put in a little more time; but they had five days to see the park, they didn't have to do everything in one day.

"Don't," Seth protested, slapping her hands away in irritation. His eyes went to the cute blond employee. Not too tired to care what she thought of him.

The next train pulled up and people disembarked in a babble of excited chatter off the opposite side. The girl opened up a cart for Seth and pushed his wheelchair up close to it. When she put the brakes on, Seth was able to get up under his own power and transfer to the seat. Leva climbed in beside him, though she was sure he would rather have had the girl there. Or any girl other than his mother. The employees moved up and down the cars, making sure that everyone was properly buckled and barred in. They were instructed to secure all phones and cameras. Leva pushed hers farther down into her pocket. She'd be devastated if she lost her phone. It would be smashed to bits if it fell from the top of the roller coaster when they went through the loop-the-loop. Everything was stored in the cloud, she supposed, but it would be a lot of work to restore it to another device. She needed to have everything at her fingertips.

"Are you sure you want to do this?" she asked Seth.

He was breathing heavily, almost hyperventilating. His skin was pale and sweaty.

"Are you okay?"

Seth nodded. "Gotta do this," he muttered. He clenched his fingers around the restraining bar, knuckles turning white.

"If you want to do a different ride… you don't have to go on the roller coaster."

"I do," Seth insisted. "I do have to go on it!" He swore. "Just leave me alone, Mom! I can do this. I'm not a baby."

"I know you're not. I'm just worried about you."

"Well, quit it. I'm fine."

"Okay."

She tried not to look at him directly. He was obviously terrified of the roller coaster, but it had been his dream for so long. He had told so many people he was going on it. It would be the first question everyone asked. 'Did you get to go on the roller coaster?' He was locked into it now and didn't see any way out.

Leva put her hand over Seth's and gave it a little reassuring squeeze. Seth moved his hand away in irritation.

There were a number of announcements, a last warning, and then the cars started to move on the track. There was a collective gasp, a held breath in anticipation, and they were on their way. Seth suddenly wasn't so irritated about having his mother next to him and put his hand over Leva's, squeezing tight. She tried to give him a smile and quick words of comfort, but the words were torn from her mouth by a lurch of the cars, and they were racing down the track, in a vortex of sound that made it impossible to talk to each other. Leva did her best just to hold on and suppress her own physical reaction to the movement.

Roller coasters weren't her thing.

It was in the loop-the-loop, the one thing that Seth had been anticipating half his life, that she felt him go limp beside her. Leva tried to turn her head to look at him, to shout out to him, but she couldn't. She was pressed back in her seat by the force of the train going around the loops, and couldn't move to help him.

By the time they got down to the bottom, to the end of the ride, Leva was screaming, yelling for help. Her yells drowned out the thrilled screams of the other passengers and everyone was suddenly looking at her, aware that something was wrong.

It wasn't the pretty blond girl that met them at the exit, but a tall, acne-scarred boy with an overbite who didn't look old enough to ride by himself, let alone be qualified to evaluate a medical emergency.

"Ma'am? Are you okay?"

Leva indicated her motionless son, his head lolling to the side.

"Did he faint? Some people experience syncope when they go through the loop," he told her in a calm voice, reciting the words that had been drilled into him in training. "Does he have any medical conditions?"

"Yes, he has a medical condition!" Leva yelled at him. "That's what I'm trying to tell you! Get an ambulance. He needs to go to the hospital!"

The boy hesitated, his eyes going to Seth and then to the other employees. "I can get some ice and a first aid worker. He'll probably be fine in a couple of minutes."

"It's always the boys that faint," a woman worker said with a laugh.

"Get—an—ambulance!" Leva insisted. "Do it now! Don't stand there laughing at him!"

She fought loose of her restraints so that she could lean closer to Seth. She thrust her fingers into his pulse, her own heart hammering so hard and fast it hurt her chest. She was relieved to feel his pulse still beating. Her body slumped and she let out her breath.

"Is he… he's not dead?" asked the boy with the acne. "He's okay, right?"

"His heart is beating," Leva said, "but it's very weak. Will somebody please call an ambulance?"

"It's on its way," an older employee assured Leva, moving in and taking charge with her calm manner. "Darcy, we're going to need to shut down the ride. See to it. We need to clear a path for the ambulance. First aid workers are here," she observed, waving to the uniformed first-aiders.

"Passed out on the roller coaster?" the male first-aider asked with unconcern. "It happens all the time. Nothing to be worried about, ma'am. He'll just be a little confused…"

He reached for Seth. Leva didn't know if he planned to slap Seth's cheeks or shake him awake, but she pushed him back angrily.

"This is a serious event!" she snapped. "He could die! Does it look to you like he just fainted?"

The man froze, looking at her in alarm. "What…?"

"Seth is a very sick boy! His heart is still beating, which is a good thing since I don't see a portable AED here. Why wouldn't you have an AED at a roller coaster?"

"We do, ma'am. But you said his heart is beating; he doesn't need one…?"

"Where is it? Are you completely incompetent? All of you?"

Someone pushed forward, holding the AED case out in offering like the holy grail. "It's here. Do you need it?"

"Not yet, but we might," Leva snapped. "Help me get him out of the car. Lay him down. Elevate his feet."

"Shouldn't we leave him there?" a girl argued. "I thought you weren't supposed to move anyone."

"This isn't an injury accident. He didn't get *hit* by the roller coaster. Get him out. Lay him down. Get blankets for shock. Don't you have blankets?"

By the time the ambulance got there—nearly fifteen minutes, Leva noted, looking at the time on her phone again—Seth was lying on the concrete, blankets over him even in the sweltering weather, feet elevated, the AED open beside him. The paramedics looked over the scene.

"What happened? What's going on?"

"He has mitochondrial disease," Leva said. "He passed out on the roller coaster. He might have had a heart attack! We've treated for shock."

"The AED hasn't been used?" the paramedic asked.

Everyone shook their heads, looking at each other for approval.

"If you thought he had a heart attack, shouldn't you have hooked up the sensors?"

Leva looked at the open AED box. She had prepared everything in the event that they needed it, monitoring Seth's pulse manually. But the AED would have monitored what kind of rhythm it was. Whether his heart was producing the right electrical impulses, not just beating.

"Doesn't anyone know how to use this thing?" she accused. "Hasn't anyone been trained in what to do?"

The paramedic moved in with his stethoscope, pulling the blankets aside and pressing it to the outside of Seth's t-shirt. He motioned for silence, and the chatter among the employees subsided. Leva held her breath, waiting for his verdict.

"It sounds okay," he said. "We'll hook him up to a monitor when we get him into the ambulance. You're his mother?"

"Yes."

"What can you tell me about his medical condition?"

"Haven't you ever heard of mitochondrial disease?" she challenged.

"I've heard of it. Not in relationship to having a heart attack or fainting riding a roller coaster. Does he have heart problems?"

"Yes, he has a damaged heart from incompetent treatment in the past."

"Should he have been riding a roller coaster with a damaged heart?"

"The doctors cleared him. They said it would be okay."

The paramedic and his partner checked all of Seth's vital signs. "He seems stable. Has he fainted before? Is he prone to seizures?"

"Yes, he's fainted. But if it was just a faint, he'd be awake by now. This is far more serious."

"Has he had seizures?"

"Yes. But this doesn't look like a seizure."

"A seizure doesn't have to look like a tonic-clonic seizure. It can be difficult to detect without proper equipment."

"We need to get him to the hospital," Leva insisted, panic rising.

"Let's do that," the paramedic agreed. He and his partner got the gurney out of the ambulance. They seemed to be moving in slow motion. Leva didn't understand why paramedics and doctors always seemed to move so slowly. On TV, it was always a rush, everybody dove in and did their part, shouting out orders, doing something to make sure that they could save the patient. In Leva's experience, it was never like that. The doctors took hours, sometimes days, to evaluate an adverse event and decide on a course of treatment. Half the time, she was the one who suggested a diagnosis and course of treatment before they could come up with something.

They got Seth onto the gurney and into the ambulance.

"Can I ride with you?" Leva asked, climbing up.

"I'm sorry, ma'am. Policy says that we can't take any passengers. You can meet us at the hospital." He told her which one and asked if she knew her way there.

Leva shook her head. "We're not from here. We came on a vacation. Something special, to celebrate that Seth was doing better. We raised the money to get here with an online fundraiser. We just got here today."

"Okay. Why don't we see if we can get a police officer to escort you over there? Do you want to get your car?"

Leva shook her head. "It's all the way over in the parking lot on the other side of the park. And I'd have to pay for parking at the hospital. It's always such exorbitant prices. Can I leave it here?" Leva asked one of the park employees. "Is it going to get ticketed and towed away if I don't pick it up today?"

"If you'll give me a description and the plate number, I'll take care of it."

Leva had to get out her wallet and check her registration to give him all the details. Her brain wouldn't work. She couldn't even remember the make. The man noted down all the appropriate details.

"Don't you worry about it. It will be there tomorrow. And if you need a ride back here to pick it up, you call this number," he gave her a hospitality card. "A service will pick you up and bring you back here. No charge. I'll tell them to expect your call."

Leva nodded. The paramedic who was going to drive closed the rear doors of the ambulance. "We're going to go on ahead, ma'am. Police will be here in two minutes. We'll meet you in Emergency."

"Okay. Thank you."

In a couple more minutes, the ambulance pulled away, lights flashing but siren off, moving out through the park at a sedate speed.

———

Leva took a picture of Seth in the hospital bed, IV in his arm again, oxygen threaded into his nose. He had machines monitoring both his brain waves and the electrical activity in his heart. He had not woken up. They were running blood tests and had scheduled brain imaging to see if they could figure out what was going on.

She used an editing app to lay the pre-roller coaster picture and the hospital picture side by side, tapped in a status update, and uploaded them to all her social networking sites with one click. Before long, everybody would know as much as she knew. Family and friends would send their encouragement.

Maybe somebody would have additional suggestions of things that the doctors should check for. Theodore Woodward's aphorism always made her shake her head: "When you hear hoofbeats, think of horses, not zebras." Seth had always been her little zebra. Diagnosing him was always just beyond the doctors' reach. A cold or flu virus would land him in the hospital for weeks. His electrolytes went up and down like a yo-yo, completely unpredictable. One day he would seem fine. Strong, acting like a normal teenager, and then the next, at death's door.

Getting a diagnosis of mitochondrial disease had felt like such a victory. Finally, an explanation for everything. But instead of being the end of their journey, it had been another starting point.

So little was understood about how the mitochondria worked, how cellular energy was created and how one little failure of an enzyme or something else in the process could disrupt the entire body. And what course of treatment were they supposed to follow? There were research programs, experimental protocols, the herb and naturopathic route. The optimum diet. Vitamins and how they affected the whole Krebs cycle and might—or might not—fix everything. Diagnosis had brought more questions than answers.

"Mrs. Wilcox?"

Leva looked up at the doctor who hovered over her. She'd been staring down at her phone, willing it to ring. Praying for someone who had a suggestion to call, text, or message her and let her know. She'd completely blocked out everything else. There was a dark cast to his skin. Black hair and dark brown eyes. A young man. Old enough to be a fully-fledged doctor, but not old enough to have his university loans paid off.

"Doctor! I'm sorry, I was somewhere else."

"Understandable. I realize how difficult this has to be for you."

"Oh, I don't think you do," Leva said, shaking her head. "By my count, this is Seth's forty-eighth hospitalization."

His eyes widened at this announcement. "Well, that would explain why my staff says they are having trouble getting me a comprehensive medical history."

He sat on the edge of Seth's bed to talk to her. Leva bit her tongue to keep from telling him how unprofessional that was. At least he had come to talk to her directly, rather than hiding behind a cadre of nurses and interns. He was trying to have a discussion with the one person who could help him, the one person who knew Seth's history like some people knew ancient Roman history or the entire genealogy of the British monarchy. Seth was Leva's obsession. She was the expert on Seth and everything that had happened since he was born.

"He's been diagnosed with mitochondrial disease," Doctor Darvish said. Leva tried to fix his name in her memory so that she would be able to record it and to ask for him again later. Later when he wasn't on duty, and the nurses didn't want to deal with Leva's questions or didn't want to pass on her thoughts and her latest research to him.

"Yes, that's right. Umm… two years ago now. We thought that once he was diagnosed, it would be easy to find the right course of treatment and get him healthy again. But that hasn't been the case."

He nodded sympathetically. "It is new country for us. Being able to diagnose it is a step in the right direction, but finding the appropriate treatment can be elusive."

"So what can you tell me about what happened today?" Leva asked. "He just collapsed. If it had just been a faint, he'd be awake by now. It wasn't heart or a seizure… so what is it?"

"Has this ever happened before?"

"Sometimes if his electrolytes are off. I told the emergency room to test."

"His sodium levels are extremely high. Can you think of any reason that would be?"

"They can be all over the place. He didn't have anything salty at lunch; I don't think. I mean, some junk food, because it was Disneyland, but nothing that should have pushed his electrolytes out of whack. Unless there's a problem with his kidneys…"

"I notice he has a feeding tube."

"He's been through so many crises when he hasn't been able to eat… I prefer the feeding tube over a central line."

"It's unusual to leave it in once the crisis is over."

"Yes. But taking it out and putting it back in multiple times is worse, it increases the chance of infection."

"He's really too old for a feeding tube."

"What does age have to do with it?" Leva demanded. "If he is in a coma like this, how do you propose to give him his nourishment? You know that IV solutions are not sufficient. He has mitochondrial disease; we can't afford to let his cells starve, even for a day."

Darvish's lips pressed together. He didn't agree or disagree. He wrote something down on Seth's chart.

"We're giving him D5W," he said, indicating the IV bag. "But I'm recommending dialysis as well. We don't usually recommend dialysis for high sodium, but cases as acute as this are very dangerous. Outcomes are not good if we don't get control of it."

Leva nodded. She swiped on her phone and entered this new protocol in her health care app.

"But you don't have any idea what might have caused this in the first place?" she asked.

"I'm afraid not. Kids with metabolic disorders can be… challenging to deal with. He hasn't had any fever or diarrhea? No confusion before the ride on the roller coaster?"

"No, he seemed fine. He was anxious about it. Tired. Sweating from the heat. I suppose he might have gotten dehydrated from all the walking around and sweating."

"That could have contributed, but I would have expected something more than that."

"And you don't think it was the roller coaster itself? We checked with all the doctors before we went, and they said it was safe."

"I can't think of anything the roller coaster should have caused other than queasiness or fainting. He didn't throw up? On the roller coaster or earlier in the day?"

"No. Not today. I wish I could point to something that simple."

He nodded and got up from the bed.

"We'll treat him, and try to avoid messing up any other electrolytes in the process. Someone will be coming to take him down to dialysis. The next time you see him, he should be awake."

"Can't I go down to dialysis with him?"

"Sorry, no. Not this time. We've got a flu outbreak, and the unit is under quarantine. No one is allowed in."

"Oh." Leva nodded. "Okay. I guess when he goes down, I'll pop over to the cafeteria and get something to eat."

He nodded and reached out his hand to shake hers.

"Good to meet you, Mrs. Wilcox. Don't you worry; we'll get him fixed up as quickly as we can."

CHAPTER TWO

How is Wilcox doing?" Jahn Darvish asked the nurse over the dialysis unit.

"His levels are normalizing. What the heck happened to throw his numbers off so far?"

"Still investigating that. Is he awake?"

"Not last I saw, but he should be awake before long. You can see if you can rouse him."

Darvish nodded his thanks and went down the row of dialysis beds, smiling at the patients as he went by. He found young Seth Wilcox's bed and shook the boy's arm.

"Seth. Time to wake up now, Seth…"

Seth's head moved slightly, but he didn't open his eyes. Darvish squeezed tighter and shook harder.

"Come on, Seth. Time to wake up. I know you're tired, but I need you to talk to me."

The muscle in Seth's arm tightened, resisting. Dr. Darvish moved to Seth's face, patting him on the cheek, each pat making Seth flinch and squeeze his eyelids closed more tightly.

"Wake up, Seth. Open your eyes now. If you talk to me, I'll let you alone, and you can go back to sleep."

"No," Seth groaned.

"Come on, son. Let's see those baby blues."

Seth's eyes blinked reluctantly open. Darvish gave him a reassuring smile and waited for a few moments for Seth to focus on him and get oriented.

"What happened?" Seth whispered.

"You had a little problem with your electrolytes. What do you remember?"

Seth brought his hand up to his face and rubbed his forehead with a frown. "I don't know. Wasn't I at Disney?"

"Yes, you were. What were you doing there?"

"My mom raised money for me to go. 'Cause that's what I've always wanted. Am I still there? Or am I home?"

"You're still in California. What was the last thing you did at Disneyland?"

Seth cleared his throat, looking around. He rubbed at the oxygen tube feeding into his nose. Not like it was bothering him, or he wanted to pull it out, just feeling with curious fingers to see what was going on.

"We had lunch. Took a break. We were going to go on the roller coaster."

"And did you?"

Seth thought about it, his eyes vague. His brain seemed to be moving very slowly. Whether that was normal or a result of Seth's screwed-up 'lytes, Darvish wasn't sure. He needed to get his hands on as much of Seth's medical history as he could.

"I don't think so," Seth said finally. He turned his head away from Darvish, letting it loll in the opposite direction to get another view of the room. He stared at the dialysis machine. "Why am I on dialysis?"

"There were dangerously high levels of sodium in your blood. I wanted to clean it as quickly as possible to avoid damage to your kidneys. Have you been on dialysis before?"

"Yeah."

Darvish made a note of this on his phone. Not on the official record, but a reminder to himself to follow up on it later.

"What did you have for lunch, Seth?"

Seth continued to stare at the dialysis machine as if mesmerized.

"I don't remember."

"Did your mom buy something? Or did she bring something with her?"

"I don't know. Maybe… I don't know."

"Tell me about your feeding tube."

Seth fingered it under his hospital robe, looking irritated. "I hate it. It gets in the way all the time. People think I'm like a freak. Who wants to be around a guy with a tube coming out of his belly? It's gross."

"I can see how it might put a crimp on relationships," Darvish agreed, giving a nod. "So why do you still have it? You don't need it, do you?"

"No," Seth plucked at it. "I don't need it and I don't want it. You could tell my mom to get rid of it."

"It's your mom's idea?"

"She says I need it when I can't eat."

"That sounds reasonable, doesn't it?"

Seth scowled. He slumped back against his pillow and hit the arm of the bed with his unencumbered hand.

"Did your mom put something in your tube?" Darvish asked. "Maybe she put something down it that she shouldn't have. Something that made you sick."

Seth stared at him without expression.

"Did your mom put something in your feeding tube today?"

Seth shook his head. "I don't remember. She didn't need to. Not when I was feeling okay."

"Has your mom ever put something in your feeding tube that she shouldn't have? Something the doctors didn't know about or approve?"

"She wouldn't do that."

"Maybe an herbal remedy or dietary aid that she read about online. Vitamins or digestive enzymes."

"The doctor has to approve everything."

Darvish nodded. "Okay. Well, you're going to be here for a while longer, so if you want to go back to sleep, you can."

Seth appeared to be more wide awake now, and not inclined to go right back to sleep. He shifted his position.

"Can you sit me up?"

"Sure." Darvish worked the controls to bring Seth up to a sitting position. "How's that?"

"Can I go back today? To Disneyland?"

Darvish couldn't help but laugh at Seth's eagerness. "Sounds like you're already feeling better. I don't think you're going to get back there today.

We'll talk about it tomorrow. Though I'm not sure the roller coaster is a good idea."

"I only have five days. I have to do everything in five days."

"We'll see how you're doing, Seth. We don't want to release you and have you collapse again. It could be even more serious next time."

"I feel fine."

"That's good. I'm glad you're feeling better. But we'll have to watch your levels and make sure that everything is stable. I don't like an episode like this just coming out of nowhere. I'd like to know what caused it."

Seth shook his head. "But I don't know. I just... things like that happen to me. Because of my mito. No one can control it."

———

It was no great surprise to Seth that when he was transferred to a gurney and back to the emergency room bed, that Leva was waiting there, ready to take his picture and post it online to update his status. It was easier than making all those phone calls, he knew, but just once he would have liked her to just leave it alone.

"Smile for me," Leva said, snuggling beside him and holding her phone out in front of them so that she could get them both into the picture. Seth rolled his eyes and didn't smile.

"I don't feel good, Mom. I don't want to smile."

"It just looks better on the posts; then everyone knows that you're doing better. People want to see you happy."

Seth waved her off, not wanting her to take further pictures. "I'm tired. You can take pictures when we go back to Disneyland."

She gave him a big smile. "All ready to go back?"

"The doctor said maybe tomorrow. So I want to sleep and get all better for tomorrow so he says it's okay."

"Okay," Leva agreed. She sat in the chair next to the bed and stroked his hair. "So you're feeling better, baby?"

"Yeah."

"It was pretty scary, you just going limp on the roller coaster like that. I was so afraid that you'd had a heart attack!"

"My heart is okay."

"It could happen," Leva protested. "All the times you've been sick, that puts a lot of stress on your heart. The doctors may say that your heart is fine, but they don't *know*. They can't see it. High sodium could have caused a heart attack too."

"I went on the roller coaster?" Seth asked. "I don't remember."

"You went on the roller coaster. So brave!"

"It's not like I'm five," he grumbled. She always treated him like a baby. Especially when he was sick.

"Shh. Go to sleep. Maybe we can go back tomorrow."

———

Jahn Darvish sat with the hospital social worker, Sia Exler, his boss, Dr. Fraser, and the hospital attorney, Samantha Dreyer, to go over Seth Wilcox's file.

"There is no way these are naturally occurring sodium levels," he said, sliding the first electrolytes report across to Dr. Fraser. "Even in a kid with a mysterious metabolic illness, there's no way his sodium levels spike that fast."

Dr. Fraser nodded, adjusting his half-glasses to review the numbers on the report. "There were no warning signs, Jahn? Diarrhea? Confusion? I wouldn't expect him to be cogent during an episode like that."

"According to the mother, nothing. Acting normally until he collapsed on the roller coaster."

"That seems highly unlikely."

Darvish nodded his agreement. "She says they had lunch shortly before getting onto the roller coaster. I think she injected sodium directly into his feeding tube."

"That would explain the rapid onset."

"Is there any other explanation?" Samantha Dreyer, the lawyer, asked. She was a striking blonde in a conservative navy blazer and skirt.

Fraser and Darvish looked at each other. Neither could come up with a suggestion.

"We're checking out other possibilities. Kidney function. Adrenals. But I think the boy was poisoned. I can't come up with any other explanation."

The social worker was flipping through printed computer pages. "This isn't the first time that he's had high sodium or another electrolyte imbalance," Sia said. "And that suggests that it is part of his disorder."

"Or part of his mother's disorder," Darvish said.

The social worker and lawyer both looked confused. Fraser's mouth twitched. "Be careful, Jahn."

"What do you mean, the mother's disorder?" Sia demanded. "You think this is genetic?"

"No, I think it's the mother. I think this has been going on for some time, and no one has been able to see the forest for the trees."

"What do you mean?"

"The mother. Munchausen by Proxy. She's poisoning him."

"I saw her earlier in the day to see what their needs were while they were away from home," Sia said. "She seemed like a very concerned, attentive mother. I didn't get any vibes."

"Munchausen by Proxy mothers are attentive. They appear very involved in their children's care, very knowledgeable, and very caring. But if they feel they're not getting the attention they deserve, the kid suddenly has a downturn."

"There's no proof," Fraser said.

"This is proof." Darvish tapped the report on Seth's initial electrolytes test. "Right there. Salt poisoning. Not a natural metabolic process."

They sat around the table looking at each other.

"You have to be sure," Samantha warned. "One hundred percent. Munchausen is being used too much these days. Judges are getting leery of it. Stories in the media about using Munchausen by Proxy to get kids away from parents when you can't actually prove abuse. I don't want that stigma attached to any of our files."

"I'll talk to her one more time," Darvish said. "Just to be sure."

CHAPTER THREE

Darvish observed Leva and Seth before making himself known. They presented a touching tableau. Seth was asleep, his pale skin almost as white as the bedsheets. Leva sat in the chair beside him, watching him as he slept. She held his hand, their fingers intertwined.

Darvis made a movement that attracted Leva's attention. Her eyes left her son and went to him.

"Hello, doctor."

"Hi." Darvish moved the rest of the way into the room and made himself look busy, taking note of Seth's vital signs and looking him over for any new developments. He was definitely looking better than he had on arrival. But he'd been pretty critical then. "How's he doing?" he asked Leva.

She parroted back his stats and every infinitesimal change over the past few hours. Darvish nodded as if this was all important news to him.

"Has he been awake?"

"Off and on. He's tired. That's pretty normal after one of these events."

"How are his spirits?"

She frowned, a crease forming above her nose.

"As well as could be expected, I suppose. He doesn't remember going on the roller coaster." She fixed her gaze on him. "Did you tell him he could go back to Disneyland? That he would be getting out of here again this week? He thinks he's going to be able to get out today."

"I told him that we would talk about it today. But I don't think we're going to be able to release him that fast. This was a pretty serious setback. I don't think he's strong enough to be released, let alone putting his body through that kind of rigor."

Leva nodded her agreement. "I would hate to go back there and have him collapse again."

"It can be hard to tell them no. I admit, I didn't want to say anything that might affect his mood negatively. His emotional state can be so closely tied to his physical health. But I'll have to let him know today that we need more time to make sure that he's stable."

"I'll let him know," Leva promised. She looked down at him lovingly, a tender smile on her face. "He's going to be crushed."

"He was pretty excited about Disney, hey?" Darvish picked up Seth's chart to note his latest vital statistics.

"It was his dream. The one thing that he wanted in life. I spent a year raising the money to get us here and made everything so special. All the little things that he had imagined, all the little extras I could think of that would make it something to remember. And then this had to happen. He couldn't forget for a week that he was sick. Just when it looks like everything is working out for him, bam! He's back in hospital."

"He's a little old, isn't he, for Disney to be such a big thing? I mean, at fourteen, there must be girls, computer games, movie superheroes… Sleeping Beauty and Buzz Lightyear are pretty juvenile."

"Have you seen all the teenagers at Disneyland?" Leva's eyebrows rose in disbelief. Then her voice dropped in tone. "Seth does have some… developmental delays. It's not unusual for a child that has had to spend so much time in hospital to be a little delayed, and with all that he's been through, we can't tell how much damage might have been done to his brain. Kids with mito sometimes have Pervasive Developmental Delays, though they don't think Seth is on the spectrum. He just… loves Disney. When he's gone through his toughest times, the days when we wondered if he'd even survive, he'd always remind me, 'it's not over yet, Mom. I haven't ever been to Disneyland.'"

Darvish cleared his throat and nodded. And now that Seth had been to Disneyland, even though it was only for a day, did that mean that he could no longer use his dream to hold off death? Darvish knew that Munchausen by Proxy mothers didn't usually kill their children, but that didn't make it impossible. They could still go too far, accidentally or on purpose. Seth was getting pretty old for Leva to still be using him as a puppet.

Hanging Seth's chart back up at the end of the bed, Darvish gave Leva a nod. "I'll be back doing rounds later. I'll break it to him then that he's not going to be able to go back to Disneyland this week."

"Thank you. He'll be devastated, but we can't exactly keep it from him any longer."

Darvish left the room. He went to the nursing station to discuss Seth's care and the possibility that Social Services would be taking him into custody. As he walked back past Seth's room, he saw that Leva had removed Seth's chart from the end of the bed and was checking it to see what he had written down. She looked up and saw him watching her. Darvish raised a hand in greeting and went on.

———

Darvish had been paged several times but had to ignore the calls as he dealt with the arrival of multiple traumas in the emergency room. When they were finally cleared, he stripped off his bloody gloves and disposed of them in the biowaste bucket. He pushed the button on his pager to quickly review the pages, then called Seth Wilcox's unit.

"It's Jahn," he said briskly. "What's up?"

"We've been trying to get ahold of you—"

"Yes. I had my hands inside of someone. What is it?"

"The Wilcox boy. His mother has just signed him out."

"I didn't approve his release."

"She knew she was signing him out against doctor's orders. She signed all the liability forms."

Darvish swore. "Who tipped her off?"

She didn't answer immediately. When she did speak, her voice was cool. "No one told her anything, Doctor. If she knew something was in the air, she just read the signals. Maybe it was something you said."

"Where is she staying? Did she give a local address?"

"She made it pretty clear she was heading home."

"At least she's not taking him back to Disney."

"No. He was pretty cut up about it, poor boy. We told Mom that he wasn't stable enough to go home. She said she'd readmit him at her local hospital. I think she will."

"Pull the information for his primary physician. We'll follow up to make sure he's being treated. We'll pass what we've got on to their Social Services department. As long as they've actually gone back, and aren't on the run."

"I'll get it for you."

———

Leva helped Seth get into his jammies and then settled into the hospital bed. Back in the familiar unit at Children's, where she knew all the doctors and nurses, and they were safe from ignorant doctors who didn't know anything about Seth's condition.

Seth was tired from the long drive, and he hadn't been able to eat much. Car trips always took a lot out of him. That's why she had arranged plane tickets on the trip to Disneyland. But there hadn't been time to make proper arrangements for the sudden trip home, and she had been forced to drive the whole way.

"Could I get a formula feed?" Leva asked Nurse Nance, her voice low. "Driving always makes him nauseated and then he won't eat."

"I don't need a tube-feed," Seth objected, not opening his eyes.

"Are you going to eat dinner, then?"

"I'm not hungry."

Leva gave Nance an eye roll. Nance nodded and gave her a thumbs-up, not answering out loud. She walked out quickly, silent in her white sneakers. With any luck, Seth would be asleep by the time the formula arrived and Leva could take care of the feeding while he was still under, without a fight.

"Just rest, Seth," Leva told him. "I know the car always makes you tired."

"It was too long," Seth whined.

"I know."

"My butt hurts from sitting for so long. Why did we have to do it all in one day?"

"You're back home now. I didn't want you to be away from hospital any longer than necessary. But they know how to take care of you here. You can rest."

"Coulda just stayed in California. I wanted to go back to Disney."

She had already listened to this refrain the whole trip back. There was no point in trying to explain it again. Seth knew that he wasn't going back to Disneyland. Not in the near future. He'd been able to be there for one day. That would have to be enough.

Seth didn't open his eyes and only murmured a few more words of complaint before he was asleep, his breathing long and slow. Nance hadn't hooked up the heart-rate and blood pressure monitor, so Leva did it herself, and watched the numbers for a few minutes.

Then she turned back to Seth and took a picture of him on her phone, to update her social media networks and let everyone know they were home.

———

When Nance returned later with the formula for Seth's feeding tube, her thin lips made her look angry, even when she forced a smile at Leva.

"Is something wrong?" Leva asked. She caught her breath. There was no guarantee that what Nance was angry about had anything to do with Seth or his care. It could have been any other patient, or even a call from home that had put Nance into a bad mood.

Nance gave no explanation. She started preparing the formula bag for use.

"I can do that," Leva offered, stepping forward to take it. She always gave Seth his feedings. Ever since he was a baby. They didn't need a nurse to waste her time doing that.

But the nurse didn't hand it to her. She continued to hook it up herself. "We've been told we have to do it ourselves."

"All tube feedings?" Leva demanded

Nance didn't answer. She hooked up the tube and watched it flow.

"You don't have to stay the whole time."

"I'm afraid I do."

Leva was stunned. It was unheard of. The nursing staff didn't have the time to babysit patients that way.

"What's going on?" she demanded. "Policy changes? Don't they know how much time you would waste having to supervise every tube feeding?"

"I'm just doing what I'm told," Nance snapped.

"Of course," Leva agreed. She didn't want to attract the nurse's ire. Nothing made a hospital stay more uncomfortable than an angry head nurse. She sat down out of the way and started to compose an email to the hospital administrators to point out the error of their ways. If they didn't respond appropriately, she might take the matter public. She'd learned a lot about advocacy in the past fourteen years. Policy couldn't take precedent over people. Seth might be getting too big to be seen cuddling with his mom now, but feeding time had always been a special bonding time between them. Ever since he was a baby and couldn't nurse, she had been able to feed him through his tube.

Nurse Nance stood there until the bag finished draining, and then cleaned up. She tucked Seth's tube away and buttoned his shirt. She looked at her watch. "He shouldn't need anything else before morning, now. Hopefully, by then he'll be feeling better."

"Yes, he should be okay by then."

CHAPTER FOUR

She probably should have guessed by Nance's behavior that there had been follow-up calls from the California hospital. But Leva brushed the episode off. They all had things to do. It was her job to make sure that Seth was getting the best care he possibly could. She grilled the doctors and nurses on his blood test results, going over his numbers carefully and noting them in her phone app. She had made calls to Seth's pediatrician and anyone else she thought he should see for follow-up care. Even after the hours she had spent driving, she hadn't been able to sleep very well in the hospital room and had eventually pulled out her phone and gotten to work.

Seth was awake but grouchy in the morning. He continued to grouse about not being able to go back to Disneyland while he poked at the pancakes and scrambled eggs that the staff had delivered to him.

"Why did I have to come back?" he repeated. "I'm feeling better. If we could check out of the hospital, why couldn't we go back to Disney?"

"You're not all better. We didn't leave because you were better, we left so that you could get care here, where they know how to take care of you properly. Aren't you much more comfortable here than you were in California?"

Seth dropped a forkful of syrup-slathered pancakes down the front of his pajama shirt. He swore to himself and popped them into his mouth with his fingers, and tried to brush the syrup off of his shirt. He looked around the room.

Leva smiled at the colorful murals on the walls, and the wide, bright windows. The service and staff at Children's were amazing. And it wouldn't be long before Seth's room was filled with the usual cards, stuffed animals, and silvery balloons of well-wishers.

"It's not any different," Seth growled. "And there's no Disneyland here."

"Well, you eat all your food so that you can get nice and healthy, and we'll try to find something nice for you to do here. What else would you like?"

Seth had crammed half of the pancakes into his mouth, so it was a few minutes of chewing before he was able to answer her.

"I want a bike like Mike got. It's really cool."

Leva shook her head. "You haven't used the skateboard we got you. You're not going to use a bike."

"Mike uses his."

"But Mike used his previous bike too. You haven't ever used a bike. There's no point in getting you such a fancy one."

"It has twenty-one speeds or something."

"Yes—"

"And the wheels come off without a wrench. And it has cool brakes—"

"We're not getting you a bike, Seth. If you want a bike, you borrow one of Mike's old ones and show us that you're actually going to use one."

"I can't help it if I get tired easily," Seth whined. "That's just because of my mito. A bike isn't as hard as walking…"

"Then borrow one of Mike's."

Seth gave a disgusted snort. He pushed his plate away. The pancakes were only half-eaten, and the eggs were barely touched.

"You need to eat more than that."

"I can't. I'm full. And I'm upset."

Leva knew that he was manipulating her, but she couldn't help reacting. He had to eat well if he were going to stay healthy.

"I'll talk to your father about a bike. We'll talk about it. Will you eat at least three bites of your eggs?"

He shook his head. "Why do you have to talk to Dad about the bike? He's not going to buy it. He doesn't care if I use it or not."

"Because we make big decisions together, even if he can't always be with you. Like I can."

"He doesn't want to be with me," Seth declared, his mouth pointing even farther down.

Leva looked for a diplomatic answer. "Your father has never been good with illness," she said. "And he has another family now. He needs to be with them. A man needs to support his wife and children."

"But we don't count."

"Well… no, it's not the same. He doesn't have custody of you, and under the Settlement Agreement, he doesn't have to pay child support or alimony. But he does need to support the family that he's with now."

Seth shook his head. He pulled the breakfast plate closer to him, inspecting it, then shook his head and pushed it away from himself again.

"I can't. It doesn't taste good. There's no salt on the eggs."

Leva laughed. "No, they can't give you salt right now, with how high your sodium was. Have some anyway. They're still good without salt. You used to love scrambled eggs in syrup."

"It's not real syrup. It's crappy hospital fake syrup."

"Come on, Seth," Leva begged, her voice high and silly, making a face at him. "Eat three more bites for Mommy."

"I told you I'm not a baby! Quit treating me like a baby!"

Leva sighed. "You don't want to be treated like a baby? Then listen up. You act like an adult and eat your breakfast, because that's what you need to do to keep your strength up, or we'll do a tube feeding." She folded her arms across her chest and looked down at Seth. "So is it a deal?"

Seth shook his head; lip thrust out in a pout.

"There will be no more tube feedings," a man's voice said.

Leva turned around to look at the man who had come into the room behind her. She scowled and shook her head. "Who are you? You're not in charge of Seth's nutritional needs."

The man walked forward and showed Leva his Social Services ID on a lanyard around his neck.

"I'm Shawn Roth. Social Services is taking over Seth's care for the time being and I am in charge of the case."

"Social Services can't just march in without cause. Seth is in my custody. He's safe in a hospital."

He handed her a folded sheet of paper with "order" written at the top. Leva looked at it, her heart sinking. But she wasn't ready to just take it.

"You don't have any right," she asserted. "I'm calling my lawyer. And my advocacy groups. You can't just walk in and take a child because he is sick. I'm taking good care of him."

"According to the hospital he was admitted to in California, he was poisoned. Probably through his feeding tube. Probably by you. He could have died from what you did to him."

"I didn't do anything to him. Seth can tell you. He's big enough to speak for himself. Tell Mr. Roth, Seth. Tell him that I didn't do anything to make you sick."

Seth was looking from one to the other like he was watching a tennis match.

"What?"

"Tell the social worker that I take care of you. I don't hurt you or make you sick. He thinks that I can't take care of you, and you need someone else to take care of you."

"Another doctor?" Seth suggested, frowning.

"No, another mother. Another family."

———

Seth's eyes followed Leva out of the room and then he turned his gaze toward Shawn Roth.

"Where's she going?" he demanded, eyes big and round.

"She's close by," Shawn told him. "She needs to make her phone calls and start getting her ducks lined up. For now, it's just you and me. We need to talk about things."

"What things?"

"Do you understand what we were talking about just now? That you're in my care now instead of your mom's? We will assign you a foster family, but for the time being, I'm in charge of your care here."

Seth nodded slowly, but Shawn wasn't sure from Seth's troubled gaze whether he understood this. He pulled the chair over and sat down. It was still warm from Leva's body.

"My name is Shawn."

Seth nodded. "Shawn," he repeated. "I'm Seth."

Shawn offered his hand. "It's good to meet you, Seth."

They shook. Seth's grip was weak, a dead fish. Shawn held it an extra few seconds, squeezing a bit, trying to get a reaction from Seth, but the boy just squirmed his hand back out of Shawn's grip, looking more petulant than ever.

"Why don't you tell me why you're in hospital?" Shawn suggested.

"I have mito. It makes me sick all the time. I went to Disneyland, but I got sick, so I had to come back here."

"What was it that made you sick in Disneyland?"

"My mito disease. I passed out on the roller coaster, but I can't remember that part."

Shawn nodded. "That sounds like quite an adventure. And then you came here?"

"Then I went to the hospital in California. But Mom said we needed to come home. So I came back here." He raised his hands in a shrug. "So here I am."

"Are you glad to be back somewhere more familiar?"

Seth looked around. "I guess."

"Good. I'm glad you're more comfortable here. Your mom said they know how to treat you here."

"Yeah."

"Is that because you've been here a lot?"

"I live here."

"You don't live at your house?"

"Sometimes. I live there, and I live here. If I'm sick."

"How are you feeling today?"

Seth considered the question without expression. Shawn wasn't sure he was going to be able to come up with an answer.

"I'm tired and want to sleep more, but it was time to get up and have breakfast. My stomach is off, and I don't feel like eating."

"It's off?" Shawn repeated.

"Yeah."

"What does that mean? You're nauseated? Full? Does it hurt?"

"I'm just… not hungry and don't want to eat anything else. Just *ick*. Out of sorts."

"Is there a medicine that makes you feel better?"

"I take lots of medicines, but none of them make my stomach feel better."

"What do they all do?"

"I don't know. Ask Mom. She knows what they do. All I know is, they don't make my stomach feel any better."

"What does your mom suggest when your stomach isn't feeling well?"

"I have to eat anyway. Or get tube-fed."

"We're not going to do tube feeding anymore, Seth. You eat what you can; we're not going to force feed you."

Seth brightened at this. "Then can I get the tube out?"

"Yes. We're going to arrange to have it taken out."

"They can't just pull it out. They have to do surgery."

"That's what I was told. But until then, we don't have to use it, do we?" Shawn said, leaning forward and lowering his voice conspiratorially.

"Yeah," Seth agreed, smiling for the first time. He leaned toward Shawn. "And how about that bike…?"

Shawn laughed. "What were you saying to your mom about a bike?"

"I need one. She doesn't think that I do. But I really would use it. Not like the skateboard."

"You have a skateboard?"

"Yes… but I'm scared of falling off of it. It isn't like a bike. I know how to ride a bike."

"Well, I don't know if we're going to be getting a bike anytime soon, but I believe you when you say you would use it. Let's concentrate on getting you better first."

"Okay." Seth nodded. "I'll get better fast so that we can get it. I'll feel better when I don't have the feeding tube anymore."

Shawn considered Seth's words. "Do you think it's the feeding tube that makes you feel sick?"

Seth's eyes went back and forth across the room. He lowered his eyebrows. Finally, he shrugged. "I don't think it makes me feel better," he hedged.

"Does your mom ever put anything in your feeding tube?"

"Yes."

"What does she put in your feeding tube?" Shawn leaned forward, eager to hear Seth's answer. He hadn't expected the boy to admit it so easily.

"Formula." Seth looked at him like he was nuts. "That's what it's for."

"I meant does she put anything *else* in your feeding tube? Anything other than formula?"

"No."

"Does she mix anything with the formula?"

"No."

"Does she put medicine in your feeding tube?"

"When can I go home?" Seth demanded.

"Not for a while. We have to get you healthy first. And then you'll be going to your foster home."

"Not a foster home. *My* home. And you're going to get me a bike."

"I didn't promise you a bike," Shawn warned, not wanting Seth to get that into his head. "I just said we have to get you healthy first, before we can talk about it. Now, Seth, I want you to focus—"

"You said I could get a bike!"

"No, Seth—"

Seth's hand shot forward and shoved the plate off of his table with enough force to keep it airborne for several feet before it went crashing to the ground. Shawn was shocked and for a minute was silent, not knowing what to say or do.

Leva returned to the room and looked in, her eyes wide with alarm. "What happened? Seth, are you okay?"

"He promised," Seth insisted. "He promised me a bike!"

Leva's eyes flickered to Shawn, and he gave a slight shake of the head. It was automatic. He didn't owe her any information. She shouldn't have even come back into the room.

"He gets stuck on an idea sometimes," Leva said. Her eyes went to the monitor showing Seth's now-racing heart rate and rising blood pressure. "Especially if he's not feeling well."

She pressed the call button beside the bed.

"Seth, I want you to take long, deep breaths," she prompted him. "Calming breaths."

"I'm not! He promised."

Leva was taking long breaths, demonstrating, and despite Seth's protests, his breathing pattern changed, matching hers.

A nurse strode into the room. She saw the plate of food on the floor, and her mouth tightened.

"What's going on?"

"Seth could use something to calm him down," Leva suggested.

The nurse looked at Shawn. He shook his head.

"Will you check his glucose?" Leva tried again. "He's very agitated. And those pancakes were dowsed in syrup. His body has a hard time handling such concentrated doses of sugar."

"Don't poke me," Seth protested. His hands clenched into fists, which he shoved under his covers.

"I don't think we need any tests," Shawn said. "I think he's just upset. He'll settle down on his own. Won't you, bud?"

Seth nodded. The nurse looked at the monitor and looked at Leva. She was obviously used to following through on Leva's requests. But she knew that Social Services was now in charge.

"It wouldn't hurt to check his glucose," she told Shawn. "It's a simple finger prick, and if his sugars are off it could be dangerous."

"Do you think they are?" Shawn challenged.

She looked back at Seth. Shawn couldn't see anything that would suggest the boy was sick. He was tired and grumpy from the events of the last few days and fixated on the idea of getting a bike, but he didn't seem sick.

"No…" the nurse hedged. "He's not showing any symptoms… but Seth's sugars and electrolytes can swing very rapidly…"

"Is he diabetic?"

"No, but his mitochondrial disease…"

"I don't want to be poked," Seth insisted again. His voice was high and emotional.

"The patient doesn't want the procedure," Shawn said. "And he's not showing any symptoms. I don't think there's any need to do it."

The nurse looked worriedly at Leva, but there was nothing that Leva could do about it. She was no longer in charge of Seth's care.

CHAPTER FIVE

Renata waited impatiently for the social worker who was supposed to be transporting her to her next home. She'd been in psych for months on end, and the hospital had not been quick to declare her stable. They knew Renata's history and how she had bounced in and out of psych since she was a toddler. They were determined not to release her until they felt she had a good chance of success on the outside. Her unique metabolism and allergies meant that the use of psychoactive drugs produced paradoxical reactions and other unpredictable results. And just when they thought they had a cocktail that worked for her, she would have a psychotic break, and they'd have to start all over again.

But they had finally settled on a regimen that they thought was working, and Renata had not had a break or a meltdown in several weeks. For Renata, that was outstanding.

Tired of waiting in her room, Renata walked out to the nursing station.

"When are they coming?"

"We can't control Social Services, Renata," Debbie said in an exaggerated, long-suffering voice. "They'll get here when they get here."

"You said in the morning, and it's almost noon."

"They told us the morning. I can't tell you anything else. They haven't called to report in or say they've been delayed. You know how it is; social workers are always running late."

"Where am I supposed to go?" Renata asked, craning her neck to look at the desk calendar to see if they had written the details down. "Foster care? Group home?"

"I can't tell you. You'll find out soon enough."

"You can't tell me because you don't know, or because they told you not to?"

"Renata… I don't mind you waiting out here if you want to. But you need to let me do my work and not grill me."

Renata watched Debbie switch to her browser and shut a couple of tabs displaying social networks. Yeah, she was working.

"Wouldn't you want to know where you were going if you were me?"

"I'm sure I would." Debbie didn't look up.

Renata sighed and turned away from Debbie to lean against the desk and watch the elevator. A watched pot never boiled. The time dragged on. George was pushing the lunch cart down the hallway, delivering dishes to each patient. Debbie looked at Renata.

"Do you want something?" she asked Renata.

"Yeah, I'll take one of those burgers," Renata retorted. They both knew that Renata couldn't take any food by mouth. She reacted so violently to food that the only nourishment they could give her was a single type of liquid formula, which was pumped directly into her stomach.

Debbie gestured to a case of Renata's formula sitting next to the nursing station, also waiting for the arrival of the social worker.

"If you're hungry, we can hook you up."

Renata sighed. "No. Not exactly hungry right now. Besides, she should be here any minute, and then she'd have to wait for me."

"Wouldn't hurt her to have to wait. She's made you wait all morning."

Renata nodded. The elevator dinged, and she turned quickly to look. It was an unfamiliar woman. Slacks instead of a skirt, but still looking very professional and social-worker-ish. She walked up to the nursing station, looking a little awkward.

"Hi. I'm here to pick up a child."

"Renata Vega," Debbie said, nodding to Renata.

"Oh." The social worker took a moment to look Renata over. A thin but vibrant teen, Latina, she looked pretty ordinary for a girl who had been in and out of psych facilities her whole life. The woman's shoulders relaxed noticeably. "Nice to meet you, Renata. I'm Bonnie Best. Are you all ready to go?"

"Been waiting all morning."

"Oh… uh… sorry about that. I was just given the assignment at the last minute, and…" she trailed off. She didn't say that she had been avoiding the job, but it was pretty obvious it was low on her list.

"You need to sign the release papers here," Debbie told the social worker. "And you need to take this with you." She kicked the case of formula.

"Okay…" She signed the papers without even glancing at the contents, then looked down at the box. "Is it heavy? Maybe I could get some help."

Debbie rolled her eyes and reached for the phone. Then she saw George as he finished delivering lunches. "George? Could you help Mrs. Best, here?"

George raised his eyebrows and looked Bonnie Best over. Then he gave a shrug and a nod. He scooped up the box effortlessly. "Lead the way."

Bonnie was talkative. Maybe to cover her nervousness. She was young for a social worker, and since she had gotten the job of transporting Renata, she was probably at the bottom of the totem pole. A real greenie. George seemed happy enough to talk to her, giving Renata the space she needed to look around and relish being outside the psych ward at last. The hospital was a bustle of busyness, everyone hurrying somewhere, the PA system cutting in every thirty seconds with another page.

They got to the outside doors, and Renata took a deep breath, walking out into the fresh air. She had a sudden rush of vertigo and thought she was going to fall right on her face. She caught George's arm as she swayed. The bright sunlight hurt her eyes and made them stream tears. The fresh air seemed cold and overcharged, and Renata felt like she couldn't get enough oxygen.

George shifted the box under his arm and put his free arm around Renata's back.

"Whoa. You okay?"

Renata took long, slow breaths, trying to calm the rapid-fire drumming of her heart. "I'm… yeah, I'm okay…"

"Take a minute. A bit overwhelming at first."

Renata felt tiny in the vastness of the outdoors. Like she was an insignif-icant speck that might just blow away. The noise of the traffic ground into her brain. She was glad she hadn't eaten because she probably wouldn't have been able to keep down her special formula. Renata continued to breathe and let the sensations wash over her. She relaxed her grip on George's arm.

"I'm fine. It was just… just took a minute."

He nodded and didn't make a big deal of it. Bonnie Best, however, was fluttering around worriedly.

"Are you sure? Maybe she's not ready to leave. I don't want to be responsible for her if she's not okay…"

"Renata's fine," George told her sternly. "It's just the first time she's been out in a while. Let her acclimatize. Why don't you go get your car and pull into the loading zone here?"

Best nodded and headed into the parking lot, looking back over her shoulder a couple of times at Renata.

Renata and George stood there waiting, not saying anything for a while.

"You be nice to her," George said.

"What?" Renata laughed innocently, but she couldn't stop the mischievous smile from spreading across her face. "What would I do?"

"I probably know you better than your own doctor. Yes, she's green, but go easy on her. Don't get her all wound up or in trouble."

Renata chuckled. George knew her too well. "I don't know if I can promise anything."

"You just got out. Don't push your luck."

He didn't want her to do anything that might threaten her freedom. But Renata had enough experience to doubt whether she had any chance at real freedom anyway.

"*Did* I just get out?" she asked George. "Or are they just locking me up somewhere else? Do you know?"

He glanced at her. "They wouldn't be announcing it to me, would they?"

Renata took in his shuttered look and sighed. George did know, or guess, and it wasn't good news. He might be happy to see her leaving secure psych, but he knew she wasn't going to like where she was going.

"Why do they even bother?" Renata asked. "What's the difference between keeping me in hospital and putting me in some residential lock-up? At least at the hospital they can deal with any medical emergencies and change my meds when they need to. What's going to happen at this *home?* They're not going to know how to deal with it."

"I don't make the rules. The goal is to get you out of the hospital, not to keep you there forever."

Renata shook her head. George was watching her out of the corner of his eye, pretending not to. But Renata wasn't going to run. She wouldn't get more than a few steps without him tackling her. Eventually, Bonnie Best pulled up in front of them in her dark sedan. Renata sighed and pulled open the passenger door. "Well, see you later."

"Not too soon, Renny."

He put her formula in the back and saw to Renata getting in and getting buckled up.

"Behave," he warned her again, and shut the door.

Best pulled the car out of the loading zone and in a few minutes, they were in traffic. Renata's mind was going a mile a minute, trying to figure out what to do. She didn't have much time, being escorted from one facility to the next. She couldn't jump out in traffic or try to run away. But she had no idea how tight the security would be at her destination. Even the hospital had tightened up security enough to keep her from escaping again over the past few months.

"I'm hungry," she told Best.

The social worker looked over at Renata, frowning. "You'll have to wait until we get there."

"But I'm really hungry. I'm starving. If my blood sugar gets too low, I could go into a coma. Didn't they tell you about my blood sugar?"

"No. They said that you can't eat. That you can only have that," Best jerked her head toward the back seat to indicate the carton of formula.

"That's what they usually give me. I haven't had anything else for months… I wish I could get a milkshake…"

"A milkshake? I didn't think you could take anything by mouth."

"I wouldn't, I'd put it straight in my tube," Renata said, tapping it under her shirt.

"Then why would it matter if you get formula or a milkshake? You can't taste it."

"It's not the same," Renata wheedled. "You know how they say when you lose one sense, it makes your other senses sharper? It's just the same with taste. With the milkshake, I can feel the cold in my belly, I can smell it, and it just… it's different in my stomach. You can tell the difference between if you eat a salad or eat pizza or something, can't you? It feels different in your stomach. The pizza is more satisfying…"

Best made a face. "Yes… I suppose so…"

"Well, all I've had in my stomach for months is that awful formula. It's not satisfying. It doesn't smell good. It's always room temperature. I just want a super-cold, sweet-smelling, satisfying vanilla shake. No… chocolate. I looove the smell of chocolate. And the way it makes me feel…"

The social worker looked at her watch. "We need to get you transferred."

"You won't even let me have a milkshake? When I haven't had anything but wretched formula in the whole time I've been in hospital? And that's all they're going to give me at the new place."

"I can't really do that."

"I hope you don't have any kids," Renata snapped.

"Why?"

"Because you'd make the worst mom ever. You won't let me have a milk-shake? Just a little, cheapo milkshake? Come on… pleeeease?"

An experienced social worker would have stood up to Renata. She would have known that Renata was a runner and a liar. And that she couldn't have anything except the formula sitting in the back seat. She would have been tough enough to stand up to a whining, pleading kid who didn't know what was best for her. But Bonnie Best was not an experienced social worker. She hadn't developed a tough skin yet. And she didn't trust her limited knowledge of Renata's medical condition and care.

Best scanned the street on either side of them.

"There's a mall just over there," Renata pointed out.

Best shook her head. "No. Hmm. How about there? The drive-through?"

Renata shrugged. "Sure, I don't care where we get it."

The social worker pulled over at the next corner and wound her way around to the drive-through window. They had to wait for a couple of cars to go through ahead of them. Renata was looking around for some pathway of escape.

"Chocolate?"

"Yeah," Renata answered absently.

"What size?"

"Doesn't matter. Small is fine."

"They have a lot of different flavors," Best pointed out. "Renata? Are you sure you don't want to try another one?"

"No," Renata scowled, irritated. "Just chocolate is fine."

Best ordered the milkshake, and in a few minutes they were up to the payment window, and Best handed it to Renata. "There you go. Enjoy."

She pulled out into traffic again and glanced over at Renata.

"Aren't you going to… do something with it?" she asked.

"I need to stop at a restroom," Renata said, staring down at the milkshake she was holding. "I have to clean up. Keep everything sanitary, you know. I can't just put this down my tube without… sanitizing the tube first."

"You need a restroom?" the social worker repeated in a tone of disbelief.

"Yeah. You know. To clean up. You wouldn't let your kids eat without making them wash their hands first would you?"

"Why didn't you say that before? You knew there was nowhere to wash up at the drive-through."

"I suggested the mall. You're the one who picked the drive-through."

Best rolled her eyes and shook her head. "You'll have to wait until we get there, then. You can… *eat…* when we get you home."

"But I'm starving! Come on!"

"I shouldn't have even gotten it. I can't stop again. You'll have to wait."

"Just stop at a gas station or mall. I'll be two minutes. I'm really, really hungry."

Best shook her head.

"Pleeease…" It had worked before, so Renata tried again.

Turning the wheel, Best made a growling sound. "No."

Renata put the milkshake into the cup holder. "You have it, then."

Best drove for a couple more minutes before turning in at a gas station. "I have to fill up. Be quick, will you?"

"Really?"

"Hurry up. Don't keep me waiting."

Renata jumped out of the car and hurried into the gas station. Best watched her all the way in. Renata headed to the back hallway. There was an 'employees only' door. Renata didn't hesitate. She went straight through the door, cutting through the stock room and out the back into the alley.

Sayonara Bonnie Best.

CHAPTER SIX

Gabriel looked around the food court and picked out the girl in the wheelchair in the main seating area. With a name like Carmel, he had not expected a blond. But he didn't see any other likely choices. He approached her.

"Uh, hey. Are you Carmel?"

"You see any other wheelchairs?"

"I'm Gabriel," he introduced himself, trying not to rise to the bait.

She motioned to the seat across from her. "Have a seat."

They both sat down and looked each other over.

"It's good to meet you," Carmel said.

"You too. The message that I got said that you had a case to tell me about."

Carmel nodded. She didn't start in right away. "You want to get something to eat?"

"No, I have to watch what I eat. Junk just makes me feel bad."

She was staring at him, her eyes intense.

"So you're really Gabriel. *The* Gabriel."

"The Gabriel? I guess so… depends on what you've heard."

"The work that you guys are doing is so cool. Really. I saw you on TV when you did that show with Kirstie Holt. I wanted to meet you. I never thought… that I'd actually get to work with you."

Gabriel smiled, feeling a wave of warmth as he blushed. "Well, I'm not exactly a celebrity, but that's cool. I'm glad to meet you too. I heard, through the grapevine, that you've been really helpful moving a couple of others through the railway."

"The Underground Railway. I love that you're doing this. It's so... romantic... noble... I don't know what to call it."

"It doesn't feel that way when it's been a week since I had a shower or I'm shivering trying to get to sleep. Mostly it's just hard work. But you've been helping out; you know what it's like."

She nodded, smiling for the first time.

"So..." Gabriel thought maybe he should have purchased at least a coffee so that he would look natural sitting with Carmel in the food court. He didn't want to prompt her again to tell him her story, but he wasn't much good at small talk, and he was there for a purpose.

"I heard about a case from a judge," Carmel offered at last. "She believes it's a case of medical kidnap, but it's not her case, and she can't interfere with it or influence the judge in charge."

Gabriel nodded. It gave him a good feeling, knowing that even social workers and judges who were forced to funnel kids into care knew about the underground railway and sometimes gave them a tip.

"The boy's name is Seth. Seth Wilcox. He has—"

"Seth Wilcox?" Gabriel interrupted, stunned. "I've met his mom. She's a huge mito advocate. They took Seth away?"

Carmel nodded. "He had an episode at Disneyland and the doctors in California started an investigation. They tried to avoid it by coming back home, where the doctors knew Seth and his history, but the California authorities pushed it through..."

"When did this happened? I remember them raising money for Disneyland."

"He's just been taken into care. His mom is afraid that he won't get the proper treatment in foster care. They've already said they want his feeding tube removed and have quashed further medical tests."

Gabriel swore under his breath. Leva Wilcox was a big name in the mito community. Social Services had made a huge mistake in interfering with Seth's care.

"What is she going to do?" he asked Carmel. "Knowing Leva, she'll sue them, won't she? She won't want to change her identity to go underground."

"Fighting it in court would take months, at least. In that amount of time, he could be dead. You know how some medically fragile kids are… while they're with their families, they have good quality of life. After a few months in care, they look like skeletons."

"Especially if they take his tube out," Gabriel said. "Don't they think he has it for a reason? Parents don't opt to have a child with a feeding tube because it makes it more convenient. It's about him getting enough nourishment! And it's twice as important for a kid with mito. It's all about cellular energy."

Carmel took a sip from her smoothie cup. "Have you ever had a feeding tube?"

"Me? Luckily, no. But sometimes they're necessary. Like with Renata."

Carmel obviously knew who Renata was too. Like Gabriel, Renata had been on the show with Kirstie. Neither had used their names at the time, but they had quickly become known.

"I talked to his mom. Leva. She's willing to consider going underground. It's the only way to get him back quickly before they can do too much damage."

Gabriel thought about it. While an advocate like Leva might normally go to the public and challenge the decision in court, that would not result in her getting Seth back right away. The Social Services investigation still had to be completed and that would take weeks or months. Then they would have particular recommendations and a plan that transitioned Seth back into Leva's care gradually, even though it had been fine for them just to rip him out of his home in the first place. They would want ongoing supervision, and if anything else happened to make them think that she was abusing him or making him sicker, they would act immediately. As much as she might want to prove to the world that she was not guilty of abuse, it was more important to get her son back.

"What are the charges?"

"They're alleging Munchausen by Proxy. They think she intentionally caused the episode in California."

"That's what they tried to use against my mom, too. What was it that happened in California?"

"Electrolytes. His sodium levels were too high. They said it was too high to have been caused by dehydration and she must have given him something."

"They'll admit they don't understand mitochondrial disorder," Gabriel said, "they don't know how it all works and how it affects every system. But one incident of blood work that they don't understand, and they're willing to say that she's poisoning him." He shook his head. "Typical."

Carmel sucked on her straw, nodding. "So, what do you think? You want to take it on?"

"I'll have to do a bit of research and see what I can find out. But… I know Leva. I can't see myself turning them down."

"Good. Should I tell the judge that?"

"No." Gabriel was aware that his tone was brittle. Too harsh. "You can't involve a judge in the operation. Anything you tell her, she'd have to report. Whatever she said to you, she would have been careful to couch in vague references. And she couldn't actually ask you or the railway for help. Right?"

"Right. I had to… read between the lines."

"Exactly. So, no. Don't say anything to her about it. She'll probably see it in the papers anyway; this one might get some press. Or she'd hear rumors through the judicial grapevine. But you never say another word."

"Got it," Carmel gave him an odd little smile. Gabriel was aware that he had just repeated himself ten times like she might not have understood him the first time. But he couldn't chance her misunderstanding. They couldn't have a judge letting the cat out of the bag.

"Which judge was it?" Gabriel got up to leave.

"Judge Dee-Dee."

Gabriel couldn't believe it at first. Then he laughed. "She's done a complete turnaround. From being a stooge to Social Services to going behind their backs on a case she doesn't agree with. That's good—I'd rather have her on our side! She could have let me go to prison, but she didn't. She made it easy for me to slip away again."

"She really admires you. She said so."

Gabriel felt himself flush again. He didn't know what to say to that.

"So I'll see you again…?" Carmel asked. "After you've looked into it, will you let me know? I'd like to help, if I could take him part of the way."

Gabriel looked her over uncertainly. He knew that she had helped out with other transfers, more on logistics and communications than the actual physical transfers. He wasn't sure what she would be capable of doing.

"Just because I'm in a wheelchair doesn't mean that I can't help," Carmel told him. "And I don't need the wheelchair all the time. Just when I get tired."

"I know," Gabriel said. "I've used a wheelchair sometimes too. It's just that… I don't know how easy it would be for you to stay undercover. Don't you think people would notice you?"

Carmel gave a bark of laughter. "Is that what you found when you use a wheelchair? Everybody notices you?"

"Well… no. I found most people ignore me," Gabriel remembered. "Look away from me and pretend I'm not even there."

"Exactly. So don't give me any grief. I wouldn't offer if I didn't think I could really help. I could do it. I want to."

Gabriel gave a noncommittal shrug. "Give me a chance to look into it first, and then we'll see about whether you can help on the actual transfer. I appreciate you bringing me the message, and being so willing to help out."

She nodded, her mouth turning downward. She obviously figured he was brushing her off and that she didn't have a chance of helping Seth out. Gabriel didn't bother trying to sort her out. If she were going to assume he had dismissed her, that was her problem. That wasn't what he had said.

———

Gabriel was always nervous going to the hospital. He felt like they were going to capture him and lock him up in secure psych again. He didn't have fond memories of the unit. Even though he had been to the hospital plenty of times before for his own medical problems, all that had been pushed aside in his mind, leaving room only for the anxiety that they were going to catch him. And send him back.

Carol Scott said that they were no longer putting the mito kids they apprehended and the other medical kidnap cases straight into psych. Judge Dee-Dee and several others had rapped social workers on the knuckles. Kirstie Holt's exposé had brought the practice to the public's attention, and someone had to take the fall.

So knuckles were rapped, but there were no long-term repercussions. Those same social workers were still on the job, out there conducting investigations and making judgments about parents like Leva and Gabriel's mother. Good, hard-working, loving parents who spent all their time and resources making sure that their children had the very best care. The same doctors who had admitted Gabriel and other kids into secure psych so that they could be demedicalized or restrained by the use of psychoactive drugs were still at the hospitals, approving care plans for other kids.

But they were no longer allowed to put them into psych without a solid evaluation, so that meant that it was easier for Gabriel and the other helpers on the underground railway to visit victims of medical kidnap, talk to them, and sometimes to get them away. Usually, they waited until kids were released from hospital and transferred to their new foster families to help them disappear. It was just less risky that way. Less chance of being charged with kidnapping.

"What unit is Seth Wilcox in?" Gabriel asked the young man behind the reception desk at the main entrance.

The man wore hospital scrubs, and his name tag said only his first name, Danny. He leaned over his computer and tapped the name in.

"Red West," he advised. "Room seventeen."

"Thanks."

The floor plan of the hospital was convoluted, due to being added on to many times over the years, the same as many of the hospitals that Gabriel had visited. And in an effort to make it more user-friendly, the units had been color coded and given a compass point, depending on which wing of the hospital they were in. It was supposed to make it easier than numbering them like most hospitals did, but most users found it to be an incredibly confusing system.

But Gabriel knew where Red West was. He'd stayed there a number of times over the years. He didn't bother following the red line on the floor, which he knew would take him to Red South rather than Red West, and instead headed for the elevator bank, where he would need to go down one floor to cross into the west wing.

He was there in ten minutes, looking at the names on the displays beside the doors. The numbers on the door were more difficult to see, as the doors were generally pushed all the way open, out of sight of the hallway. He found Seth's name and peeked in.

A wave of *déjà vu* took him back to when he had lain in a bed in that very room, staring out the window at the uninspiring view of the east wing. How many weeks had he been there, as they tried to figure out what was wrong with him so that they could treat him properly? They had been the ones to finally diagnose mitochondrial disease, which had been a life sentence instead of the reprieve Gabriel had hoped for. It seemed like a long, long time ago.

The boy in the bed was dark blond, his hair spiky. He was thin and fretful-looking. He turned his head as Gabriel entered the room. Gabriel checked the other bed and found it empty. He turned back around to face Seth.

"He was released," Seth said, indicating the empty bed. "If you're looking for him."

"No. I was just checking to see if we were alone. How are you, Seth?"

"I don't feel very good." Seth made a little *urp* of a belch and swallowed. "But… I never feel very good. Who are you? You're not a doctor or a nurse here."

"No," Gabriel agreed, smiling in a way that he hoped was reassuring. Seth could undoubtedly tell that Gabriel was too young to be a doctor or a nurse, just a few years older than Seth was himself.

"Then who are you?"

"My name is Gabriel."

Gabriel waited for it to sink in, wondering whether Leva had ever mentioned him to Seth. Had she told him about the underground railway, taking kidnapped kids to freedom? Back to their parents, where they were safe and cared for?

Seth showed no recognition of the name. He turned on his side and punched his pillow, looking for a comfortable position. Gabriel remembered how it was, how sore he would get lying in a hospital bed all day, shifting position a hundred times and never able to get comfortable.

"How long have you been here?"

"I don't know. A week. More or less." Seth shifted again, sighing loudly. "I went to Disneyland, you know. I should still be there. I never got to go on all the rides."

"Yeah. What happened while you were there?"

"I blacked out on the roller coaster. Not because I was scared or I fainted," Seth made sure Gabriel wouldn't think that he was a wimp. "My blood levels were messed up. So I had to go back to hospital."

"That sucks."

"Yeah. Mom said this is my forty-eighth time in hospital. I practically live here."

"That's a lot. I always hated having to go to the hospital. It was more comfortable at home, where I had my own stuff and could watch the shows I wanted or use my computer. Here, the channels and the wifi always stink."

Seth nodded in eager agreement. "And if you want to play games, you have to go to the game rooms. And wait for everybody else ahead of you. And then they probably don't have any games you want, and the controllers don't work." Seth sighed in exasperation. "But they won't even let me leave my room right now."

"Why not? Aren't you well enough to get around?"

"Yes, I say I am. But Social Services says I have to stay put until they're sure that I'm strong, and no one is doing anything to hurt me." He leaned toward Gabriel, his eyes getting bigger. "They already said my mom can't stay with me. She can't even visit without a guard in the room. So who else do they think is going to hurt me if I go into the game room?"

"It does seem sort of stupid," Seth agreed.

"It is. Stupid." He flopped back again.

"When was your mom here last? Are they at least letting her visit you?"

"Only when they say. And with a guard in the room. And she's not allowed to touch me, not even to clip my toenails." Seth's eyes filled with tears of frustration. "What do they think is going to happen? They won't let her feed me, so how do they think she's going to hurt me?"

"I don't know," Gabriel admitted. "I don't think she's going to stab you with the nail clippers."

"Yeah!" Seth laughed at that. "What's she going to do? Stab me with nail clippers?"

Gabriel shrugged and shook his head, rolling his eyes dramatically. "What's she going to do?"

They both subsided into silence. Gabriel rubbed the back of his neck.

"Has she ever done anything to hurt you, Seth? Put anything in your feeding tube or hit you? Given you something that made you sick?"

"No. She wouldn't do that."

"Yeah. They thought that my mom did too. They took me away when they said that they thought she was hurting me."

"Really?" Seth's expression brightened at this. "But she didn't, did she? She took care of you when you were sick. That's all. She just took care of you."

"Yup. She never hit me. Never gave me any foods that would make me sick. It was just my mito."

"You have mito? I have mito!"

"I know you do," Gabriel said, smiling. "I think that's cool that we both have it, don't you?"

"Yeah, cool."

"Having mito sucks. But I know that your mom has done a ton of research. She talks to a lot of other moms and doctors so that she can figure out how to keep you the healthiest she can."

"How do you know that?"

"Because I have mito too, so I read whatever people are posting about it. I've read a lot of what she has to say and I've even met her."

Seth was staring at the TV, mesmerized by the images that flashed across it. Gabriel wondered what Seth had heard and what just went straight over his head. Mito could cause attention problems, in addition to the social difficulties that went along with pervasive developmental disorders. Which meant that sometimes Seth was 'on' and could communicate at an age-appropriate level, and other times he was gone, too distracted to carry on a conversation, or too foggy from medications or mito to put his thoughts into coherent words.

"I'm feeling better," Seth said suddenly, surprising Gabriel.

"Are you? When did you start feeling better?"

"Well, the doctor in California did dialysis, so I felt a lot better after that. But when we had to drive here, I got really tired, and I didn't want to eat or talk to anyone."

"You drove all the way at once?"

"Yeah."

"I'd be tired too. I don't like driving more than a couple of hours at a time."

Seth nodded.

"But then you felt better when you'd had some rest? Are all your bloods good now?"

"Yeah. Since Mom had to go away, I've been feeling better."

Not surprising, Gabriel thought. It would take a while to recover from such a bad episode and driving wouldn't have made it better. A few days in bed would have Seth feeling a lot better.

"I'm glad to hear it. Has Social Services told you what they plan on doing?" At Seth's blank look, Gabriel offered further details. "Are they going to put you in a foster home? A group home? How long are they going to keep you here?"

"The doctor said I could go home soon."

"Did he? And where did the social worker say that you would be going? Where will home be?"

"Home," Seth said, shrugging. It didn't sound like he understood he wouldn't be going back to his own home. He would be going somewhere else.

"A foster home?"

"No. Back to my home," Seth insisted.

"They won't take you back to your home because they're not giving custody back to your mom. They want to stay in control. So are they going to put you into a foster home?"

"I don't know." Seth shook his head and rubbed his temples. He looked over at his bedside table and Gabriel tried to anticipate what he wanted.

"Water?"

Seth hesitated, looking for something else, and then he nodded. "Yes. Water. Have to keep hydrated. They took me off of IV." Seth showed Gabriel the gauze taped to his hand, where they had removed the IV needle.

Gabriel handed Seth the cup of water with the straw in it. Seth took a few sips and handed it back.

"That's not enough to stay hydrated," Gabriel countered. "The nurses will be getting after you."

"Yeah." Seth gave a little grin. "They keep coming in and telling me I have to drink more. Don't want to have another episode." His mischievous smile widened, and he shook his head in amusement. "I'm not going to have another episode."

"I hope not. That isn't much fun."

"No. But it's kind of fun to bug the nurses."

"Oh, I see. You're a bit of a troublemaker, are you?"

Seth's eyes flickered back to the TV. "It's more interesting than the daytime soaps."

Gabriel nodded and laughed. He picked up Seth's chart at the end of the bed and flipped through it, trying to decipher all the notations. It looked like Seth had been doing pretty well the last few days. His blood levels were all perfect. Vitals were normal. It had been a rapid recovery. That was a testament to all the work that Leva had done to keep Seth's body functioning at the highest level possible.

———

Renata waited impatiently for Gabriel to show up. It seemed like a lifetime since she had seen him face-to-face. They talked on the phone as often as he could manage it, but it had been so long since she had been with him that it seemed almost like a dream. A different lifetime.

Ray hadn't told him who Gabriel was looking for, so when he stepped in and looked around, he was scanning the coffee shop patrons for a girl with a book, rather than looking for Renata. His eyes skimmed over her the first time, and he was looking at the other side of the cafe for his contact when he made a sudden pivot and looked back at her, his brain processing what he had just seen. Gabriel's eyes riveted on her, and then he was pushing his way through the crowd toward her.

"Renata?" He couldn't believe what he was seeing. "Is it really you?"

He didn't wait for her reply before throwing his arms around her. It wasn't a bear hug like Nick would have given her, his arms were gentle, and he didn't pull her into him. She appreciated that he didn't want to hurt her or break any bones by mistake, but the hug was too tentative. Gabriel had never been very demonstrative. She hugged him tight, closing her eyes for a moment and fully appreciating the human contact. It had been way too long since she had hugged anyone.

Gabriel pulled back from the embrace to look at Renata's face. "When did you get out? I can't believe it's really you!"

She gave him a wide smile. They pulled apart and sat down across from each other.

"I'm on the lam," Renata informed him, so he wouldn't have to ask or guess.

"You escaped from hospital?"

"I was released from hospital. I escaped from Social Services."

"Oh, good. If they released you, you're stable. You're feeling good?"

"I'm feeling great. The fresh air, the open sky, the people…" Renata looked around the crowded coffee shop, her chest tightening. It wasn't paranoia that took over when she looked around at everyone; it was anxiety. Plain old agoraphobia after being shut up in hospital, spending most of her time in a single room. She tried not to let it show. She was happy to be out. She was happy to be free and able to interact with dozens of people. Hundreds of people. So many crowds.

She looked at Gabriel's face. He was watching her far too carefully.

"It's great," Renata assured him.

"What about meds? You'll need to keep on taking them, to stay stabilized."

Renata dug into her pockets and pulled out two plastic bottles full of viscous liquids. They had eyedropper tops.

"I'm good, see? All set with a thirty-day supply."

Gabriel nodded. "And in that time, we can figure out a new source for you. There has to be a doctor who will prescribe it for you."

Renata nodded, unworried. Gabriel looked at her, then at the floor beside the table. Then back at her again.

"This is it? No backpack? No supplies?"

"Just the clothes I'm wearing."

"We'll get you fixed up." There was a slight frown on his face as he considered what she would need and where they could source it. Renata wasn't worried about clothes or sundries. She could easily shoplift what she needed.

"It's the formula that's the problem," she told him. "I couldn't bring any with me. Left a whole case there in the social worker's car."

Gabriel brightened. He bent over his own backpack and dug around, eventually pulling out a can of powdered formula and what bags and tubing she would need for the first couple of feedings.

Renata was floored. "Where did you get that?"

"You had it with you before you went back to hospital. I kept some with me, because I didn't know when I'd see you again, or when you'd need it."

"You've been carrying my formula around with you for months? Just in case?"

Gabriel nodded, grinning.

"You think I don't know how precious space is when you're living out of a bag? What a blockhead!"

It was meant affectionately, and Gabriel's wide smile did not falter.

"The rest is in a locker," he informed her. "Your bag, all the formula you had when you had to go back to hospital, everything. We can go get it anytime."

Renata let out a sigh. She hadn't realized how much it had weighed on her. Wondering how she was going to get her hands on a food source quickly enough. How she was going to live when she had left the hospital with nothing but the clothes on her back and the meds in her pockets. But Gabriel had everything she needed. And not just what she needed, but her *own* stuff. Familiar and comfortable.

"You should have ditched it a long time ago," she told him. "What are you doing paying to store a bunch of junk that you can't use? I can replace all that crap. Aside from the formula."

"Well, now you don't have to." He looked as satisfied as the cat that swallowed the canary. He was practically purring.

"You're the best, Gabe. Honest, I don't deserve a friend like you. You're unbelievable."

Gabriel melted, laughing and looking away in embarrassment. "You hungry now?" he asked, indicating the formula. "You want to get hooked up?"

"Starving," Renata admitted. She hadn't eaten at the hospital and hadn't thought that she would be able to eat anything for a day or two, working through the logistics of finding a doctor who would prescribe the formula and then getting the prescription filled without attracting the attention of the police or Social Services. And fasting was bad for someone like Renata, her cells already starving due to mitochondrial disorder. She grabbed the equipment and formula.

"I gotta get water; I'll be a couple of minutes."

Gabriel nodded. "Come back out, though. Don't make me eat alone."

"Yeah." She knew he was remembering that one breakfast they had enjoyed together when the manager of the restaurant—not even a fine restaurant, but a fast-food joint—had tried to kick her out or force her to take her formula in the bathroom, disgusted by her hooking up her feeding tube in public. Gabriel wanted her to know that he didn't expect her to eat in the bathroom, just to mix her formula and return to the table.

She did, and when she got back, he had a drink and a sandwich for himself. A few people watched Renata covertly and whispered behind their hands when she hooked up her feeding tube. It was a bit of a shock after being sheltered by the hospital culture for so long. But she did her best to ignore the curious eyes and just focus on catching up with Gabriel.

———

Gabriel was elated that Renata was out of hospital. They fell back into a daily rhythm as if they had never been apart and the intervening months had just been a dream. And she was well, better than he had ever seen her. Her paranoia and anxiety were minimal, her mood fairly stable. She was taking her meds. After all of her sedentary time at the hospital, with enforced mealtimes, she had filled in, regaining the weight she had lost when they had initially run away, and more, so that even though she was thin, her cheeks were round and her figure a bit curvy instead of stick straight. It was everything that he could have hoped for her.

"So tell me about this girl," Renata said.

Gabriel was shaken from his reverie. He looked at Renata in confusion, having lost the thread of their conversation. He couldn't even excuse himself saying that he'd been distracted by the zoo exhibits, as he had no idea what they had walked by so far.

"Carmel?" Renata prompted.

They had been discussing Seth and his potential transfer. Gabriel blinked and refocused.

"Oh. She's seventeen, I think. She uses a wheelchair when she's out, but doesn't need it all the time. She'd still be able to use the bus or walk short distances."

"She mito?"

"No. Lyme disease. She had it for years before it was diagnosed, so she has a lot of damage they can't reverse."

Renata nodded. "Pretty?"

"What?"

Renata raised an eyebrow. "I said, 'Is she pretty?' Why are you stalling?"

"I'm not... I'm just... I suppose so. I didn't think about it."

"Uh-huh. Didn't take any notice, huh? How long has she been working with the railway?"

"Long time. She's helped with a couple of transfers. But only on the communications end, not directly."

"You trust her?"

Gabriel took a quick glance at Renata. Was it her paranoia, or something else? Was she just curious, trying to get a picture of Carmel, or was she really worried about something?

"Yes. I don't have any reason not to. She's never given us bad information. The transfers she's been involved with didn't have any problems."

"Okay. Let's meet her."

They both looked around, eyes open for Carmel. She was supposed to be near the giraffe barn. They had picked an exhibit fairly close to the entrance, since none of them had the energy to walk long distances. Gabriel wasn't sure whether Carmel would be in her wheelchair or walking around. He looked from one person to the next, trying to isolate her.

"That one?" Renata pointed to a blond in a wheelchair, pushed up to the edge of the giraffe exhibit barrier. The barrier was too high for her to see over it while she remained in the chair.

"Yeah, I think so," Gabriel picked up his pace a little and approached her. "Carmel?"

She turned around and gave him a nod. "Hey. You made it."

Renata took a few seconds to catch up and fall in beside Gabriel. She looked Carmel over and then looked at Gabriel as if accusing him of something.

"And this is…?" Carmel asked.

"Oh. Renata. Renata, Carmel. Renata is—"

"I know who Renata is!" Carmel laughed. "Nice to meet you. I'm glad to see you're free."

Carmel offered her hand. Renata gave it a quick shake and looked back at Gabriel. Gabriel wasn't sure what she wanted or what she had to be irritated about.

"Is there somewhere we could sit?" Renata suggested.

Carmel motioned to an observation area with a roof to keep off rain and a park bench to sit on farther down the exhibit area. "Over there?"

They walked to the bench and sat down, Carmel wheeling herself along beside them and parking.

"So what do you think about the situation?" Renata asked Gabriel. "Is Seth a good candidate?"

Gabriel nodded. "Sure. It's a clear case of medical kidnap; they don't have any proof that Leva has done anything. Seth has had plenty of similar episodes before; it's not an anomaly. He's had a chance to talk to social workers and doctors and police. He denies that Leva put anything in his tube. He told me the same thing. He's in good enough health to travel soon.

Leva's willing to assume an identity and go underground so that she can have him back right away. Seems like a good chance."

Carmel listened to Gabriel's evaluation and didn't have anything to add.

"Reasons against?" Renata asked.

Gabriel thought it through. "If she really did have Munchausen by Proxy," he said. "But I don't see any evidence that she does. And Seth is old enough to say if she's trying to hurt him. If she was poisoning him, he'd know it."

"How?"

Gabriel looked at Renata, then at Carmel for help. "She couldn't exactly hide it, could she? Especially if she was putting something in his tube. She'd have to do it right in front of him."

"She could hide it in a supplement. Mix it in with his formula."

"He'd still know if she was tampering with the bags. They're supposed to stay sealed until use. He'd know if she was opening them up to put something else in them. Right?"

Renata shifted, thinking about it.

"I don't think she could do anything without him knowing about it," Gabriel repeated. "He said she's not. It's just his mito. His own doctors never thought she was doing anything. Just the doctor in California who didn't know Seth's history. The doctors who treat him regularly know that it's just his mitochondrial disease."

Carmel was nodding. "Judge Dee-Dee said that there were no previous allegations. She's never been investigated before. And he's been to the hospital a lot. If it was because of abuse, they'd know."

"Okay. As long as you're sure."

"You know Leva." Gabriel looked at Renata, having a hard time believing that she would distrust the woman. "You don't think she's Munchausen, do you?"

"I don't think you can tell by looking at a person," Renata said sharply. "And just because her son has mito, that doesn't mean she can't be abusing him too."

Gabriel gave a small shrug. "I suppose. But she's such an advocate… she's so well-known in the community. Don't you think that people would start to get suspicious that something was wrong if she was hurting him? I mean… she documents everything. Everything. If there was a pattern of abuse, someone would have picked up on it."

"Okay, Gabe. If you're sure. We'll start working on a plan. And if Carmel wants to be involved," Renata flipped a hand at her, "she can help."

Carmel looked at Gabriel, looking uncertain whether to be pleased she would be allowed to help or offended by Renata referring to her as if she weren't even there. He gave her a weak smile that he hoped was reassuring. He cleared his throat.

"So I guess you and I should go see Seth next. Talk to him about getting away. We can get the lay of the land and decide the best way to get him free."

CHAPTER SEVEN

Gabriel guided Carmel up to Seth's hospital room. They didn't attract any attention. Being in a wheelchair in the hospital is just about as good as an invisibility cloak. Anyone who noticed them quickly looked away, not wanting to be caught staring at someone in a wheelchair.

"So why do you want to help?" Gabriel asked as they worked their way through the maze of hallways and underground walkways.

"Why do you?" Carmel returned. "Because there's an injustice being done… and I can't just stand by and ignore it. And I'm hoping maybe some of the karma will rub off on me, and someone will find a way to help me someday too."

"Help you…?" Gabriel's eyes were concerned and Carmel could immediately see that he was wondering if she needed to be rescued from an abusive situation herself.

"With my Lyme disease," Carmel said quickly. "Help to find a way to reverse the damage that's been done. So that I can feel better. Be physically able again."

"Ah," Gabriel nodded. "Got it."

"I just want to help. I want to be a part of the solution."

"You've been a big help so far. I'm glad that you want to help."

Carmel didn't know her way around the hospital as well as Gabriel, but it was familiar to her. She had spent some time there, though she hadn't usually been sick enough to be admitted. Mostly they took care of her at home.

They arrived at Red West, and Gabriel gestured to Seth's room. Carmel rolled in ahead of Gabriel. Seth was sitting up in his bed flipping TV channels. He turned to look at them as soon as they entered.

"You again," Seth said, looking at Gabriel. He peered down at Carmel from the high bed. "I don't know you, though."

"I'm Carmel."

"Carmel? Like in a chocolate bar?"

Carmel shook her head. "Not caramel. Carmel."

"What's that?"

"It's just my name."

"Oh." Seth looked back at the TV. He sighed peevishly. "There's never anything on."

"I know," Gabriel agreed. "Hey, Seth, do you remember what we talked about the last time I came here?"

Seth didn't look at him. "No. Just about… going home?"

"That's right. Are you getting excited about going home?"

"No."

"Because it's going to be a foster home instead of back to your mom?" Gabriel suggested.

Seth shook his head. "I just don't want to go home. I want to stay here."

"Why do you want to stay here?" Gabriel sat down in the visitor chair.

"I don't like going back and forth," Seth said. "I just want to stay here. And the food tastes better."

Gabriel chuckled. "The food tastes better? Your mom isn't a very good cook?"

"No," Seth said frankly. "She has to spend a lot of time looking after me, so she doesn't have a lot of time to learn to cook. She'd be better if she had more time."

"Yeah, that makes sense. But you must get tired of being here and want to go home again."

"I want them to bring me my TV from home. And my other stuff. Then it would be good."

"Why would you rather be here than home?" Carmel asked. "Other than the food?"

Seth stared at her for a few long moments. He had blue eyes, with little flecks in them. He stared at her intently.

"It's better here," he said eventually. "They have everything they need to take care of me. When I go home, I just get sick again and have to come back here. It would be better if I just stayed here all the time."

"But you'd like to go back to your mom, wouldn't you?" Gabriel suggested. "You want to be with her again. Did you know… we can help with that?"

"I can't go to my mom," Seth said. "It's against the rules. But she can come and visit me. As long as there's someone to watch her."

"I know. But we could take you to your mom so that you could be with her all the time. Wouldn't you like to do that?"

"No."

"You don't want to go back to your mom? Forget what Social Services said. We know ways to help kids get back to their parents."

Seth looked at the TV again. None of them said anything for a while. Seth found a cartoon and watched it without blinking. Carmel looked at Gabriel.

"Is he… okay?" she whispered.

Gabriel looked at Seth and decided it was safe to answer. "He has some delays. But his IQ is normal. Just… some attention and social issues."

"You won't take him if he says he doesn't want to go, will you?"

Gabriel sat back in his chair, chewing on his lip. "I think he really does want to; he just doesn't understand the situation yet. They've been brainwashing him. But no… I'm not going to take him against his will. They'd make kidnapping stick if we ever got caught."

"You could tell him you were just going to take him home to get his TV and other stuff."

"Lying to him would still be taking him against his will. We just have to make him understand that we're taking him to his mom, get him to agree that he wants to go to her."

Carmel nodded. "I think that's going to take some doing."

Gabriel sighed. His eyes were distant as he considered how to handle Seth. "If we do transfer him, it's going to have to be different from the others. Usually, we take a few days to a week. Get the kid out of town and make sure we lose any tails. Leave the parents in place so that Social Services isn't tipped off to the fact that we're taking them out of town. Arrange the reunion when it's safe. But with Seth…"

Seth looked over at Gabriel, hearing his name. Then he decided Gabriel wasn't talking to him and went back to watching TV.

"We can't have him changing his mind because we take too long. I think we need to get Leva out of town first, make sure she's in place, and then take Seth directly to her. We can't be sleeping rough or traveling an extended length of time with him. As soon as he gets tired, he's going to start whining that he doesn't want to go, and then we're putting ourselves in the position of taking him against his will."

"We have to reunite them within a few hours."

"Yeah. I don't see any other way. He's not going to have the patience to travel around for a few days."

Carmel nodded. "This is going to be a tricky one."

———

———

Carmel took a few deep breaths to calm herself down. She needed to stay relaxed and focused. She couldn't walk into Seth's unit looking worried or anxious. She had to look like she was just there to visit a friend. Just like people had come to visit her when she'd been in hospital. She had just as much of a right to be there as anyone else.

She wheeled her chair past the nursing station. The two nurses at the computer, one sitting and one standing and bending over, looking over the first nurse's shoulder, didn't give her a glance. Carmel pushed herself into Seth's room. He was sitting on the edge of his bed, bare legs dangling over the edge. He looked at Carmel.

"You're finally here. You took a long time!"

Carmel hoped that her smile was reassuring. "Have you been waiting long?" she asked. "I'm sorry."

"You said you'd be here at eleven-thirty. It's almost twelve."

Carmel looked at the cheap clock sitting on the nightstand. It said eleven thirty-five.

"Sorry," she apologized again. "So, are you ready to go see your mom?"

This was the test. If he didn't freely agree to go, they couldn't take him. He had to agree, and he had to understand where they were going.

"Yeah," Seth agreed. He ran his fingers through his hair, further mussing his already disordered blond spikes. "It's been forever since I saw her."

That had been Gabriel's doing. Arrange it so that Leva wasn't visiting him every day, so that Seth had a chance to miss her. He didn't have any motivation to go to her if she were always there for him in spite of the Social Services investigation. Leva hadn't been happy about being pulled back, but she agreed. It had apparently worked.

"Great," Carmel approved. "Do you remember what we're going to do?"

Seth nodded. "Wait until lunch is delivered. Walk beside the lunch cart when it goes past the nursing station. Go to another floor to change into my clothes."

"Good. Put your things in this backpack." Carmel pulled out a backpack emblazoned with the local NBA team.

"That's my team!" Seth cheered.

"That's what I hear," Carmel agreed. She held it open on her lap while he took his clothes and a few personal items from the narrow closet and stuffed them in.

"Can we go now?"

"Wait until they bring your lunch. It won't be long now."

He returned to his bed and flipped restlessly through channels on the TV. "I'm tired of staying in bed. I'm feeling better now; I don't want to stay in bed anymore."

"That's why we're going to go to your mom now. She won't make you stay in bed all day, will she?"

"No," Seth agreed. "She only makes me stay in bed if I'm really sick."

Carmel did up the backpack. "You're feeling pretty good now?"

"I'm all better now."

Seth looked at the door, impatient for the lunch cart to arrive.

"It will just be a few minutes now," Carmel assured him. "Just watch TV for a little while."

He sighed loudly. The time passed excruciatingly slowly. They should have been taking lunches around, but seemed to be running late. Finally, Carmel heard the familiar noise of the lunch cart coming down the hall.

"So just act like you're going to eat lunch like normal," she told Seth in a low voice. "We'll go after the cart is past your room."

"I *know*."

It was a few minutes before the lunch cart got to Seth's room. He kept looking anxiously toward the door. A harried-looking nurse came into the room and slapped a tray down.

"There you are, Mister Seth." Her eyes flickered over to Carmel. "You have a visitor today?"

"I'm going to see my mom today."

Carmel bit her lip and kept her face flat and expressionless, showing no reaction to this news. She and Gabriel had agreed not to tell Seth to keep his plans a secret or to tell lies to cover them up. He would just end up making them suspicious.

"Are you?" The distracted nurse made a couple of notes on Seth's chart. "She's coming for a visit, is she?"

"No," Seth disagreed.

The nurse didn't even look at him. Just flashed a smile, and went back out to the hallway. Seth looked at Carmel.

"*Now* can we go?"

"Just give it a minute." Carmel was worried about a nurse taking lunches around instead of an orderly or volunteer. The nurse would know that Seth was supposed to remain in his bed in his room and not be wandering the halls. The whole point of waiting until the lunch cart went by was to screen them as they walked past the nurse's station. The tall shelves filled with lunch trays would camouflage them from view.

It was up to Carmel to make the call to go ahead or to delay for another day or two.

If they were challenged, Carmel could claim that they were just going for a walk around the unit and that she didn't know Seth wasn't allowed. Seth might or might not say something to make them suspicious. They couldn't do anything to Carmel, but they might increase security precautions if they thought there were a plot afoot.

Carmel heard the cart stop at the next hospital room.

"Okay. Let's go."

Seth moved more quickly than she had expected. She had to tug on his sleeve to slow him down.

"Not so fast. Just walk slowly."

He gave her an irritated look, but did as he was told. They walked past the next couple of rooms, the second occupied by the nurse distributing lunches. No one stopped them. They continued their leisurely progress out of the unit and Carmel breathed a sigh of relief. They weren't in the clear yet, but getting out of the unit without being stopped was the first milestone. Getting past the nurses was the biggest difficulty she and Gabriel had identified.

They made it to the elevator, and as planned, went down to another floor and found a restroom for Seth to change into his street clothes. Then they took a wandering route outside to where Gabriel was waiting.

"How did it go?" he asked immediately.

"Pretty smoothly. It was a nurse taking lunches around, but no one tried to stop us."

"Great. You ready to go, Seth?"

Seth looked at Gabriel. "Where's your car?"

"We're going to take the bus and walk for a little while." Gabriel looked back at Carmel. "We'll split up here and I'll meet you like we planned, right? Text me if anything looks suspicious."

"Okay. See you there."

Gabriel started walking, motioning Seth to follow him.

"You don't have a car?" Seth was whining as they walked away.

———

The name of the boy who was escorting Leva was Nelson Schmer. A pretty unfortunate name, Renata thought. Schmer was bad enough to start with, without coupling it with Nelson. The kid sounded like a nerd without even meeting him. He was to make contact with Leva at a rare diseases conference she was attending and to bring her to the 'railway station' that Renata was managing. Leva had been warned to get all her papers in order and to be ready to move, but hadn't been told when she would be contacted or where she would be meeting Seth. Each step along the railway was supposed to be blind so that one volunteer could not expose the others if questioned.

One benefit of helping on the parent's end of a transfer instead of the kid's was that they didn't have to depend so much on public transportation. Leva would sell her car and rent a new one using her new identity, making it harder to trace her. Nelson would stay with her to direct her to Renata's station. Which, as it turned out, was a gas station convenience store. Renata watched for them, not knowing what kind of vehicle they would be arriving in.

She didn't want to be hanging around for too long, attracting the attention of the employees. She had a coffee in the restaurant attached to the gas station, and then went and browsed the convenience store shelves, keeping an eye out the front window. If it took too long, she would move on to the gas station across the street. If there were a problem and they still didn't show up, they would do a reset and arrange a new meeting place.

A white Focus pulled up to the pumps, and a dark-haired teenage boy jumped out. Renata couldn't make out the driver's face through the glare on the windshield until the woman opened her door and got out. Renata recognized Leva Wilcox. Nelson hadn't gotten out of the car to pump gas like Renata had originally assumed, but was making a beeline for the convenience store. He hurried through the entrance and darted past Renata, looking around for the restrooms.

Renata watched him disappear into the back hallway, then turned her attention back to Leva. Leva paid at the pump, hopefully with her brand new credit card, pumped her gas, and then walked into the convenience store.

Her eyes went around the store and landed on Renata. She didn't say anything, unsure whether Renata was her contact.

"Nelson's in the restroom," Renata offered.

Leva's expression relaxed and she stepped up to Renata.

"Hi. Was he… okay? I don't think my driving is that bad, but he seemed a little…" she searched for a word, "car sick…?"

Renata gave a chuckle. "No, it wasn't your driving," she said. "He didn't tell you anything about himself?"

"No, not really. Mostly he just asked about Seth."

Renata nodded and didn't fill her in. It was up to Nelson how much he wanted to reveal about himself. Some volunteers wanted to remain completely anonymous; others liked to share more. Maybe Schmer didn't want his contact to know anything more than his name.

They waited, pretending to browse the snack racks. Leva looked at her watch.

"Am I supposed to wait for him? Or are just you taking me on the next leg?"

"He's supposed to be coming along. We'll give him a few more minutes."

"Is something wrong, do you think?"

"Give him some time," Renata said. "We're not in a hurry yet."

It took him long enough that Renata *was* getting anxious about the gas station employees watching her and making too many glances toward the restrooms. She had Leva move her car away from the pump and considered whether they should order something in the restaurant while they were waiting.

Finally, Nelson made his way back through the convenience store. His face was pale and glistened with a thin sheen of sweat. He looked at Leva, then at Renata. "You must be Renata."

"Must be," Renata agreed. "Are you okay?"

"Yeah." His stomach made a jump, and he covered his mouth with his hand for a moment. He took a long breath in and let it out again. "Just need to take something for my stomach."

"Can I get you something?" Leva offered. "A ginger ale or motion sickness pills?"

"No. I got something in my bag. Thanks."

"Ready to go then?" Renata asked.

"Uh… yeah. I'm good to go. In just a minute."

They went out to the car. Nelson grabbed his backpack from the passenger's seat to get his medication out. Leva's eyes were concerned and didn't leave his face. He shook a couple of capsules with greenish contents into his hand, and with a sip from his water bottle, swallowed them down.

"What kind of herbs do you take?" Leva asked, tearing her gaze away from Nelson and getting into the car. They all got into the car to continue the discussion, Nelson motioning for Renata to take the front seat.

"It's more of a weed than an herb," Nelson said with a weak smile.

"What does that mean?" Leva asked, then it clicked. "Oh… you mean… medical marijuana?"

Nelson nodded.

"Oh. I've heard it's good for nausea."

"About the only thing that does any good."

"How long does it take to work?"

"It's pretty quick," Nelson said. "We can go, you don't have to wait."

Leva put the car into drive and pulled out. She glanced a couple of times at Nelson in the rear-view mirror.

"Are you… on chemo or something?"

Nelson sighed. His face was getting red. "No… it's called CVS. It's a chronic condition. They don't really know what causes it. But the pot is about the only thing that helps it. I can usually keep it under control, but sometimes if I'm more stressed… it can get worse again."

Leva stared at him in the mirror. "Well… it's good that you have it under control."

It was obvious that she wanted more details about Nelson's illness, but had decided it would be too rude to ask. There was a silent pause that made everyone feel uncomfortable.

"Take the next exit," Renata instructed. Leva's gaze snapped forward. She nodded and inched the car into the exit lane, focused on getting to her son. Renata checked her watch to calculate how long they had before arriving at the next station and which route they should take.

———

Gabriel was tired but tried to keep Seth occupied, kicking a soccer ball back and forth and trying to stump Seth with movie trivia. Neither of them ran to intercept the ball; they just did their best to aim a kick at the other and to block or kick it if it got close enough. Carmel sat nearby in her wheelchair, the sun shining down on her blond hair, while she watched them and occasionally looked around for anyone acting suspiciously.

Seth was much better at the movie trivia than Gabriel had expected. He often fired back additional facts in response to the questions Gabriel posed and Gabriel wasn't well enough informed to accept or reject them. Gabriel lifted his knee to block the ball, letting it drop back to the ground in front of him.

"Who's your favorite Batman?"

"That's not trivia," Seth objected. "There's no right answer!"

"No, I know. I'm just curious."

"Ask me a real question!"

"Gabriel," Carmel called. When he turned to look at her, she pointed to the edge of the field, at three figures walking toward them.

"Ask me a real question," Seth insisted again, not to be distracted.

"Seth," Leva called to him.

"Mom, I'm just—" Seth suddenly realized who was there and dropped the argument with Gabriel. "Mom!"

Leva jogged toward him. "Seth! I missed you so much!"

He kicked the ball wild, far wide of Gabriel, and ran over to her. Gabriel shook his head and trudged after the ball. He returned to the small group, smiling.

"Everything go okay?" he queried, looking around carefully, especially in the direction they had arrived from. "No trouble? No one following you?"

"Smooth as silk," Renata said.

Gabriel nodded a greeting at Nelson. Then he turned to Carmel. "We should probably split," he said. "Too many people here. Renata, you want to run through plans with Leva? Make sure she's got everything she needs?"

Renata nodded, but she was scowling at Carmel.

"You don't need me anymore?" Nelson asked.

"No." Gabriel took a second look at Nelson. "You doing okay? You look…"

"A bit rough," Nelson admitted. "Let's just say I think I'll be walking for the next few days. No more car rides until my CVS settles down again."

Gabriel nodded sympathetically. "Sorry about that. Maybe just communications next time."

Nelson nodded. "Maybe," he agreed, holding one hand against his stomach.

Gabriel took hold of the handles of Carmel's wheelchair. They had decided that the best way for her to get across the grass was for him to push at the same time as Carmel rolled her wheels so that neither of them had to do all the work. Renata stared at Gabriel as he went past her.

"How about you?" she demanded. "Everything went smooth for you?"

"Yeah, fine," Gabriel agreed. "Let's get together once Seth is settled and I get Carmel home."

"You don't need to take me home," Carmel protested. "I can get there on my own."

"I know. I'll let you handle it yourself. I just want to make sure you get off safely. This is your first field operation."

She rolled her eyes, but let Gabriel push her up over the edge of the sidewalk, where she could maneuver more easily.

"I'm almost an adult," she pointed out. "I can handle myself."

"Get in touch with me," Renata ordered Gabriel, her voice stiff. "I'll get a new burner and give the number to Ray. Call me once your fledgling is back in the nest."

Gabriel agreed. "But we shouldn't always use Ray as the intermediary. Someone else next time."

"What's wrong with Ray? I know I can trust him."

It was odd to hear Renata say that she trusted anyone. It gave Gabriel an uneasy feeling. Things weren't quite what they should be. He didn't like it. But he forced a smile.

"I trust him too. We just can't expose him so much. We should use other methods."

Renata stared hard at Gabriel, then nodded.

"Call me," she repeated.

CHAPTER EIGHT

The transfer had been so quick that it left Gabriel feeling uneasy. They had followed all the usual precautions, except for the acceleration of the timing. But the shortened timeline left him feeling uncertain whether they had been tracked or followed.

After ensuring that Carmel had gotten home safely, he switched to a new burner phone and called Ray.

"Hey," Ray greeted cheerfully. "What did you do to put a bee in Renny's bonnet?"

"I don't know… she seemed upset about something at the reunion. But I'm not sure what."

"Wouldn't have anything to do with a pretty blond, would it?"

Gabriel sputtered. "*What?* What are you talking about? Carmel?"

"Is that her name?"

Gabriel felt his face flush. "There's nothing between me and Carmel! She was just helping with the transfer. She's the one who got the transferee out of the hospital."

Ray just laughed.

"Did she say it was because of Carmel?" Gabriel demanded. "That's what she was mad about?"

"She didn't say," Ray said, snickering. "I just got the feeling…"

Gabriel shook his head. "What's her new number?" he sighed.

Ray gave it to him. Gabriel could still hear the smile in Ray's voice. Gabriel hung up and hesitated before calling Renata. Did he really want to deal with her if she were ticked off with him? He worried about it for a few minutes before deciding that he was making it worse by overthinking it. It would be less stressful actually calling her than having to think about it. So he took a steadying breath and called her.

"Gabriel?" Renata answered the phone with his name.

"Yeah, hi."

"Gabe…" Her voice didn't hold the same hard tone that it had at the reunion. Instead, she sounded worried. Almost on the edge of panic. Gabriel's mind went immediately to her meds. Was she still taking them? It hadn't been long enough for her to go off the rails already. It would take longer than that for all the psychoactive drugs to clear her system, and then for the paranoia to start building up again. "Gabe, something is wrong. I think we messed up on this one."

"What happened?" Gabriel's throat tightened. "You weren't followed…?"

"No. No, nobody seemed suspicious or anything. I don't mean that I think that we're going to get caught. Or they are. It's just that…" she trailed off.

"What?" Gabriel coaxed.

"It's Leva. I don't get a good feeling about her."

Gabriel sat down on a bus bench, his knees suddenly weak. "We checked it out. She's never even had a complaint against her before. None of the doctors who treat Seth regularly thought that she had anything to do with his illness. He has mito. The California doctors just didn't understand that."

"No… have you seen them together? Seen them interacting with each other?" Renata demanded. "There's something bad in that relationship, Gabriel. There's something wrong with her."

"She just hasn't seen him for a while. She probably felt awkward being watched. Afraid that you would judge her because of the investigation."

"I'm not stupid," Renata growled. "I know all that. But I've seen this before. My mom was poisoning me, remember? I see the way she looks at him. It's not normal. She plays the doting mother, but she's not. I think it was true. I think she is the one making him sick."

"He has mito."

"What do you know about his diagnosis?"

Gabriel considered. "Well… nothing. Just that he was diagnosed."

"Muscle biopsy? DNA sequencing? Clinical signs?"

"I don't know. I'm sorry. I didn't get those details."

"What if she just talked them into a mito diagnosis? What if he doesn't really have it?"

"Why would she do that?"

"Because she's sick. Or what if he does have mito, but she has to make him sicker? She decides he's not getting enough attention, so she does something else to him?"

"Renata…" Gabriel tried to think of what to say. "I didn't come across any evidence that she's hurting him. I think… maybe you're just stressed from the transfer. You need a break."

"A break? I just got out! I'm not imagining things, Gabriel! I'm not being paranoid. I'm telling you; there's something wrong. I think we made a mistake."

Gabriel tried to think of what to do. "Where are you?"

"Why?"

"Are you still with them? Or close by?"

"I had to leave. Couldn't hang around there any longer without it seeming awkward. But I'm still watching the house. If she continues to run with him, they could end up anywhere, and we wouldn't be able to find them again. So I'm watching…"

"How are you going to keep up if they drive away?" Gabriel challenged. "There's no point in staying there right now."

"If they drive away, I'll drive after them," Renata said. Her voice was tight. Gabriel opened his mouth to ask her how she planned to do that, when she didn't have a car or a driver's license, then decided he didn't want to know. Renata didn't have quite the same scruples as Gabriel did, and if she thought that Seth were in danger, she would feel completely justified in hot-wiring or jacking a car and going after them.

"I should come back and meet with you. You can tell me what happened, and we'll be close by and can work together if she tries to run farther."

There was silence over the phone line. Gabriel cleared his throat, uncertain. "You mean it?" Renata finally asked.

"Yeah. Is that okay? I can come?"

"Sure." Renata gave him some directions. "Text me when you get closer and give me the all-clear."

"Okay." The sky was already getting dark. It had been a long day. "Are you camping there overnight? I'm not going to get there before nightfall."

"Yeah. Maybe you'd better wait until morning. We don't need you keeling over because you did too much and didn't get any sleep."

Gabriel considered. He would get there before midnight, but his body was already complaining about how much he had done. Doing the full transfer in a day, playing soccer to keep Seth busy, and then taking Carmel all the way home again had already been too much. Renata was right. If he traveled all the way back to Renata, he might end up passed out on the bus or in hospital.

"Will you be okay on your own? You need to sleep too. You can't stay up all night watching the house."

"I'll go to sleep when they do. Seth is going to need to go to bed pretty soon. When the lights go out, I'll sleep near the car, so I'll hear it if she decides to run with him during the night."

"Okay. I'll bed down soon and I'll see you in the morning."

———

Gabriel arrived at Leva's new house. Her car was in the driveway, but Gabriel couldn't see any sign of Renata. He walked over to the car and walked around it, looking in the bushes and beside the house for her. Had she changed her mind and left? Been picked up by the police for vagrancy? She hadn't texted him back when he had given her an update that he was close and hadn't been followed.

He looked at the house, trying to decide what to do. Renata wasn't there. But he should still follow up on her concerns. After pacing back and forth a couple of times, Gabriel was startled by the front door of the house opening. He turned quickly to look at it.

"Gabriel?" Leva frowned at him, raising a coffee mug to her lips. "I wasn't expecting to see you again. Is everything okay?"

Gabriel nodded. The movement felt unnatural. She would know that he was lying. That something was wrong.

"Just checking in to make sure everything looks okay?" Leva asked.

"Yeah. Sorry, I didn't mean to scare you. Just... making sure there's nothing suspicious… we like to keep track of transfers for a few days." It was a complete lie, of course. Once a transfer was done, they stayed as far away as possible, not doing anything that might attract the attention of police or neighbors or make anyone think that there might be something wrong. "Just to make sure they are settled in and don't need anything else."

"Oh. No one told me that."

"No. We try to keep it quiet."

Leva studied him for a moment. Gabriel was sure that she could see right through him. Finally, she nodded.

"You want to come in for a few minutes?"

"Yeah, if I could. Just to make sure everything looks… safe. We want to make sure there are no security risks."

Leva stepped back, motioning for Gabriel to enter the house. Gabriel went up the sidewalk and into the house. He took a quick glance around.

The house was nearly empty, of course. They had just arrived the day before, and Leva had to leave all her furniture and most of her possessions behind to go into hiding. There were a few boxes in the living room that had been transported in the trunk of the car. They had suggested blow-up mattresses for the bedrooms until Leva could get beds. There were a table and some plastic outdoor chairs in the kitchen.

The smell of coffee made Gabriel's stomach growl.

"You drink coffee, right?" Leva asked pleasantly.

"Yes. Please."

Gabriel sat down at the table. She poured him a mug. Gabriel studied Leva, imagining that he had never seen her before. If he were seeing her for the first time and didn't know anything about her or her advocacy, what would he see?

Leva was of medium height and build. Brunette. She had an open, pleasant face. Remarkably few lines, considering the amount of hardship she had been through with Seth. He knew that she had been married to Seth's father for a few years, but like many families with chronically ill children, they hadn't been able to stay together. The stresses of constant illness, emergencies, and hospital stays had torn the family apart. So many of the kids that they helped out had only a single caregiver. Usually a devoted mother, worn out with the stress and the work.

Leva looked fresh and pleasant. She had been up for a while. Showered, dressed, hair styled, makeup done. She wore slacks and what looked like a nurse's smock. Very practical and not unattractive.

"How is Seth?" Gabriel asked, after a long sip of the hot coffee.

"He's still sleeping. He probably won't be up much before noon, with all the excitement yesterday. You can peek in on him, but don't wake him up. If you want to talk to him… you'll have to wait or come back."

"I'll bet he was glad to be home."

"Delighted. I can't thank you enough for all that you've done for us. Putting yourself and your network at risk to help us."

Gabriel nodded, his face warm.

"I know that it caused you some problems, with me being so well-known and worrying over whether Seth would cooperate. But you pulled everything off famously. Not a single hitch."

"I was worried," Gabriel admitted. "Every transfer has its challenges and this one was no exception."

She shifted, watching him, waiting for something.

"Maybe I *will* peek in at him." Gabriel stood up and walked to the bedrooms. Leva had put Seth in the large master bedroom and had taken the smaller bedroom for herself. Seth looked peaceful, his hair mussed and his blankets held up at his chin. His breathing was long and even. He looked healthy, just like any other teenager. He had on different pajamas from what he had been wearing at the hospital.

Gabriel didn't know what he was looking for. Something had made Renata uneasy, but had it just been her paranoia? Maybe she wasn't quite as stable as she had led the hospital to believe. Maybe the old anxiety was still there, just more carefully hidden. She would see danger wherever she looked.

Seth went to the bathroom and took a quick glance around. The pajamas that Seth had worn at the hospital were hung over the shower rod, obviously hand washed and hung to dry in the absence of a washer and dryer. Leva would have to get all of those things eventually, but for now, she was making do. Seth took a quick glance at the contents of the medicine cabinet. A few prescription meds. Tylenol. Toothpaste. Epsom salts. Under the sink were an array of first aid supplies and feminine products. Seth closed the cupboard again and straightened up. Leva was watching him from the hallway.

"Is something wrong, Gabriel?" she asked.

"No, sorry. Just having a look around." He gave a little chuckle. "Sort of like a surprise social worker visit. Don't worry; everything looks great. I'm sure it won't be long before you have everything set up comfortably and decorated…"

"Yes. We'll do what we can. Although finances are a definite issue right now. I can only do so much with the credit card. Then I'm going to need to raise some funds."

Gabriel knew that Leva didn't work. She sometimes got donations from the people and organizations that she advocated for, honorariums, but they wouldn't go far to support a family. She had previously raised private funding for Seth's care through online crowdfunding. Did she still have access to those monies, now that she had had to take on a new identity? In order to do more crowdfunding, she would have to get a following. She would have to post their pictures online and tell their story. People might recognize them. Without the funding, she would have to work, and she couldn't work a full-time job while taking care of Seth. He spent half of his life in hospital and needed her constant attention.

"What do you have in mind?" he asked.

She didn't answer at first, her eyes closing part way while she considered. "It won't be easy," she said, not answering his question. "I'll need to be creative. But we'll manage. You don't need to worry about us."

"I can't help wondering. I always worry about my transfers and how everything works out."

"But they manage, don't they?" Leva said. "We all have to figure it out. It's better to have a little hardship and be together."

Gabriel nodded. He walked past her and back into the living room. He glanced in at Seth again as he passed the master bedroom. The boy was still. He hadn't moved.

Gabriel forced a smile. "Well, I suppose this is goodbye. You'll pass the word on to me if there's anything else you need? Or just to let me know how it's going?"

"Of course." She smiled, a little thin-lipped. "It was so nice of you to drop by. Tell Renata 'hi' for me, next time you see her." She looked Gabriel over. "Such a nice girl."

Had she seen Renata hanging around? Had Renata telegraphed her concern? Did Leva know that Renata was the reason Gabriel had come back to check on everything? Or was it just a casual comment, completely innocent?

"I sure will."

Leva escorted Gabriel to the door and let him out. He didn't look for Renata when he stepped out. If Leva saw Renata there, she would be suspicious. Instead, Gabriel walked to the end of the private sidewalk, turned onto the city sidewalk, and marched off down the street. He could feel Leva's eyes on him until eventually, Leva shut and locked the door with a thump and a click. Gabriel glanced back over his shoulder to make sure that she was inside, and he was safe.

Gabriel turned the corner and looked around for a bus stop or convenience store; somewhere good to meet Renata if she hadn't abandoned her purpose.

"You went inside?"

Gabriel jumped at Renata's voice in his ear. He hadn't even seen her coming.

"Yes, I went inside. She saw me looking for you and invited me in. I figured that was the best way to get a handle on what's going on. To see if there is something wrong."

"What did you find out?" Renata took Gabriel's arm and they walked along aimlessly.

"Everything seems fine. I couldn't find anything wrong."

"Did you see them together?"

"Seth was sleeping. He's exhausted after yesterday. I am too. Wish I was still sleeping."

"You need to see the two of them together. That's when it makes sense. Or doesn't make sense. That's when you can see something is wrong."

"Leva seems loving and competent. I didn't see anything harmful in the house. She has all his medication. There's food in the house. Coffee. I don't know what else to do."

She walked arm-in-arm with Gabriel, at a slow pace that wouldn't wear either of them out too quickly.

"I'm tired too," Renata admitted. "Maybe that's all it is. Maybe it's just the letdown after a transfer is done."

"I always feel that too. Disappointed. Worried. Anxious. Anti-climax. I keep thinking about Katt, and how just when we thought we were safe, it all fell apart." Gabriel took a long breath in and released it. "But those are just normal feelings. When you're expecting trouble, and everything is fine, you feel sort of… restless. Disquieted."

"Yeah."

"Seth is going to be okay. We did a good thing. He's safe with his mother. Now they can live their lives together."

Renata nodded. Her lips were tight, the skin around them pale. Gabriel look down at her.

"What?" Renata demanded.

"I'm just wondering. About your mom. Did you ever hear anything from her, when you were in hospital?"

"No. She's in prison. She can't get ahold of me."

"Maybe she could. If she has phone privileges. She could call the hospital and ask for you."

"I suppose. But she didn't have any way of knowing that's where I was. For all she knew, I was in a foster family somewhere."

"She would probably hear through the grapevine. Someone would let her know how her daughter was doing. If she *did* contact you… would you talk to her?"

"She tried to kill me!" Renata looked at Gabriel in disbelief. "Why would I want to talk to her? I don't ever want to see her again in my life!"

"What was it like? When they arrested her and took you away. You must have been confused. And upset."

"No, I wasn't."

"Why not? I would have been. I was," Gabriel amended. "I was really freaked out, scared, and confused when they apprehended me. And I wanted to be with her. Didn't you still want to be with your mom?"

"No, of course not." Renata shook her head. "It was different for me. My mom really *was* trying to hurt me. It's not the same as it was for you, when there wasn't a real reason for taking you away."

"But you didn't know that at the time, did you?" Gabriel still didn't believe that Renata's mother had been poisoning her. It was just Renata's paranoia, combined with all the accusations and her physical illness. He didn't believe that Renata's mother had really been hurting her.

Renata looked at Gabriel, shaking her head. "Gabriel… I was the one who reported her."

Gabriel stared at her in shock. "You reported your own mother?"

"Wouldn't you? If your mother was trying to kill you, don't you think you would say something? You wouldn't just stay there and let her do it, would you?"

"Well… I guess… I don't know. I wouldn't want to report her, but…"

"You wouldn't want to die."

Gabriel was silent, thinking about it. He tried to wrap his mind around what it would be like to suspect your own parent of trying to murder you. He hadn't realized that it was Renata's paranoia that had led to her mother being investigated. Hadn't Social Services looked at her file to see that she was diagnosed with paranoia before they had involved the police?

"It would be hard for a kid like you, or like Seth," Renata said. "You love your mom and are attached to her. I never bonded with my mom. I'm not gonna let anyone kill me. I'm not one of those people who keeps enabling their abusers and staying where they are being hurt." She lifted her chin proudly. "I take care of myself."

"Wow."

"I've been there. That's why I look at Seth and Leva, and I know… And he doesn't want to report her. He's too scared of losing her. We can't just stand around and not do something to help him."

Gabriel shook his head. "I thought we did help them. I thought that's what we were doing. If she really is doing something to hurt him… I just can't understand it. I don't know what to do next."

"We could report them. Make an anonymous tip."

"But if you're wrong… then you're wrecking everything that we just spent all that time and effort on for no reason. And Seth is going to go into foster care and be sick and bullied and miserable. You'll send Leva to prison for no reason. We can't take the chance of being wrong."

Renata turned them around so that they were walking back the direction they came. Back toward the house again.

"I just have to make sure they're still there. That they haven't taken off again."

Gabriel didn't pull away from her. If he argued or separated from her, she would go right ahead and report them and destroy everything they had just accomplished. She needed to see that they were still in place and that everything was fine.

———

They still hadn't moved on from Seth's house. Gabriel could see that they were going to be camped out there another night. Renata was too concerned to leave yet, worried that something was going to happen. Hoping for evidence that she could show Gabriel to convince him that Leva really was abusive.

Gabriel sat down on the curb several houses down from Seth's to eat, hoping that a boost in his blood sugar would either help him figure out what to do, or help him relax so that he wouldn't be lying awake all night.

"You could talk to Carmel," Gabriel said. "She talked to Seth alone too. Maybe he said something to her that would help us figure out whether there is something wrong." He didn't want to figure it out so much as to put Renata's fears to rest.

"You think I should talk to Carmel?" Renata repeated, her voice rising. "Just what is blondie going to tell me that I don't already know. You think she's an expert in child abuse? In poisoning? Maybe she's some kind of psychologist and has accessed all Seth's childhood memories!"

Gabriel caught himself staring at her with his mouth open. He snapped it closed, shaking his head.

"I just thought… she might be able to reassure you."

"I don't need to be reassured, Gabe. I'm tired of talking about it. You won't see it. I don't want you or Miss Lyme Disease to talk me out of it! I want to do something! You want to sit around waiting until she kills him?"

Gabriel shook his head wordlessly.

"We just put an innocent kid back into the hands of a monster! We're just as guilty of putting him in danger as Social Services was in taking you away from your mom and putting you into the mito clinic. Why can't you see it?"

"I think… you're feeling anxious. What could you see in the few hours that you were with the two of them that the hospital staff didn't see in the months he has spent there? If it's that obvious, why hasn't anyone else ever reported her?"

"I guess everybody else is blind and stupid. That's all I can think of."

Gabriel breathed slowly, trying to keep from reacting to her and getting angry himself. A yelling match wasn't going to solve the situation.

"I guess… you have to do what you think is best," he told Renata finally. "I'm going to go find somewhere to sleep tonight."

Renata blinked. "You're not going to stay with me?"

"No. You can stay here if you want, if you think that's what you have to do. But I have to get a better sleep tonight and I'm not going to get that here."

"You're used to sleeping rough. What's the difference whether you sleep here or in a park or alley somewhere?"

"We're just going to get picked up for vagrancy here. People don't like you sleeping in their yards. You got through one night; I don't think you want to tempt fate sleeping here another night. But it's up to you. Go ahead, if you like."

"You just don't want to be with me."

"I'm not helping you by being here; I'm just making things worse. I think it's best if I just leave."

She closed her eyes and then turned her head away from him.

"Okay. Fine. I'll let you know if anything happens."

"Yeah." Gabriel got up, rubbing his stiff joints. "Let me know."

It didn't sound like she was planning on calling any anonymous tips in yet. Hopefully, when a day or two passed without anything happening, she'd be able to relax and leave it alone. They could move on to the next job and not stay stuck in one place.

CHAPTER NINE

Sleep didn't come as easily as Gabriel had hoped. He had been looking forward to spending the night with Renata. Cuddling up and sharing body heat like they had when he had run away. Instead, he was alone again, like most other nights. His body was restless, and he couldn't lie still and find sleep like usual. The ground was hard even though he was used to sleeping outdoors.

When he did drift off to sleep, it was a shallow, disrupted sleep, full of dreams that made him feel more tired rather than rested.

He rose before dawn and after packing up his things and taking care of his immediate physical needs, he tried calling Renata. There was a possibility that she'd still be asleep, but it wasn't very likely. She would also need to make sure she was up and wouldn't be discovered by early morning commuters.

Renata's phone went directly to voicemail.

Had she turned it off? When they had been on the run together, she had only turned her phone on when she wanted to call someone else. She kept it off the rest of the time to avoid being tracked. Even if she bought a burner phone, she wanted to be sure that no one could use it to GPS track her. She would use it a few times, shutting it off when not in use or expecting a contact, and then toss it and get a new one. Gabriel followed a similar protocol, though he usually kept his phone on between uses, relying on the fact that only one or two people knew his number.

After Seth's transfer, Renata had kept her phone on so that he could call her.

Had she been picked up by the police, and they had shut it off?

Or had it run out of battery power and she hadn't been able to recharge it yet?

Or did Renata just not want to talk to Gabriel? She was pretty mad about him not staying with her.

"Come on, Renata. Turn on the phone." He closed his eyes, concentrating on her as if he could telepathically command her, and she would obey. She would call him and her anger would be gone. They'd laugh at her paranoia and jealousy, and everything would be back to normal again.

How long would it take before she finally realized that Seth was okay and Leva taking care of him was the best thing for him?

————

Gabriel called Carmel later in the morning.

He felt a little twinge of guilt doing so. Renata would be on the rampage if she found out that he was calling her. But how would she find out? Gabriel knew that he wasn't calling Carmel with any silly, romantic ideas. He wasn't interested in her that way. He just needed someone to talk to and bounce ideas off of. He could just as easily have called Ray, who they'd been calling too much lately, or Nelson, or any one of a dozen people whose numbers Gabriel had memorized. But Nelson needed his rest to recover, and Gabriel didn't want to talk to just anyone. He wanted to talk to someone who had been involved in Seth's transfer. He needed reassurance.

"Hello?" Carmel's voice was cautious. He'd changed phones since he'd called her last, and she'd have no way of knowing it was Gabriel.

"Hey, it's me. Is it safe to talk?"

"Gabriel!" She had to be by herself, or she wouldn't use his name. She sounded pleased. "I didn't expect to hear from you again so soon. Do we have… another job?"

"No. Just… following up on the last one."

"Oh. Okay. Everything going okay?"

"I guess. Our friend thinks there is a problem." He didn't want to name Renata aloud.

"Our friend? What problem is she worried about?"

"She thinks… the caregiver might be guilty."

There was silence from Carmel. Gabriel had been expecting an immediate protest. A laugh. But it didn't come.

"Do *you* think she is?" Carmel returned finally, her voice worried.

"No. I don't. Do you?"

"I don't know…" Carmel's voice was thoughtful. She trailed off.

"I didn't find anything in the investigation," Gabriel told her. "There's nothing suspicious in her background."

"Yes… but… Seth didn't want to go home. Not to start with."

"That doesn't mean anything. Once he understood that the only way he could see his mom again was if he went with us, he was fine." There was no immediate answer from Carmel. "Right?" he prodded sharply. She had been the one who escorted Seth from his hospital room. Only she knew what he had said before that. Seth had been eager to see Leva when Gabriel had been with him.

"Yes, yes, he was fine with it then. I wouldn't have taken him out of his room otherwise. Like you said… once he understood it was the only way to see his mom, he was okay with it."

Gabriel scratched the back of his neck.

"We did the right thing," he said.

"We followed all the precautions," Carmel said, but her voice was not confident. She obviously had doubts of her own, no matter what she said to him.

Both Renata and Carmel seemed to have doubts. Was it women's intuition? Simple nervousness over not being directly involved in a transfer before? Gabriel didn't know whether to read anything into it.

A car rolled past Gabriel. Dark sedan. Tinted windows. The kind of car that plagued his nightmares, and which he always avoided when he saw in real life, fearing a visit from one of the clinic doctors, or an undercover cop or judge. Or a hired gun. Gabriel looked around for an escape route. No one had anything on him. No way to trace him. Nothing new to charge him with. He had skipped out of the last foster home before he could face the minor charges against him, but he was pretty sure that they would just go away. The car wasn't looking for him, but it was best to avoid it anyway.

"I'll think about it, then," he said to Carmel. "Talk to you later."

He hung up the call, even though he heard that Carmel tried to answer him. After a few moments fighting paranoia, he powered off the phone. It was probably a coincidence, the dark car showing up while he was talking to Carmel on the phone. And likely the car was nothing to do with him. It wasn't anyone actually looking for him. But just in case…

He waited for the car to circle around, but it didn't. It kept driving in a straight line down the street until it was out of sight. But Gabriel couldn't shake the uneasy feeling it left him with.

———

Gabriel didn't go back to see Renata, but after a while, he did turn his phone back on in case she tried to reach him. He busied himself instead with other tasks. Checking in with contacts to see what the reports were from their various cells. Going to the library to research others cases, looking up laws and diseases he was unfamiliar with, running background on parents, judges, doctors, and social workers. There was always plenty to do, and it was easy to lose himself in research, forgetting about his worries and his own health issues as he delved deeper.

He didn't stay at any one desk or computer for too long, keeping an eye out for anyone who might be paying too much attention to him. He didn't think the police were looking too hard for him, but there were other enemies to be wary of too. The doctors at the mito clinic or other research programs that he had stolen kids away from. Each child was worth tens or even hundreds of thousands of dollars in grants. And there were other parties on the take. The car with the tinted windows had spooked him. He wondered whether he was being reasonable, or whether he was developing paranoia like Renata.

His mind was drawn reluctantly back to her. Were her worries about Seth just her paranoia? She had been right about so many things in the past. Just because she was paranoid, that didn't mean she wasn't right.

Gabriel shifted gears and typed in a search on electrolyte imbalances.

———

It wasn't Renata who called Gabriel.

It was Nelson Schmer.

"Hey," Gabriel greeted. "How are you feeling?"

"Getting better. Gabe... I had a weird call from the last transfer's mother."

"Leva?" the name slipped out before Gabe could stop it. Nelson was right to be discreet and not mention names over the phone. "Whoops. What did she have to say?"

"She was asking me questions about cannabis. Whether it was good for all nausea, or just CVS and chemo. And whether I had any... er... non-medical sources."

Gabriel frowned. He switched the phone to his other ear.

"What's going on? Why would she be asking that? Is he sick? Did she say?"

"No, I tried to find out, but she wouldn't say anything. Just kept posing 'hypothetical questions.' It kind of weirded me out. I mean before, she's always used doctors and hospitals, right? Advocating for whatever services or medications she thinks he needs. Using political pressure and public opinion to convince the doctors to listen to her...?"

"Yeah."

"Then why would she be calling me about cannabis? Why wouldn't she be trying to talk the doctors into prescribing it, if that's what she thinks he needs?"

"Because it would take too long and she needs it now," Gabriel divined. "And she doesn't want to go up in front of a judge for an emergency order when she's just gotten her identity established. Seth must be pretty sick. I'm going to head over there."

"Yeah, good idea. You think I should go too? If he's throwing up and she can't stop it, I am the expert."

"This is an emergency. You'll have to get a ride over," Gabriel pointed out. "That won't trigger you again?"

Nelson gave a little groan. "I know. I'll have to chance it."

Gabriel gave him the address. "I'll meet you there."

CHAPTER TEN

Normally, Gabriel walked and took the bus. It was rare that he would call on a volunteer on the railway to help him or to take a cab or some alternate mode of transportation. He didn't like to put other people out or to have to dig into his spare funds. Not when walking was free, and he could take the bus as many times he liked on a monthly pass.

But it was an emergency, as he had told Nelson.

It could be nothing. It could just be curiosity or hypotheticals, as Leva had indicated. Or she could be asking for someone else, a friend in her networks. There was no guarantee that there was anything wrong with Seth.

But between Renata's and Carmel's reservations, and the weird conversation with Nelson, panic set in. Gabriel needed to get back to Seth's, and he couldn't wait for the next bus. It might be too late.

The woman who picked him up went by Rose. It wasn't her first name or her last name, but it must have meant something to her. She was a retired social worker, her hair steel gray. Her face was stern, but her manner was motherly and compassionate. Gabriel thought she must have been a good social worker in her time, being able to balance those traits.

"Hop in," she invited Gabriel. "Let's burn rubber."

Gabriel obeyed, and she was pulling out before he even had his door closed. Somebody along the grapevine that had gotten her the message to pick him up had apparently lit a fire under her. Gabriel held on to the door handle and tried to do up his seatbelt one-handedly as the car leaned first one direction, then the other. It was a good thing that Nelson wasn't riding with Rose. Gabriel felt a little carsick himself.

In fifteen minutes, they were pulling in to Seth's crescent. Gabriel made a halting motion to Rose. "Stop here. I'll get out and walk the rest of the way. I don't want to attract the attention of anyone in the house."

"Do you want me to stay?" Rose asked.

"No. I'll be fine."

"Are you sure?"

Gabriel nodded. He got out of the car and headed toward the house, looking for Renata or Nelson.

Renata popped up from behind a car one house away. She beelined to Gabriel, her eyes concerned.

"What is it? What's happened?"

"Probably nothing," Gabriel said. "I just wanted to check on Seth."

"Nothing?" Renata repeated, as Nelson climbed out of a cab and joined them. "What's going on?"

Gabriel motioned to Nelson. "Fill her in. I'm going inside."

Both of them watched him speechlessly as he hurried up the walk to the front door. Gabriel took a few deep breaths. He had to be careful not to use up all his energy at once. Running to the door wasn't going to help anything. Letting panic take over and adrenaline flood his body was the worst thing he could do if he wanted to conserve his energy. He breathed in and out slowly and knocked on the door.

There was no answer. Gabriel waited. He looked back at Renata and Nelson, standing in front of the neighbor's house. Renata would know if they weren't home. If Leva had taken the car or called an ambulance, Renata would have told Gabriel instead of standing there waiting for someone to answer the door and let him in. Instead, she was watching him, waiting anxiously for the door to open. Gabriel pressed the bell several times and knocked harder. He saw a shadow through the frosted glass beside the door. He looked straight at the peephole, waiting for Leva to open the door for him. There was the sound of the deadbolt being turned, so slowly Gabriel wanted to scream. Then the handle turned, and the door cracked open. Leva looked out at him through one inch of space.

"Gabriel? What are you doing here?"

"I need to see Seth."

"Another surprise visit? You guys are worse than social workers."

"Yeah, well, I'm concerned."

"He's sleeping. It's not a good time."

"Leva. I talked to Nelson. I know you were asking him about cannabis. What's going on?"

"Nothing." She stood there for a moment, her mouth twisting as she tried to settle on an answer. "Seth has been nauseated. Probably just the flu. But I can't afford to let him get dehydrated. You know what will happen."

"Nelson came so that he can help Seth. We don't want him to get sicker either."

Leva peered past Gabriel but didn't open the door any wider to be able to see Nelson.

"I shouldn't have called him," she said, with a little shake of her head. "I wasn't trying to alarm anyone. It's nothing. I'm just being cautious."

"Let me in. I want to see him."

Leva shook her head. She looked like she was going to close the door again, then suddenly cocked her head like she had heard something.

"I have to go take care of him. Come back another day."

"I want to see him now. If you don't let me in, I'm going to call the police."

"You wouldn't do that. You don't want to see the police any more than I do."

"What are you trying to hide?"

"I'm not hiding anything. I just want to be left alone to take care of my son."

But despite her words, she swung the door wide, allowing Gabriel to enter. Gabriel hurried in before she could change her mind. But she didn't bother trying to close it behind him, she left it ajar and led the way to Seth's room.

"Mom," Gabriel heard Seth's weak voice, followed by several choking coughs.

Gabriel tried to keep his breathing even and fend off panic. Seth was sick. It wasn't just a hypothetical. He had known that, but now there was proof. He followed Leva into the room, though she looked at the last minute like she was going to try to bar him from entering. She stood in the doorway blocking him, then gave in. She approached Seth.

"I'm sorry, baby," she crooned. "I had to get the door. Look who came to see you."

"Sorry," Gabriel echoed. "I just had to check to be sure that you were okay."

Seth's breathing was labored. Gabriel wasn't sure whether it was just from throwing up—the acid stink of fresh vomit hung in the air, making Gabriel gag—or whether there was something else wrong on top of that.

"Poor Seth," Leva soothed, moving in to wipe Seth's face clean and to hand him a couple of tissues. She picked up the basin on the bed, swapping in an empty one, and went into the attached bathroom to dump and rinse it. Gabriel watched her move around Seth, plumping pillows and murmuring to him, and suddenly he saw what Renata had been talking about.

Leva was dressed like a nurse, and as she attended to Seth, soothing him, cleaning him, and taking his vitals, she smiled. Instead of a panicky or worried mother, she was perfectly serene, in her element.

Seth's eyes closed. His face was nearly as white as the sheets he lay on.

"No more," he said. "Please…"

"I know, honey. Throwing up makes your tummy and your throat hurt. Gabriel said that Nelson was coming, he'll be able to give you something to make you stop throwing up."

Gabriel opened his mouth to protest. Nelson wasn't there to give Seth cannabis. He might be able to make suggestions about things that they could try, but he wasn't going to give Seth a prohibited substance, just because Leva wanted him to.

But he left that argument for Nelson instead.

"When did he get sick?" he asked Leva. It couldn't have been that long ago. Gabriel had been there just the day before. But Seth had been asleep then. There had been no way for Gabriel to know how he was doing. All he could do was judge by appearances.

Appearances had changed. Seth's eyes were sunken. He looked like he had lost weight. His skin looked dry and papery, like an old man's. Seth was still breathing heavily, taking desperate gulps of air.

"How long has he been sick?" Gabriel repeated, raising his voice.

"Seth is always sick."

"He wasn't like this when we brought him back. What happened?"

"He's always been like that. Everything can change in an instant. He'll be happy and playing one minute, riding the roller coaster at Disneyland, and then next minute he's passed out, in a coma."

Gabriel thought about Seth after Disneyland. His electrolytes out of balance. Way out of balance, so much that the doctors didn't believe it could be natural.

"Did you give him something? Some medication, maybe? What's happened?"

"This is just the way it is with Seth."

Gabriel sat on the edge of Seth's bed and felt his forehead—cool to the touch—and then felt Seth's pulse.

"Seth. Stay awake. Did you have something to eat? Did you take something?"

Seth's eyelids fluttered. He made a growling noise in his throat but didn't answer.

"Did he eat?" Gabriel asked Leva. "Help me out here. He's throwing up, so he must have had something to eat. What was it?"

Seth's pulse was weak and irregular. Gabriel didn't like it.

"Seth. Wake up. Stay with me."

Then suddenly Seth was throwing up again. Leva dove in with one of the empty basins just in the nick of time, raising Seth up slightly and turning his head, so that he didn't baptize the bed or aspirate his own vomit.

"Get it all out," Leva urged. "Once it's all out, you'll stop throwing up, and you'll feel so much better."

Gabriel struggled, not wanting to turn away from the scene, and at the same time, not wanting to have to see and smell the throw-up. He would be sick himself.

"Do you want to dump this for me?" Leva suggested, thrusting the bowl into Gabriel's hands.

He gagged, just about throwing up himself having it right in front of his face. But he took it from her and walked it into the bathroom. He saw it as he dumped it into the toilet. White and frothy. Some streaks of bile and blood. But white and frothy like Seth had drunk a milkshake.

"Does he still have his feeding tube in?" Gabriel asked as he returned with the emptied and rinsed bowl. Leva was sitting on the bed with Seth, cuddling and washing him. Murmuring in baby talk.

"Yes, they didn't get a chance to take it out yet," Leva said, parting Seth's pajamas to show Gabriel the tube.

"Did you use it today? To give him formula?"

"He wasn't feeling very well," Leva said. "He couldn't get anything down. So I gave him formula. He needs the nourishment. He's looking so frail."

"And he's throwing up the formula," Gabriel said.

"Yes… he is sicker than I thought. I thought he just didn't feel like eating."

Seth moved his head back and forth. "Tastes bad," he complained.

"Do you want to rinse your mouth?" Leva asked. She picked up a cup of ice water from the nightstand. "It does leave a nasty taste, doesn't it?"

"No," Seth protested, turning his face away from the cup. "No, tastes bad."

"The water tastes bad?" Leva laughed. "The water tastes like water. Just the same as always."

Seth closed his eyes, and he didn't stir when Gabriel gave him a little shake.

"Don't go to sleep, Seth. Seth… stay with me! Seth!"

Gabriel couldn't rouse him again.

"He's tired," Leva said. "He spent most of the night throwing up. He's exhausted. Just let him sleep."

"I don't think so," Gabriel growled. "Something is wrong. He needs to go to the hospital and to see a doctor."

"It's too dangerous," Leva said. "They'll recognize us. They'll know who we are. There are bulletins out. I've seen them on TV. We can't take the chance."

"If you don't take the chance, Seth is going to die. He almost died at Disneyland, didn't he? He needs a doctor. Right now."

Leva shook her head, looking indecisive.

"Your ID will hold up," Gabriel assured her. "They're not going to know who you really are. They'll be too busy treating him to stop and think about it."

"It's so soon…"

Gabriel ground his teeth. "He needs a doctor now. I'm calling an ambulance."

Leva stood there and watched him do it. She gave him the address when he couldn't recall it. Gabriel tried to explain what was going on in a way that would allow the paramedics to treat Seth properly when they got there, without making Leva think that he suspected her.

"He's been throwing up. He's probably dehydrated. His pulse is weak and he fainted. He might… he had an electrolyte imbalance recently that was very bad."

———

It seemed like it took forever for the ambulance to get there. Gabriel stayed close to Seth, monitoring his pulse and breathing, though he wasn't sure what he would do if either of them stopped. He wouldn't have the strength or endurance to perform CPR or rescue breathing. Leva hovered over him, attending lovingly to her son, making sure everything was in order.

When the paramedics arrived, Gabriel was pushed back out of the way so they could look Seth over. When Gabriel looked around the room to see if he could glean any other information from their surroundings, he saw Leva taking pictures with her phone of the paramedics working over Seth. She was still smiling faintly, the corners of her mouth just barely curved up. Could he fault her if her natural expression was pleasant? People often had inappropriate responses to stress or grief. He really couldn't know anything from just looking at her. If he could, the doctors would have figured it out years ago.

Renata and Nelson didn't enter the house, but they were standing outside when Gabriel followed the gurney out. Gabriel noticed that Leva had picked a home with easy access for the paramedics. No steps or narrow doorways to fit the stretcher through. Renata and Nelson were both pale and grim-looking. Renata shook her head, biting her lip as she met Gabriel's gaze.

"I *told* you."

"I know. But there was nothing I could do. Not until she did something."

Renata's eyes followed the gurney to the ambulance, and she watched them load it in. "How bad is it?"

Gabriel swallowed. "I think it's pretty bad. She didn't want to take him to the hospital because of their new identities. So she left it, instead of taking him in like she normally would."

"We caused this."

"We didn't cause it," Nelson disagreed. "She's been doing this for years. We're here. We're making sure he gets taken care of."

"If it wasn't for us, he wouldn't be here today." Renata's voice rose in anger. "He'd still be in hospital, or in foster care, and she wouldn't have access to him. There was a reason she could only see him under supervision!"

"I know," Gabriel agreed softly. He put his arm around her, wanting to comfort himself as much as her. He needed to hold her and know that it was going to be okay. Seth would survive his latest encounter, and it would all be okay. He wouldn't be any worse off than he had been before they returned him to Leva. It had only been a couple of days. A couple days couldn't make that much difference in the scheme of things.

Renata stiffened at first; then her shoulders relaxed, and she pressed herself against him. "If he dies…"

"He's not going to die. She's always been careful not to kill him before. She's always gotten him to the hospital on time."

"But that was before. When she wasn't afraid that taking him to the hospital would blow their new identities. We made it worse by making them fugitives."

"Their new identities are sound. She could have gone to the hospital, and no one would have found out. It wasn't our fault."

"It was."

She pressed her face against his chest, and Gabriel rested his chin on the top of her head. When had he gotten so much taller than Renata? He didn't remember being that much taller than she was before.

"You want to go to the hospital, so we can find out how he does?" Nelson suggested.

Gabriel nodded. He couldn't just wander around wondering. He needed to be right there and know the instant the doctors had any information. He looked around. He shouldn't have told Rose to leave.

The ambulance pulled out and Rose's car nosed in beside them. She rolled down the window.

"You guys need anything? Give you a lift somewhere?"

Gabriel stared at her. "I thought you left. What are you still doing here?"

Was she following him? Was she reporting their movements to someone else? People with dark cars and fatal needles? Gabriel shook off the thoughts.

It wasn't the time for paranoia. She was there to help them. He had just wished that she were still there, and she had appeared. That was a happy coincidence, not bad news.

"I just thought you might need me again," Rose said, her stern face impassive. "So?"

"Yes," Renata agreed. She looked at Gabriel, tilting her head toward the car. "We need to get there quickly. Can't wait for other transportation."

"You're right," Gabriel agreed, but he let the other two get into the car before he forced himself to slide into the back seat next to Renata. Nelson rode shotgun, which Gabriel hoped would help him not to get carsick. Renata held Gabriel's hand, looking out the window and not speaking.

"I should call the authorities," Gabriel said. "Shouldn't I? Let them know he's there, and have them arrest Leva. If they will. We still don't have any proof that she did anything to him. Just our own suspicions."

"He's not supposed to be in her custody. They can charge her with kidnapping."

"Not when she didn't have him against his will," Gabriel sighed. "Maybe custodial interference."

"I don't care what they call it!" she snapped.

"Yeah. Sorry."

She squeezed his hand. "I'm just wound up. It's not your fault."

Gabriel breathed out, trying to calm his heart, which was still beating much too rapidly, burning through his energy reserves. He dug into his backpack for a snack.

The hospital wasn't too far away. Leva had looked specifically for a house that was close to the hospital, knowing that they would need it sooner or later.

Probably sooner.

———

When they took Seth from the ambulance, Gabriel saw that he had on an oxygen mask and had two v-fib pads stuck to his bare chest. That scared Gabriel, but at least he had managed to get Seth help in time to use them. Seth was whisked away, and Leva had to go to the admitting desk to fill out his paperwork. A serious-looking white-haired doctor approached the teens, with a clipboard in hand.

"You were with Seth before he was brought in?" he demanded.

"I was. Just for a few minutes," Gabriel agreed.

The doctor's eyes went to Renata and Nelson, then back to Gabriel again. "You were the one who called the ambulance?"

"Yes."

"What happened? What was it that made him sick?"

"I don't know. He has mitochondrial disease. A little while ago, he had an electrolyte imbalance that just about killed him. Maybe it's the same thing again." Gabriel couldn't help looking at Leva at the admitting desk. He didn't know how to tell the doctor that it might be something to do with her. Had she poisoned Seth or was Gabriel just imagining things because of what paranoid Renata had said? Now that he was away from Seth and Leva, he started to wonder if he had just been imagining things. Renata gave him a fierce look but didn't say anything.

"Were you guys taking anything? Experimenting with drugs?"

"No!" Gabriel was shocked. "We wouldn't do that!"

"Kids do. You need to tell me now so that we know how to treat him. It's imperative that we get it out of his system, if he's taken something. He is in respiratory distress, and while he hasn't had a heart attack, there are problems with his heart rhythm and he could still have a cardiac event."

"I didn't give him anything," Gabriel repeated. "He didn't take anything. I don't know… if his mom might have given him something. Maybe some med that wasn't prescribed… that would make his sodium too high…"

The doctor studied Gabriel, frowning.

"She was asking me about cannabis," Nelson inserted. "Asking me if I had a source I could put her onto. Because he was throwing up and she hoped it would stop the nausea."

The doctor's attention turned slowly over to Nelson.

"So you gave him cannabis?"

"No! I didn't give him anything. I didn't even go into the house. She just talked to me on the phone, and that's what she was looking for. So maybe she got someone else to bring her something. Or maybe she decided to try some other remedy. I don't know."

"There wasn't enough time," Gabriel disagreed. "Between when she called you and when we got to the house. She wouldn't have had time to get it from someone else."

"Do you have cannabis on you right now?" the doctor demanded.

Nelson swallowed. He shot a glance at Gabriel, eyes widening a little. "Yes. I have CVS; I have a prescription. But I didn't give any to Seth."

"CVS?"

"Cyclical Vomiting Syndrome."

The doctor continued to stare at him; then he finally turned his attention back to Gabriel again. "What makes you think his mother might have given him something?"

"She was—is—under investigation by Social Services. They thought she might have given him something to cause the last episode. I didn't see her do anything, but I know she gave him formula in his feeding tube today because he was throwing it up. And she just seemed… strange… I think… she likes taking care of him when he's sick."

"You saw her give him this formula? What kind of formula?"

"I didn't see. I just saw… you know… when he threw up, it was like milk. She said she'd given him formula, but I didn't see her do it. I don't know… if she gave him anything else."

"Was he conscious at all?"

"Yes, when I got there. I called the ambulance when he passed out."

"Did he say anything? Give any clue about what had happened?"

Gabriel shook his head. "No… he didn't say anything… he said he didn't want to throw up anymore. And that… the water tasted bad."

Gabriel pondered that. Why would the water taste bad? As Leva had said, water was just water. It didn't usually have much of a taste. Seth had complained in the hospital that his mom's cooking didn't taste good, like the food at the hospital did. Did it taste bad because she wasn't a good cook, or because she was putting something in his food? Something that would make Seth sicker? And when he refused to eat, she would use his feeding tube. And give him what?

The doctor wrote a few notes. "I'll call a social worker. Then we'll be ready if the tests suggest she's given him something."

A doctor who looked way too young to have finished medical school hurried up to them. "Results from the boy in curtain two," she announced breathlessly.

The doctor who had been talking to them took the lab sheet from her, and his eyes flicked over it. "Why didn't you take this directly to treatment?"

The young woman looked crestfallen. "I thought you'd want to see them right away, and to give orders…"

"What course of treatment would you suggest?"

"Administer calcium gluconate, intravenous fluids, maybe get him into gastric lavage and dialysis?"

"Bingo. Get in there."

She hurried back away, lab coat flapping behind her. The doctor turned back to Gabriel.

"It's not his sodium today."

"What is it, then?"

"Magnesium."

"Too high or too low?"

"Too high. Way too high."

Gabriel shook his head and rubbed his temples. "Maybe she gave him milk of magnesia to stop the vomiting?"

"She'd have to give him an awful lot. Possible if she put it through the feeding tube. Did you see any in the room?"

"No," Gabriel admitted. There hadn't been any medications in the bedroom. Not out where he could see them.

The doctor wrote notes on his clipboard. "Most of the children that get magnesium poisoning are toddlers eating bath salts."

Gabriel felt a chill. "Like Epsom salts?"

The doctor looked up. "Yes. Epsom salts are magnesium sulfate."

"She had Epsom salts in the bathroom."

The doctor's brows drew down and his lips pressed together. "We need to get the police over there... see if there's any evidence before she has a chance to clean it up."

Gabriel nodded his mute agreement.

Renata punched him in the arm. Not just a friendly nudge, but a punch that was intended to hurt. Gabriel yelped and pulled away from her.

"Ouch! What was that for?"

"I told you! I told you she was poisoning him, and you didn't believe me. Admit you thought I was just paranoid!"

Gabriel rubbed his arm. "I didn't know. None of us have anything but suspicions. I did everything I could!"

She aimed another blow at him, but Gabriel stepped back, avoiding her.

"Cut it out. You didn't know either. You didn't suspect anything until you saw the two of them together."

"I wondered before I ever saw them at all. *You* were the one who was sure that Leva couldn't have done anything. She was an angel. Could do no wrong. You were so sure!" Renata was shouting.

The doctor and Nelson stared at Renata with wide eyes. Gabriel took a slow breath, trying not to react to her anger and make it worse. She was just upset. Like he was. Upset that Seth had been hurt and that it had happened on their watch. She was reacting to the same guilt as Gabriel was. A horrible feeling in the pit of his stomach that he had been blinded by Leva's image and that he'd been wrong.

When no one said anything, Renata seemed to realize the attention she was attracting. She relaxed her body language and looked away from Gabriel, trying to compose herself.

"If there's anything we can do to help…" Gabriel said to the doctor.

"There's nothing more you can do at this point. Calling the ambulance and providing your insight… that's the most you could do for him."

The man tactfully took his leave, letting Gabriel sort Renata out. Gabriel watched him go back toward the treatment area through a set of swinging doors. Gabriel didn't want to look at Renata or Nelson.

"We need to go," Nelson said. "The police are going to have more questions. Including who we are."

"I want to make sure he's okay," Gabriel said hesitantly.

"We can't stay here."

"You can come back later," Renata said. "Nelson's right. We can't stay right now. But the cops won't stay here all day. You can check back in later."

Gabriel nodded. Renata put her hand on his arm. Her touch was gentle. She wasn't trying to hurt him anymore. Renata tended to get angry fast and get over it fast. Gabriel took longer. He was still building up to being angry. Guilt, betrayal, confusion, he felt all of those. But he wasn't angry yet.

"You look tired," Renata said. "You'd better find somewhere to recover before you crash."

Gabriel nodded. He'd eaten, but if he didn't sit down and get control of his racing heart, he would end up in trouble.

———

The three of them found an urban park nearby with short-clipped green grass where mothers pushed children in strollers, twenty-somethings sunbathed, and office workers stretched their legs and got a breath of fresh air or a smoke. They sat in the shade of a group of trees. The soft, warm grass was inviting, and within a few minutes, Gabriel stretched out on it and closed his eyes, feeling like a cat that had found a spot on the windowsill. The sun shone through his eyelids and warmed his body. He found himself drifting while Nelson and Renata talked.

"Hey," Renata shook him. "You okay?"

"Yeah," Gabriel assured her. "I'm just going to have a nap, recharge the batteries."

"Your sugar's okay?"

"I'm fine. Just feeling a bit sleepy. Didn't get much rest last night."

She grunted. "You should have stayed with me."

"Uh-huh."

He let the heaviness take over his brain. It wasn't a long nap; he didn't think so, anyway. When he awoke, he felt relaxed and refreshed. He rubbed his eyes and rolled over to look at Renata and Nelson.

"Hey, sleepyhead," Renata greeted.

"Hi. That felt really good."

"You must have needed it."

"Yeah." Gabriel sat up and rubbed his eyes some more, blinking in the bright sun. "Has anyone called Carmel? She'll be wondering what's going on. She was involved in this transfer too."

"She's your girlfriend," Renata said. "Why would we call her?"

"Whoa!" Gabriel held up his hands. "She is not my girlfriend. We have never gone on a date or done anything together other than work. I don't know her personally at all, just through the railway."

"You seemed pretty cozy with her."

"Cozy?" Gabriel shook his head. "You're crazy. We are not together and she is not my girlfriend. In any way."

Renata leaned back in the grass, a small smile of satisfaction on her face.

"We haven't called her," Nelson said. "I guess you should."

Gabriel shrugged. "Do you want to?"

"You go ahead. I barely know her."

"Neither do I," Gabriel said. But he picked up his phone and considered it. He looked at Renata. "You want to call her?"

"Why would *I* want to call her?"

"You don't sound like you like me talking to her. You could talk to her if you don't want me to."

"I don't want to talk to her. You go ahead. It doesn't matter to me."

"You sure?"

"Why would I care? You said there's nothing between you, and I believe you."

Gabriel looked at Nelson. "You're my witness, right? She said she doesn't want to call Carmel. She wants me to do it. She said she doesn't care."

Nelson just smiled and looked away, not getting involved. Gabriel gave Renata one last look to make sure she didn't object. She shrugged widely and motioned for him to go ahead.

Gabriel dialed Carmel's number.

"Hey, it's Gabriel."

"Oh, hi! Are you okay? You hung up sort of quick the other day; I wasn't sure if maybe something was wrong."

"I'm fine." Gabriel glanced at the nearest road, remembering the car that had shown up the last time he had talked to Carmel. It didn't even have to mean that she had betrayed them. But it might mean that they were bugging her phone. "You remember talking about our transfer? That things might... not be right?"

"Sure, of course."

"He's back in hospital. And we've... given the doctors a heads-up."

Carmel swore. "No! Judge Dee-Dee was so sure. I didn't think she could be wrong about it."

"I think she was. We don't have proof. No one saw her doing anything. But I think it was her, and the doctor's going to have the police follow up, see if they can find anything at her house. His magnesium is high, and we think... I saw Epsom salts at the house. She might have..."

"Or might not have," Carmel pointed out.

"I know. That's what I said. We don't have proof. Maybe the police can find something."

She breathed for a minute. "I'm sorry, Gabe. You must be pretty disappointed. You... really admired her."

"Yeah, I did. She was such an advocate for mitochondrial disease. I didn't think... I didn't think that the doctor's suspicions could be true. I couldn't see it."

Renata was listening in on Gabriel's side of the conversation and he caught her nodding in agreement.

"I just thought... you should know," Gabriel finished. He wasn't sure how to end the conversation. Maybe Carmel didn't really care about the developments. She was done the transfer and back home again, back to her own life.

"Yeah. I'm glad you called. I wondered how things went after your last call. Thanks for telling me."

Gabriel said goodbye to her and ended the call. He looked out to the street again, looking for any suspicious vehicles. Renata followed his gaze.

"What?"

"Nothing. Just making sure."

"Making sure what?"

"That we weren't followed… under surveillance."

Her eyes narrowed. "Why? What makes you think that?"

Gabriel tried to wave it off.

"Nothing. It's fine."

"Don't lie to me." Renata searched the street herself. She took a long look around the green space, eyes alert. "Come on. Spill."

"Last time I talked to Carmel, a car went by… it was nothing. Just a dark car with tinted windows, it went by, and I wasn't sure…" He trailed off. "I'm just being overcautious."

"You think she's a leak?"

"No. Just… being careful. Just in case."

The three of them sat there, looking around suspiciously. Renata was the first to break.

"I can't stand sitting here anymore. I'm all creeped out now. Let's go back and see how Seth is doing."

CHAPTER ELEVEN

Gabriel waited impatiently while Nelson scouted ahead. As the only one among them who didn't have any warrants or Social Services interest, it was safest for him. But Gabriel found waiting excruciating. It was one thing if he had to move slowly himself, but having to wait on someone else while he stood around made him itch like a hundred bugs were crawling over his skin.

"You told *me* to chill earlier," Renata said. "I could tell you the same thing now."

"I don't need to chill. I just need Nelson to get his butt moving and find out how Seth is and if we can see him."

"He will."

"How long does it take to find his hospital room?"

"Longer than thirty seconds. And you know he could be somewhere else having tests done, too. How many times were you in a room within a few hours of being admitted to emerge?"

Gabriel groaned. "But admitting will tell Nelson if Seth hasn't been assigned a room yet. We won't have to wait while he traipses all over the hospital."

"Be patient," she advised. "Come sit down and talk to me."

Gabriel considered the seat next to Renata's. In a waiting room full of patients, two more people sitting and waiting didn't stand out. But if he continued to pace like an agitated squirrel, people would begin to take notice. He forced himself to sit down. The chairs were uncomfortable, as if whoever had purchased them had no idea people would be sitting in them for hours on end. They were hard and slippery and had no head support if a person wanted to lean back and go to sleep. Gabriel tried to settle into a comfortable position. Renata gave him a wry smile.

He hadn't expected to have to wait an hour for Nelson. But the time dragged on and on and seemed to go more slowly the more he looked at his watch.

"Gabe," Renata said softly as he looked at his watch yet again.

"I know, I know. A watched pot."

"No. Look."

Gabriel followed the direction of her eyes and saw the police escorting a woman from the elevators toward the doors. Leva. Gabriel felt a sinking feeling. He swore softly under his breath and turned away from the scene so that the police and Leva wouldn't notice him sitting there. It was his fault. His fault that Leva had had access to her son again, and his fault that she had been rearrested. He should have just left well enough alone. He should never have interfered with the case.

"I know," Renata said. He looked at her face and saw his own emotions reflected there. He nodded.

Gabriel's phone vibrated in his pocket, making him jump. Renata giggled. Gabriel pulled it out and looked hungrily at the screen. It was Nelson, finally.

He's in.

Nelson gave the unit and room number. Gabriel got up eagerly.

"Be careful," Renata warned. "Just because they left with Leva, that doesn't mean there aren't any others around."

"Nelson wouldn't have texted me if it was dangerous."

"He might not know."

Gabriel had to concede the point. So they went cautiously, not taking a straight approach, keeping their eyes out for cops, social workers, or anyone else suspicious. But they didn't see anyone else to be concerned about on the way there. Gabriel took a peek into the hospital room and saw Nelson standing beside Seth's bed. Seth was hooked up to oxygen, an IV draining clear fluid and a monitor.

Gabriel entered the room. "Is he awake?"

Seth opened his eyes and regarded Gabriel. "I don't want to go home."

"I'm not taking you home this time. I'm sorry. I didn't know she would hurt you."

Seth looked at him steadily. Gabriel sat down on the edge of the bed. There was only one visitor chair, and Renata had already taken it.

"Why didn't you tell me she was hurting you, Seth? I asked you."

"My mom doesn't hurt me," Seth objected. "She's never hit me."

"But it hurts you when she gives you things she shouldn't, and they make you sick."

Seth shrugged, his eyes closing again.

"If you told me she puts things she shouldn't in your tube or gives you food that's been tampered with, I wouldn't have taken you back there," Gabriel persisted. "Why didn't you tell me?"

"My mom loves me." His eyes opened again. "She does everything she does to help me get better."

"She poisons you!" Renata snapped. "She's not trying to help you; she's trying to hurt you!"

He shook his head, a small movement. "She tries to make me better."

"Why do you think the food and the water taste so bad? It's because she's putting things in them that she shouldn't."

"No… she wants to make me better." One of Seth's hands snaked to his face, and he rubbed his eyes. "Medicine tastes bad."

"She made you sick. You know that what she gave you in your water and your feeding tube made you sick."

Seth looked toward the door. "The police arrested her. They put her in handcuffs and took her away."

Gabriel's heart ached for Seth. Did they have to arrest her in front of him? Seth sounded so forlorn. Even if Seth knew in his heart that Leva was trying to poison him, trying to make him sicker instead of making him well, he still loved her.

"She needs to go to jail," Renata said. Her voice was hard, and Gabriel knew she was thinking of her own mother. "She needs to be locked up for trying to hurt you. She could have killed you. If Gabriel hadn't gotten to the house and called the ambulance, you would have died."

Seth rubbed his eyes again, keeping his hands over his eyes for a few minutes.

"Can I just stay at the hospital now? Can I live here all the time?"

"They'll find a family for you to stay with," Gabriel told him. "They'll take good care of you and you'll be able to get better and not be sick so often."

Renata shot Gabriel a look. He knew the statistics. A child was five times more likely to die in foster care than with his own family. But that wasn't Seth. Some kids were in so much danger from their bio parents that they had to be removed. They all agreed that staying with Leva could be fatal for Seth.

———

He slept soundly that night, an aftereffect of the adrenaline and the stress of the previous few days. He could finally rest, knowing that Seth was safe and once more on the road to recovery. How much of Seth's sickness was real and how much was from being poisoned by his mother, Gabriel didn't know. And the doctors had no idea how much permanent damage there might be to his kidneys or liver.

Did he really have mito or was it all just Leva's abuse?

Renata shifted and stirred restlessly. She rolled over and looked at him. "You awake already?"

"It's late," Gabriel pointed out, looking at the light of dawn creeping into the sky. They should have already been up and moving on, getting out of the park before the police showed up to roust them.

Renata blinked a few times, turning her head to gaze at the sky and take this in.

"It is late. Why'd you let me sleep in?"

"We both needed it. You have a good sleep?"

"Yeah." She snuggled against him, their bodies both cozy in the shared warmth. "Really good. I've missed this."

"Me too."

"We're going to need to get up."

"Mmm-hmm."

Renata looked around. "Maybe the cops won't roust us here. Maybe we can stay here a while longer."

Neither of them made a move to get up.

Renata chuckled and pressed her face against Gabriel's chest.

As much as Gabriel would have liked to stay there all day, warm and cozy with each other, he couldn't stay still as the sky got lighter and his body announced its needs. He rolled over, relinquishing the blanket, and got stiffly to his feet. Renata slid out the other side of the blanket.

"Thank goodness," she said. "I have to pee!"

"Me too," Gabriel agreed.

They went opposite directions and reconvened a few minutes later, working out the kinks from sleeping on the cold ground.

"I guess it's back to real life," Renata said, massaging the back of her neck and shoulders. "We should replenish our funds. See what news is on the grapevine."

"Sounds good. Food next? I'm starving. I must have burned through a lot more fuel than I thought yesterday."

"Stress hormones will do that. Lead the way."

With Renata, Gabriel didn't have to pretend that he bought all his meals, like he might with Carmel or one of the other railway volunteers who lived normal lives the rest of the time. Dumpster-diving was a fact of life for the homeless. Renata stood close by, screening him from view as he checked out the garbage can near the entrance to a submarine sandwich store. He preferred subs to the greasy food at most of the fast food joints. In a few seconds, Gabriel grabbed several likely-looking wrappers containing uneaten portions of sandwiches, and the two of them retreated to a bus bench down the block to eat breakfast. Renata watched Gabriel unwrap and check out each sandwich as she hooked up her formula. Gabriel caught her eyes on him.

"I bet you're glad yours is all sealed and pasteurized."

"Actually," Renata spoke kindly, "hygiene theory suggests that you're healthier if exposed to plenty of microbes, rather than avoiding them. Parents try to keep their little ones sterile, and then they get sick as soon as they're exposed to anything as adults."

"Well, no problem there," Gabriel said. He broke away the chewed portion of a sandwich, leaving only the untouched half behind. But it had still been handled by someone else. Maybe even coughed and sneezed on. He'd learned not to care. It was more important to get the nourishment his body needed than it was to avoid bugs.

They ate in comfortable silence, watching the traffic and pedestrians go by. Gabriel started to formulate a plan in his head. They needed to get to a different neighborhood. It was too dangerous staying so close to the hospital, where the doctors and now the police knew that they had been. They needed more money, as Renata had suggested. That would mean spending most of the day panhandling. It still wouldn't yield a lot, but he'd have some emergency funds to fall back upon.

"I think I should ditch my phone," he said. "Pick up a new burner."

Renata raised one eyebrow.

"I don't suspect Carmel," Gabriel said uncomfortably. "Not really. I just think I've used it too much. I need to get rid of it before somebody *does* start tracking it."

"But there might be a problem with Carmel?"

"Could be. I don't think there is. But she was the one who suggested Seth's case, and it turned out she was wrong. He was being abused."

"But the information came from Judge Dee-Dee to start with."

"So Carmel said."

Renata considered that, sucking her cheeks in. She nodded.

"And then there was the car. It was probably just a random car, not surveillance. But it showed up right after I called her... Gotta be a coincidence, because they couldn't have gotten someone to me that fast..."

"Unless they already had your general location and were waiting for you to make a call to pinpoint you."

Gabriel's skin crawled. "Yeah. So I need to get a new one."

Renata nodded in agreement. "You got the money now, or is that what we're raising funds for?"

"I have enough to start with." Gabriel pulled out his phone and powered it on to wipe it. He glanced at the usage information. "This one was just about out of minutes anyway. Good timing."

He did a system wipe, then popped out the SIM card and broke it in half, tossing one piece in the garbage and putting the other in his pocket to dispose of later in another location. He threw the phone down on the pavement and stomped on it, taking several tries to bust it up to his satisfaction. Gabriel picked it up and attempted to turn it back on, then nodded and threw it out.

———

Renata finished touching base with her contacts and hung up the phone.

"Leva's being transferred back to face additional charges. And Social Services is going to send Seth back to the Children's."

"I guess there's no reason for us to stay around here, then. Do you want to go home?"

Renata nodded. Her mouth quirked up. "Don't you think it's funny that we talk about home when we're homeless?"

"Well… I guess. Even living on the street, I still think of the valley as home. It's not that much different than being here or any other city… but I'm familiar with where everything is. That's where most of our contacts are. It's just… more familiar."

"And you know your mom is there, even if you can't see her."

"Yeah, I guess there's that too. I need to set something up to meet up with her again one day soon… I miss her. They're probably not still surveilling her… do you think?"

"Every time the authorities figure out that you're involved in a transfer, they're going to show renewed interest in finding you. And she's the best opportunity they have to do that."

Gabriel grunted.

Sometime. He'd see her again sometime.

CHAPTER TWELVE

Their plan for 'business as usual' lasted only a few days. Gabriel started to feel like he was getting back on his feet. He wasn't so tired. They fell into a comfortable routine. Renata seemed to be stable and happy. It was all he could have hoped for and more.

Renata gasped and stopped so fast that Gabriel just about tripped walking beside her.

"What? What's wrong?"

Renata pointed to a newspaper box. They could see the big headline through the window. And a picture. One column of the story showed, the rest of it cut off.

Gabriel stared in blank disbelief.

"Is it an old paper?" he asked, not understanding.

"No!" Renata was bent over, reading what she could through the window. "Leva was out on bail. She wasn't supposed to be anywhere near Seth."

"Didn't they have anyone at the hospital? A guard? Some kind of security?"

Renata shook her head, her eyes still on the words on the paper.

"She just walked in and took him. They didn't have any idea. She was wearing a nurse's uniform."

Gabriel pressed his temples, feeling like his brain was going to explode.

"They knew that she already spirited him away once," Gabriel omitted their part in the caper. "How could they not know that she was going to do it again?"

"Maybe they figured we wouldn't help her, and she wouldn't be able to do it alone." Renata jerked on the handle of the newspaper box, but it didn't open. "You've got change," Renata snapped, "buy a paper."

Gabriel slotted money into the machine and opened it up. Renata grabbed two copies and handed Gabriel one of them. He let the door shut and wondered if he dared put the fee for the second paper into the box while she stood there. He chickened out and didn't. Renata was already holding her paper in front of her face, engrossed.

"I can't believe this. I can't believe they let her get in there and just walk out with him."

Gabriel made a noise of agreement. He scoured the article for some suggestion of where the police or Social Services thought Leva would go. She didn't have any family. Just Seth. She had plenty of friends in the mito community who would be sympathetic to her story that she was being persecuted by the authorities just for trying to care for her sick son. There were dozens of people who might be willing to flout the law and help her out.

"What are we going to do?" Renata asked.

"I don't know. What *can* we do? She's not with us this time."

Renata flipped through the pages of the paper, looking for a continuation of the front page story or a shorter side piece.

"So what? If we can hide people, we should be able to find them too. How many people in our network know Leva? If we put the word out that we're looking for her, someone is bound to know something. She can't just disappear into thin air. We know all the exit routes. We know she has to establish a new identity. We've been through this before. There are only so many people she can go to for help."

"She has a car. She can leave town and then look for someone to help her with the identification."

"There's an APB out on the car. She'll have to dump it and get a new one. And that means she's stuck in town a little longer. She won't leave town before she has an identity. It will be too hard to find someone who will trust her. She knows people here. She knows what has to be done."

Gabriel wanted to argue with her. He couldn't see what would stop Leva from fleeing town. And the state. Get as far away as possible, and then find a way to get herself established.

But if Renata were right, they had a much smaller footprint to search. There were only so many sources of good identification papers in town, and his contacts knew them.

"Seth is still sick," Gabriel said, looking at the newspaper. "She won't be able to take him far. Traveling makes him worse."

"Being alone with her makes him worse," Renata snapped. "What are we waiting for? Time to make some phone calls."

Gabriel ignored her impatient tone. She wasn't mad at him. She was just eager to find Seth again and to rescue him. Again. From his mother. Again. How many times were they going to repeat the same scenario?

He caught Renata looking at him, her face slack, mouth slightly open. "What?"

"How many times…" she repeated. Gabriel hadn't even realized that he'd said the words out loud. She put her hand on his arm as if to stop him from some action. "What if she decides that it's not worth it? What if she decides that it's too dangerous? She knows that if she gets caught again, she's not going to get out on bail. I don't know how she managed to make bail this time. If she gets caught again, there's no way she'll ever get another chance."

Gabriel wasn't sure where Renata was going with it. Or maybe he just didn't want to admit that he did.

"What if she decides to kill him this time, Gabriel? It happens sometimes, doesn't it? I know Munchausen by Proxy parents rarely kill, but it still happens. She's desperate. She's going to lose him. If she decides the authorities are getting too close…"

"You think she'll kill both of them? Him and herself?"

Renata nodded. She gripped Gabriel's arm tighter. "We've got to find them, Gabe."

Gabriel didn't answer. He just pulled out his latest phone and started dialing.

———

He reconnoitered first, taking a walk up and down the block looking for any suspicious vehicles or watchers. He did a turn around the block, walking through the alley behind the building. Everything seemed to be as usual. Gabriel went back to the front of the pawn shop.

The owner was behind the counter. No assistants or additional staff in sight. Merrick was a big man, overweight; even his stubby fingers were fat. And yellow from chain-smoking, which he did in the store despite the by-laws. But Gabriel had seen him at work. His fingers were as deft and nimble as a child's. Merrick glanced up when the chimes rang, then went back to whatever he was writing in the log book. Gabriel approached the counter, pretending that he was looking at the watches under the glass top.

"Something must be going on for you to come visit me in person," Merrick remarked.

Gabriel looked up from the watches. He shifted his weight from one foot to another. He might just be a teenager, but Merrick knew who he was, knew that Gabriel had sent business his way. So he showed him the respect that he would show any adult business associate.

"I'm wondering if you've done any paper recently," he said. "Probably a rush job, for a mother and teenage son."

"I can't share confidential information," Merrick said. "You understand that. You wouldn't want me sharing any of *your* clients' information."

"Well, she actually is one of ours. We've just sort of… lost her…"

"That was careless, wasn't it?"

"It's important that we get in contact with her. The boy could be in danger."

Merrick studied him.

"What kind of danger would he be in? Mothers with children that are in need of my services are usually running from something. They already know where the danger lies."

Gabriel hesitated over what to say. He didn't want to take the chance of spooking Leva if word got back to her that someone was looking for her. But Merrick and those like him wouldn't help Gabriel if they thought that Leva and Seth were safe where they were.

"Actually… we think that *she* is a danger to him."

Merrick's eyes widened in surprise. "I thought you said that you had sent them."

"Initially, we did. But then we became aware of… other facts."

Merrick drummed his fingers on the countertop. "This is all very… unusual. You know the way I operate. Discretion is paramount."

"I know. And I normally wouldn't expect you to say anything. It's just that… I know he could be in danger. Serious danger. From her."

Merrick stared off into space for a long time, then shook his head. "I don't think I can help you. You'll have to look elsewhere."

Gabriel sighed. "Should I be asking other artists?" he asked. "Or did you handle this job?"

Merrick's eyes were inscrutable. "I can't help you."

Gabriel expected he was going to get a similar response from everyone he asked. He could only hope that whoever had forged papers for Leva and Seth would have a conscience and let him know somehow where they were headed.

He wasn't holding his breath.

———

Gabriel made the decision to reunite their extraction team. All of them had talked to Leva or Seth at some point along the way. If they pooled their information, maybe they could figure out where to start looking.

So far Gabriel's investigation into new identification had not panned out. No one would admit to having heard anything from Leva. Which either meant that she was lying low, or that she had persuaded them to keep her secret. Gabriel didn't have the money to pay for bribes. If Leva had paid them enough money to keep their mouths shut, Gabriel didn't have anywhere near enough to open them again.

"She probably isn't trying to get identity papers yet," Nelson argued. "If Seth was still sick when she took him from the hospital, she wouldn't want to leave him alone or in someone else's care while she chased around after paperwork, would she? She'd just hunker down somewhere and take care of him until he was stable."

"Maybe," Gabriel agreed. He had no evidence to counter the theory.

"He complained at the hospital about getting sicker traveling," Carmel said. "He doesn't like to travel at all when he's sick. And it sounds like he was still pretty bad."

"Where did you get that?" Renata demanded. "The paper said he was sick, but it didn't say *how* sick."

Carmel hesitated. She looked at Gabriel, then back at Renata.

"Come on, spill!" Renata insisted. "You need to let us know what you've heard, and from whom. We need to pool everything."

"Well… it's not official."

"We don't need official," Gabriel assured her. "If you're hearing rumors through the grapevine, that's just as important as what we're getting through public media. Maybe more so."

"It wasn't through our network. I was… talking to Judge Dee-Dee."

There was silence as they all considered this and looked back and forth at one another. Gabriel tried to compose a question in his mind. He needed to get as many details from Carmel as he could. But Judge Dee-Dee was not on their side. Not completely. And if Carmel were in cahoots with her…

"She called me," Carmel confessed, without anyone posing the question. "She thinks that the underground railway is helping Leva again."

"Why would she think that? We turned her in!" Gabriel's voice was loud in his shock and anger. "We found out that Judge Dee-Dee was wrong and we went back in and called the ambulance and made sure that the doctors knew it was Leva. We made sure they called the cops. Doesn't she know that?"

"I told her," Carmel said in a small voice. "But I guess the official report said that it was Leva who called the ambulance and the doctor who reported her. Judge Dee-Dee thought that we were helping her. I told her we weren't." Carmel looked down at her hands in her lap, not meeting their eyes.

"There must be a recording of my call," Gabriel said. "All she has to do is listen to it to hear that I was the one who called."

"She didn't know until I told her. I don't know if she's verified it since. She probably has."

"How sick did she say Seth was?" Nelson asked, trying to circle back around to the original question.

Gabriel stopped arguing and closed his mouth, waiting for the answer. Carmel looked reluctant to say anything else. She looked at each of them before going on.

"They're pretty worried about him. He was still being treated for magnesium poisoning. He was still on oxygen and IV."

"Let's assume she's still here," Gabriel said finally. "I've been assuming she would go out of state, as far away as she could, but that's all the more reason for her to stay here. If everybody is looking for her elsewhere, she'd be safest sticking close to home. Just like what we usually do… stay in the city for a few days until they assume that we already slipped through their fingers and then leave once security is relaxed."

"How does that help us?" Nelson asked.

Gabriel closed his eyes and thought.

"She needs medical supplies. Even if they're staying with a friend. She needs money. Probably a lot of it. She can't live on the street and be invisible like us. Not with him needing that kind of care."

"Maybe if Judge Dee-Dee thinks we're helping her, other people do too," Carmel said. "Can't we use that to our advantage?"

Everyone looked at Carmel with suspicion.

"Other people will think that we're still on Leva's side. So if they know where she is, they might not have a problem telling us, like they would the police."

"But Leva knows," Gabriel pointed out. "She'd set people straight pretty quickly."

"*Does* she know?"

"How could she not know?" Renata snapped. "She was right there when Gabriel turned her in."

"When Gabriel called the ambulance," Carmel corrected. She raised her eyes to Gabriel. "What did you say in front of her? That you knew she did it? Did you tell the dispatcher that she was the one who made him sick?"

"No… I told her that they wouldn't get caught if I called the ambulance. I just told the dispatcher that I thought his electrolytes were off, like at Disneyland, not that I thought she did anything. I didn't tell anyone it might be her until we talked to the doctor."

"So maybe she thinks we're still on her side. We could reach out to her. Say that we would help her to get out of town again."

"We'd have to know where she was to reach out to her."

"We can put the word out to her friends and our volunteers. If we can get word to her that we want to help…" Nelson suggested.

"Do you think she'll believe it?"

"Psychopaths like her always think they've got people snowed," Renata said. "They think they're smarter than anybody else."

"Psychopaths?" Gabriel repeated skeptically.

"You look at how she's fooled the doctors all these years. You think she's going to worry that some teenagers are going to figure it out? She'll underestimate us."

"I hope so."

"Put the word out," Renata instructed, taking them all with her gaze. "Reach out to your top contacts. Have them fan out. Gabriel… you know Leva's contacts the best."

"I don't really know them…"

"You knew who Leva was, so I know you are familiar with the community. You need to reach out to others. People you think are safe, who Leva would trust. You're a teenager with mito. Trade on that. They'll trust you because you're one of them."

"You are too."

"I don't know the players. I'm not part of that community. You're the one who has been keeping up with them." She shook her head. "I've been completely out of touch with anyone outside of our group for months. You need to be the one."

CHAPTER THIRTEEN

When they split up to go their different directions, Gabriel headed for the library. That was the easiest place to get online and start contacting people. There were internet cafes, places where he could rent a computer. But the library was free, and he could stay there for as long as he needed to, within the hours they were open.

His phone was off. He didn't want anyone to be able to trace him. Especially not now, knowing that Judge Dee-Dee thought that they had spirited Leva and Seth away again. If they were going to make Leva believe that they were on her side, they couldn't tell anyone else otherwise.

Logged into one of the library computers, Gabriel opened up several social media sites where there were mito support groups. Some of them were full-fledged organizations, with their own officers and websites. Others were just ad hoc groups of mommies or teens, gathered together in one place to ask questions and offer their support. He started looking for Leva's trail. People that she had posted to online. The friends that asked her questions or exchanged messages with her the most. People she had given advice to on legal or medical issues.

He felt sick reading them. Had they all thought that she was an angel, as Renata had put it? Did they all think that she was the perfect mother, so well-educated on all her son's health issues, helping out others, advocating for protection of their rights? There were pictures of Seth in various ambulances and hospital beds. A few of him smiling at the camera or playing video games, but mostly he was unconscious, grimacing in pain, or staring vaguely out of the frame of the picture like he was only barely aware of what was going on. Gabriel read through her descriptions of his illnesses. A positive word about his recovery over a few days, and then weeks of hospital and doctor's reports. Tirades about officials who didn't know how to care for him properly or who didn't provide the accommodations that he needed. Rants about his feeding tube and the doctors who wanted to remove it, saying that it was unnecessary. And every time, people flocked to her to agree and offer their support. Of course he needed the feeding tube. Anyone who suggested otherwise didn't understand what it was like to take care of a child who might starve to death. They couldn't leave his health in jeopardy at the times when he just couldn't be forced to eat. Sympathies were offered about doctors who didn't know anything about mitochondrial disease, and that was ninety-nine percent of the profession. Had anyone ever suspected that Leva wasn't everything she pretended to be? Wasn't there anyone who had seen through her posting online when Seth's health was in dire straits?

He started a list of the names that he saw the most often. Many were familiar to him from his previous time on the various forums. Gabriel liked to keep up on the latest research and advances on mito, and he tried to keep an eye out for kids who might be in danger or who were already having problems with Social Services. If any mito kids were kidnapped, he wanted to know about it. It was hard to remind himself not to be distracted by anyone else's stories. He needed to stay on track and focus on those who might give Leva shelter if she asked them. That was his only goal.

The list grew. But that was good. The more people in the community that he could make contact with, the better their chances of finding Leva and convincing her that they could help her again.

Once he had the list of names, the next step was to figure out the best way to reach each of them. He didn't have logins on all the sites, so there wasn't always a way to message them. And while a few made their emails prominent for everyone to see, most guarded their privacy. He could do searches and background checks on their names. He could search directories for their numbers. Some of them would be easy to find, but many of them would not be.

It was going to take time, something Seth might not have.

Renata updated Gabriel on everyone's progress when they met up again in the evening. It wasn't difficult. No one had made any discernible progress. They had reached out to dozens of volunteers in the underground railway, but so far no one seemed to have any idea where Leva and Seth might be staying. They were keeping well-hidden.

"Well, we didn't expect to find them the first day, did we?" Gabriel asked. "We knew that this would take some time. The police have more resources than we do and they haven't found anything yet."

"They may have resources, but they don't have access to the underground community. Their databases aren't going to tell them where she has decided to go. Their APBs won't do any good when she swaps cars. And we already told her to do that, so she's going to know. She can dye and cut her hair. I don't know why she didn't before. She can dye Seth's too. Or shave him bald and say that he has cancer instead of mito. Anyone would believe it."

Gabriel laughed. "You have a devious mind."

"I know I do." She smiled proudly. "How do you think I've managed to escape so many times?"

He gave her a hug around the shoulders. They walked along the street, taking their time and relaxing before retiring for the night. Gabriel was exhausted after the long day. He had just started to feel like himself again, and the stress of Leva and Seth disappearing again and worrying about whether Seth would survive until they got him back were taking their toll.

Gabriel glanced at the road and tensed. Renata felt his body go rigid and turned to see what he was looking at.

"You see it?" Gabriel murmured.

Renata nodded, turning her head away but still watching the dark car with tinted windows out of the corner of her eye. It didn't slow down as it passed them, which was a good sign, but Gabriel wasn't much comforted by that. They both watched it pull into the turn lane, make a right turn, and disappear out of sight. Renata looked behind her as if she expected it to already be pulling up behind her again.

"I don't see any others," she said. "If they're tailing us, there should be more than one car. So that if we make the one," she gestured in the direction that the car had gone, "they can still keep eyes on us from another car."

"But the second car wouldn't have to be the same kind," Gabriel pointed out. "Just because one has tinted windows, the other could look just like any old car. A classic Volkswagen Beetle. A Prius. A motorcycle."

They watched each of the vehicles that he had named pass them and continue down the street.

"Yeah," Renata agreed. "It could be anything. You haven't noticed any of these other vehicles earlier today? Or over the last few days?"

Gabriel shrugged helplessly. "I don't know how I would. I only noticed the sedan because of the tinted windows. I don't notice cars."

"Was it the same one as you saw before?"

"I don't have a clue. Could be. Or it could be something completely different. I just saw one before, and it kind of freaked me out."

"We'd better move on. I was ready to bed down for the night, but I've changed my mind. We need a change of scenery. Shake any tails."

Gabriel nodded his agreement. He wouldn't be able to lie down and go to sleep with his heart pumping so fast. He'd be up all night, feeling like a bug under a glass.

Renata led the way, looking behind her and studying the cars going by them frequently. She didn't point out any one particular vehicle, so he trusted that she hadn't noticed any that passed them more than once. There were so many; Gabriel didn't know how she'd be able to keep track and notice any patterns.

It was silly for him to freak out because of seeing one car with tinted windows. Two, if he counted the other one. There had to be hundreds of cars with tinted windows in the valley. Maybe thousands. He was only noticing them because he was on high alert. There wasn't anything to be worried about.

"So how did you do?" Renata asked brightly. "With your research into the online mito community? Find anything interesting?"

He recognized that she was trying to distract him, but was glad of it. He hadn't had a chance to make his report yet. Though she was bound to know that the fact that he hadn't said anything meant that he hadn't made any progress either.

"I have a lot of names. Some of them chatted online with Leva every day. I sent messages or emails to some of them, but I don't know how long they'll take to get back to me, if they will at all. Or if they'll tell Leva… or what they'll tell her."

Renata shrugged. "At least we're trying."

"I still have more to track down and get messages to. Not everyone makes it easy to get a private message to them."

"They shouldn't."

"Uh… no, I guess not."

"People don't pay enough attention to online privacy. They think there is no harm in just letting it all hang out there. Let everybody know their business. Contact information, health, what they like and don't like, it's scary how much of their lives they just put out there for anyone."

Gabriel nodded. But his mind was far away. His feet were on autopilot. He didn't have to think about where he was going, just to stay with Renata. He looked over his shoulder at the traffic again, expecting to see another car with tinted windows. But everything seemed normal.

———

Renata sighed in relief as they sat down on the bus. She felt safer there than on the street. Less exposed. Not as easy to follow. They obviously couldn't perform any evasive maneuvers on public transit. A bus was incredibly easy to follow, going slow and making stops along the way to give any pursuers a chance to catch up again, following a predictable route. But it also meant that it was easier to see any followers. Regular traffic should flow right by them without slowing down. A pursuer would have to slow down to stay with the bus, stopping if the bus got ahead of schedule and had to wait before going on.

She kept a close watch on the traffic beside and behind the bus. No one seemed to be going too slowly. They were in the clear unless their stalker had enough sense to know the bus route and where Renata and Gabriel would want to stop. Then they could get there ahead of them.

Gabriel was nodding in the seat beside her. She smiled with affection. Gabriel was a good guy. She was lucky to have found him, and that he put up with her eccentricities even through hospitalizations and epic tantrums.

His body was slumped in the seat, sliding a little as the bus turned corners and stopped and started along its route. Renata gave him a little nudge to wake him up and keep him from falling out of his seat.

"Gabe. Hey, Gabe."

Rather than sitting up straighter, he listed farther to the side. Renata grabbed his arm to pull him upright, squeezing it and giving him a little shake.

"Gabriel. Wake up. Are you okay?"

He didn't respond to her. Renata studied his face. It was hard with his dark complexion to tell when he wasn't feeling well. She held his hand and looked at his nails. They had a dusky blue color. Renata touched his face and found his skin cold.

She swore. She realized that she couldn't remember the last time she had seen him eat something. He probably had a snack while he was doing his research at the library, but if he had forgotten himself and been too involved in what he was doing, he might have forgotten. Add the adrenaline of possibly being followed on top of that, and he'd obviously depleted his glucose reserves.

Renata swore again. She glanced around the interior of the bus, considering her options. If she couldn't help him quickly, it would mean a trip to the hospital, and that put him in danger of being recognized and arrested. She pulled the backpack in Gabriel's lap closer and turned it around. She checked the pockets on the outside and found a roll of fast-dissolve glucose tablets. Renata wasn't sure whether he would be able to absorb enough orally to bring him to, but it was worth a try. She couldn't exactly make him eat or drink while unconscious. Glancing around to make sure she wasn't being observed, Renata thumbed a tablet out of the roll and pushed it into his mouth, positioning it under his tongue. Watching him, she put her fingers over his radial pulse, waiting for some sign that it was working—or that it was not. His pulse and breathing remained even, and she thought that the blue was starting to leave his nail beds.

The bus passed the stop that they had intended to get out at, but Renata wasn't worried about that. They could transfer and go back, or take the bus around the route a second time. She was too concerned about Gabriel's condition to worry about them attracting attention by staying on the bus too long.

"Is he okay?"

An old woman was leaning across the aisle, studying Gabriel closely. Renata looked her over. The woman didn't seem suspicious of them, only concerned about Gabriel.

"He's just tired," Renata said tersely. "It's been a busy day."

Gabriel shifted his position, leaning his head against the window of the bus as if to verify Renata's words. Renata breathed a sigh of relief. That was a good sign. She gave the old woman a glare until she looked away and left them to their own business. Renata took out another glucose tablet and placed it in Gabriel's mouth, where there was only a smudge of the first tablet remaining. Gabriel's lips pursed and smacked, and he shifted position again. Renata pulled him closer so that he was leaning against her instead of against the window.

"That was a close call," she murmured in his ear. "What if I hadn't been here?"

He wasn't yet aware enough to give her a response. But before they reached the end of the line, Gabriel's eyes opened and he looked at her, confused.

"It's okay," she told him. "You were hypo. You passed out."

Gabriel made a sucking sound, finding the remains of the glucose under his tongue. He didn't respond to her words. For a long time he just sat there, his eyes going back and forth trying to piece everything together.

He cleared his throat. "Give me one more of those." He sucked on the glucose. "I passed out?"

"Yeah."

He swore and pulled his jacket tighter around him. "Man, I'm sorry, Renata. I didn't mean to…"

"I'm just glad to see you conscious again. You up to walking for a few minutes? We should get off of the bus before people get too suspicious. I don't think the driver's noticed we've been on so long, but he will if he starts another lap and we're still here."

Gabriel rubbed his eyes.

"Yeah. I can walk. We don't want him calling the cops."

Renata pulled the bell cord and looked out the window, planning out an alternate route. The bus slowed, and she got up. Gabriel didn't move. Renata grabbed his jacket and gave it a strong tug. "Come on, get up. You may be a lightweight, but I can't carry you."

Gabriel got to his feet. He wasn't particularly steady, especially with the lurching of the bus as it slowed and pulled over. Renata kept holding on to his jacket, keeping him upright. The bus stopped and waited as they walked to the back door to get off. Normally, Renata would have been to the door by the time the bus stopped, but she didn't want Gabriel to end up flat on his face. She gave him a little push ahead of her when they reached the doors, and followed him out, still holding ont o his jacket. They stood there for a minute, and then Gabriel started to walk.

"I'm okay." He turned his head and looked at her. "It's okay. You can let go now."

Renata felt a little silly still holding on to him. She let go and watched him like a hawk to make sure he wasn't going to pass out again or trip and fall.

"You should get something else inside you," she advised. "Just glucose isn't enough to keep you going. You need complex carbs."

"Yeah. We'll find something along here. I don't have a lot in my bag right now. Don't want to take the chance of running out."

"You'd better restock. We can't take chances."

Gabriel nodded. "Need more money. In the meantime…" He motioned to the shops that lined the street they were walking down. There were plenty of coffee shops, sandwich places, and family-run international restaurants. It wouldn't take them long to find something that he could eat.

———

They had been talking about casual, unimportant topics. Carefully avoiding the subject of Leva and Seth, which had already been talked to death. Suddenly, Gabriel snapped his fingers.

"That's it! I just remembered!"

Renata turned to him. "Remembered what?"

"Remembered what it was I was thinking of. Before I, uh, fell asleep on the bus."

She didn't correct him on the details. She just nodded encouragingly. "Okay… what?"

"Leva. When I look at her online profiles, she's everywhere. She's posting all the time. Night or day, anytime anything happens, she's taking pictures and posting them, ranting about the doctors, asking for prayers or money for procedures. She's constantly online."

Renata made an expectant motion with her hand, waiting for the revelation. "Sure. Narcissistic. Looking for attention. That's why she poisons him; so that people will think she's important. Sympathize with her and admire her for being so long-suffering and strong."

Gabriel gave a knowing smile.

"Well, what?"

"She's not going to be able to turn that off. She's not going to be able to go from getting accolades all day long to getting nothing."

"You're saying she's going to poison him again? Make him worse?"

"No… I didn't mean that." Gabriel frowned at that thought. "What I mean is, she's going to have to be online. She can't just leave those groups alone. It's like a drug. She needs them."

"So she'll be on them again," Renata agreed, thinking it through. "But she knows the authorities are looking for her, so she can't use her old accounts. She has to set up new accounts. New names and avatars to go with her new identity."

"Right. She has to be there. There I was online half the day today, writing down everybody who has been interacting with her… and I probably saw her somewhere along the way. I just didn't recognize it."

"Because it's a new account. Not one that has been posting for months or years."

"Yeah. She wouldn't put her picture on it. She can't use her real name. She can't even take a picture of Seth unless it's from an angle that ensures no one can recognize him."

"So how do we find her? How do we know who she is?"

"I'll have to look again tomorrow… I'll still keep trying to get into contact with her through her old friends, but I need to be looking for her too. She'll probably stick pretty close to the real story, right? Do you think?"

"Probably. Unless she decides to shave his head and say that he has cancer. An easy way to disguise him, and at the same time make people feel sorry for him. She'll say…" Renata tried to get inside of Leva's mind and imagine her story. "She'll say she's a single mom, handling this all on her own. That her son has just been diagnosed. Or maybe she'll just list symptoms and announce his diagnosis after she's been settled there for a few weeks. She won't be able to post their pictures for a while, so she'll have to either use a stock photo or give an excuse for not posting. Say, his father is trying to find them or something. That would be a good story because it gives her an excuse for not giving any identifying information."

Gabriel was nodding, his eyebrows drawn down. "Yeah. That's good. I'm sure she'll be there. She won't be able to stay away. She's practically the queen bee on those forums. That's where she gets all her validation."

"It's a good idea," Renata agreed.

———

In the morning, Renata accompanied Gabriel to a different library. She didn't plan to stay there, but to make visits to a few places that Leva might need to frequent for medical supplies instead. Gabriel was glad that he was just going to be staying in one place. The library was quiet and relaxing. He didn't know where Renata got the energy. He would need to bank a few days before he could traipse around town interviewing people.

But she wanted to see if there was anything new in the news, and the library was a good place to catch up on that. There were newspapers scattered on the various study tables when they walked in. Renata immediately grabbed one as they made their way over to the computers. She flipped a few pages.

"Not front page anymore," she commented. "That's good. Page five now."

Gabriel fired up the web browser and began tapping in a few searches while she read through the newspaper article.

"Trail is getting cold," Renata said, "and I don't see any sign they are progressing at all. No new leads announced. Plea to the public. Please call the authorities if you know anything about their whereabouts."

"Is that what they're relying on? Tips? No evidence?"

"Not that they've announced," Renata said, and closed the paper again, folding it over a couple of times. "How about you? Anything interesting?"

Gabriel pressed play on a news video, and they both leaned in close to be able to hear it, keeping the volume down so that it wouldn't disturb other patrons. The library was quiet so early in the morning. No school kids or families. Just homeless and other early birds. Businesspeople or writers. Retirees.

The news anchor recapped the story of Leva's charges and Seth's disappearance, showing a security video of Leva arriving in the unit, then leaving a few minutes later pushing Seth in a wheelchair. Dressed in a nurse's uniform, she looked completely at home and legitimate, and no one stopped her. She was just a nurse taking him off to his next series of tests. Gabriel shook his head. After Seth had been taken from the hospital once, he would have thought they would put a guard on him. Especially after Leva got out on bail. Apparently, no one had communicated that fact to the police or the hospital.

Renata punched him lightly in the shoulder to get his attention, and Gabriel realized that his mind had wandered, but the video was still playing. It had switched to an interview with Judge Dee-Dee, and Gabriel was immediately alert. He inched the volume up a little, glancing around to make sure that it wasn't bothering anyone.

"It has come to our attention that Leva Wilcox may be being aided by an underground organization that has been known to assist with parental kidnappings in the past," Dee-Dee said gravely. Her picture disappeared, and in its place, pictures of Gabriel and Renata were posted. Renata swore quietly. Gabriel felt his stomach tying in knots.

"No, no, no… we *told* her we're not involved…"

Gabriel's and Renata's pictures stayed up for a few seconds longer, and then were replaced by a carousel of pictures of medically kidnapped kids they had helped escape, and anyone else in the organization who was known to have been involved. Gabriel turned his attention back to Judge Dee-Dee's voice, which was still playing in the background as the pictures were being displayed. "You may remember a report by Kirstie Holt last year about the alleged practice of medical kidnap, taking custody of medically fragile children away from their parents and putting them into foster care to give them proper medical care. Gabriel Tate and Renata Vega were part of that exposé, detailing their experiences with the system."

"Do you know these youth personally?" the anchor asked.

"Gabriel has appeared before me. Renata has not been in my courtroom, but I was made aware of her when her mother appeared before me." There was a pause while Judge Dee-Dee considered what to say. Her voice was quiet and serious. "If Gabriel and Renata are involved in this parental kidnapping, as I think they may be… I believe that they have been misled as to the facts of the case. I don't think that they would participate if they knew all the details that have come to light in the last couple of days."

The video ended.

Renata swore steadily under her breath. Gabriel looked at her, letting out a deep sigh.

"She should know we're not involved," Renata growled.

"We're going to have to let her think we are."

"Why?"

"Because we need Leva to think she can trust us. We can't go public with the fact that we're trying to find her to get Seth back. If Judge Dee-Dee thinks we're involved… then I guess that's good. If she puts out warrants for our immediate arrest… even better. The more she suspects us, the better the chances are that Leva will trust us. Right?"

The twisted logic made immediate sense to Renata's paranoid brain. She sighed, conceding the point.

"I just don't like Judge Dee-Dee thinking that we're still helping Leva when we're not. I mean, she trusted us to rescue Seth when she thought Leva was innocent, but she doesn't trust us to bring him back when it becomes obvious that Leva's guilty. I think she should know."

"We'll tell her when it's all over."

Renata laughed. "Not face-to-face, I hope."

"Yeah… probably not a good idea."

————

When Renata left, Gabriel trolled through the various social networks, groups, and discussion forums. The most helpful were the forums which listed their newest members with a hot link. Gabriel was able to view anyone who had signed up since Seth's initial transfer, and to start a list. Hopefully, he would see some of the names or themes appearing on other boards. Or the same photos being used. He did a few reverse image searches to see if any of the avatars tracked back to stock photo sites, but didn't find anything. There were quite a few users who used cartoonish pictures or pictures of animals instead of pictures of themselves or their kids.

He took a break from trying to figure out Leva's new online identity and instead checked for messages in the new email accounts he had set up to contact Leva's friends. Only a couple had responded, and only to say that they didn't know where Leva was. Did that mean that others had been suspicious of him? Had counted it as spam? Or had they quietly passed the information on to Leva to let her decide what to do with the information? All it would take was one person passing his information on to her. If they could just get her to believe that they wanted to help Seth, they could make contact and get her back in the hands of the police.

Gabriel went back to the social networks and paid close attention to the introductions. Would she try to pass herself off as someone completely new? Or would she try to use code words and phrases to let people know who she was?

Mothers with girls or young children were out. Gabriel was sure that Leva would still want to refer to Seth as her teen son. She wouldn't pretend to have a younger child or a girl. He started to write down the names of those who said they had a teenage son. The mito forums were the best bet. There wouldn't be a lot of intros over the past week to sift through. Mito was a rare disease, which made for a small, close community.

Gabriel read over the same introduction a few times.

I'm new to all of this. The doctors have just said that my son might have mito. He has always had medical problems, but they have never been able to tell me what was wrong with him. Anyone else here with teenagers? I'm a single mom and could really use the support.

Her avatar was a duck. Gabriel scrolled through, looking for other posts by her. For a newbie, she was surprisingly active, commenting on quite a few threads and demonstrating more knowledge about the ins and outs of mito than her initial introduction suggested. She hadn't posted any pictures. Gabriel pictured Leva sitting looking down at the photo album on her phone, itching like a junkie to post some of her pictures of Seth. From what Gabriel could tell, Seth was probably still looking pretty rough. And if he started feeling better, Leva could take care of that.

Gabriel had already created a profile on the board. No avatar, just the default user silhouette. Bob Smith. He clicked on Melanie Bruce's profile picture to open up a private message to her. He sat for a long time staring at the computer screen, trying to figure out what to say to her.

Melanie, I am a teenager with mito like your son. Can I help you? GT

Was it enough? Too much? If it were Leva, she would immediately know that GT was Gabriel Tate. Even if she hadn't known his last name before, it was all over the news now. He offered his help. If it wasn't Leva, she might wonder why Bob Smith was signing GT, but there was nothing else in his message that should make her suspicious. If it was just a single mom who was new to mito, and not Leva, he might be able to help her in other ways, just reassuring her and giving her some insight into handling the diagnosis.

But it had to be Leva.

He was sure that Leva wouldn't be able to stay away from her old stomping grounds. She needed the accolades. It was her crack cocaine. And hers was the only introduction by the single mom of a teenage boy. Most of the other new members had toddlers or preschoolers. Gabriel was glad that they were being diagnosed so early. It was always better to know what they were dealing with as early as possible.

Gabriel pressed 'send message.'

———

There was only so much that Gabriel could do at the library. And Renata had made sure that he was going to meet her for lunch. He could see right through the demand. She wasn't looking for company so much as she wanted to ensure that Gabriel stopped and ate and didn't let his blood sugar get too low again.

And he was pretty sure that she knew he knew.

She was absolutely right. He knew better. If he had done that while he was alone, instead of with her, he would have ended up in the hospital, and they might have identified him. Or worse, he could have blacked out somewhere where there was no one to see him and get him medical attention. He could have gone into a coma and died.

So he wiped his trails on the library computer, picked up his bag, and left to find Renata.

While they had agreed to meet at a nearby park, he didn't have to go that far. Renata was sitting on the pavement panhandling just outside the doors of the library. She was lucky that the library security hadn't sent her on her way.

"Hey. You ready to go?" he asked her.

Renata got to her feet and rubbed her bottom tenderly. "Ouch. Yeah, I'm good to go."

She picked up her cup and emptied the loose change into her hand, then put it in her pocket.

"You have any luck?"

"Yeah, pretty good, actually. This is a good place."

"You weren't there the whole time, were you? They usually kick people out pretty quickly."

"No, not the whole time. But a while. They 'suggested' that I move on, but they didn't make any noises about calling the cops, so I took my chances for a while longer."

"You've got guts. Where do you want to eat?"

"I figured we need to top up your snacks." Renata jingled the change in her pocket.

"You didn't need to do that for me." Gabriel was embarrassed. Panhandling was hard work, and he'd been sitting in a comfortable chair in front of a computer screen in a climate-controlled room the whole time she'd been working. Well, not such a comfortable chair, but Gabriel knew it was more comfortable than sitting on concrete. He'd spent enough hours doing just that to know.

"You were working too. Division of labor. Next time you can do the dirty work."

"Well… okay. But that means you have to let me."

They walked down the street. Gabriel wasn't familiar with the area, but Renata seemed to know where she was going, so he followed her lead. He assumed that she had reconnoitered the area before begging. Something he should have done as well, even if it were just via Google Maps on the computer.

"I might have found her," he announced.

"Leva? Where is she?"

"Well, virtually, not physically. Though I wonder if I can trace her IP address to find out where she's posting from…?"

"So you think she's already back online? Tell me about it. Did you send her a message? Tell her we want to help?"

Gabriel filled her in on the latest developments.

CHAPTER FOURTEEN

Gabriel spent a restless night. His brain was spinning like a hamster wheel as he went over the things that Melanie Bruce had posted online. Going over all that she had said again and again. He tried to analyze the meaning of each word and turn of phrase. Where was she? What was she doing to Seth? Was he stable or had she made him worse but couldn't take him to the hospital for fear of being arrested again? How long could she resist the temptation to poison him *just a little more?*

He didn't make any progress. His brain got tired, going over it all again and again without advancing any theories. He was too tired to think, too wired to sleep. Gabriel tossed and turned, looking for a more comfortable position. He needed sleep. He couldn't function properly without it.

Renata's arm went around him. "Settle down. I can't sleep when you're so restless."

"Sorry."

"It's okay. Just try to relax and be still." She rubbed his back. "It will all have to wait until morning."

"I know. I'm just… I can't shut my brain off. I can't stop thinking about what she might be doing."

"Right now, she's sleeping. Everyone is. We'll deal with it in the morning. Maybe she'll send you a message back."

Gabriel's brain spun even more. "I hope so."

Renata settled against him, her body warm and comforting. Gabriel lay with his eyes open for as long as he could, willing his eyes to get so tired that he wouldn't be able to keep them open. The night was cool and clear. They hadn't been disturbed by any other homeless or by punks looking to have some fun.

It was a good night for sleeping, especially with Renata there to make him feel comforted and relaxed.

———

It figured that as soon as Gabriel finally succeeded in getting to sleep, that someone would come along and disturb them. They had been able to avoid any contact with the police for quite a while, and it was bound to catch up with them.

Gabriel awoke to a hard smack on his arm and was immediately awake and alert, ready to defend himself. He expected to be facing a man with a baseball bat. The blow to his arm had been hard and painful. But it was a cop. Gabriel shook Renata before the policeman could hit her too.

"We'll move on," Gabriel said without prompting. "I'm sorry. I didn't think we were disturbing anyone here."

Renata stirred and rubbed her eyes. Her body was still soft and relaxed against Gabriel. He gave her another shake.

"Cops," he told her, trying to wake her up the rest of the way.

Renata's body went stiff. She propped herself up on one elbow. "What's going on?" She turned her head, looking at the policeman. "We're allowed to sleep. What's the deal?"

"Get up," the cop said. Gabriel couldn't make out his facial features in the dimness of the street lights that reached them. "You can't sleep here."

"Yes, we can," Renata argued. "It's our right."

"Not here. Up you get. Get a move on it."

Gabriel sat up, threading his arms through the straps of his backpack and pulling the blanket off of Renata. He started to fold it. Renata seemed intent on arguing the cop down, but without the blanket or Gabriel's body against hers, she was grudgingly forced to move.

"We're allowed to sleep here," Renata insisted to Gabriel. "He can't force us to move."

"Maybe someone complained."

"Doesn't mean he gets to violate our rights."

She helped by folding up the groundsheet and in a moment they both stood in front of the cop.

"Is there somewhere safer to sleep?" Gabriel asked, hoping that his cooperation would persuade the cop to leave them alone and not spend all night harassing them. "Somewhere we'd be out of your way?"

"I'll take you to a shelter."

The cop was older, white-haired, gruff. Gabriel still couldn't see his name badge, but at least the guy wasn't beating on them. They had both dealt with cops in the past who wouldn't leave them alone while they picked their things up. Cops that would continue to kick them and whale on them with a nightstick until they were on their feet, and maybe not stop even then. This one was at least showing them some respect.

"We're not going to a shelter," Renata argued. "If we wanted to go to a shelter, that's where we'd be already. So thanks, but I don't think so."

"You kids aren't allowed to be sleeping out here like this. You're at risk. We take care of our homeless here. Provide services. Let me get you somewhere safe tonight."

"No," Renata repeated. "You can't force us."

The cop grabbed her elbow, and he pulled her a step closer to himself. "That's enough of your attitude. You're coming with me. We don't want anyone sleeping on the street."

Renata tried to jerk away from him, but he wasn't letting her go.

Gabriel looked at the sky, noting the position of the moon. "Why bother?" he said. "We'd only be there a couple of hours before they'd be waking us up and kicking us out. Why not just let us stay where we like? We're not causing any trouble."

"They'd give you a hot shower and meal, and whatever counseling you need to get back on track. They have an addiction program, school alternatives, job training. Everything you need to get off the street permanently."

And they had police bulletins on outstanding warrants. They cataloged and tracked everyone who went through their doors. They would coordinate with Social Services to get them put into residential care, unless the police wanted to put them in jail.

The cop was being nice, but firm. He had already decided on a course of action, even if it didn't comply with the current policies that said Gabriel and Renata had the right to sleep on public property, as long as they were on their way before the early-morning commuters had to see them. They were lucky that he hadn't recognized them as the couple who were supposed to be complicit in Seth's kidnapping. Those pictures were all over the media.

"We don't want to go to the shelter," Renata repeated. "It's nice of you to want to help, but we don't need your interference. We were doing just fine without you."

"Fine?" the old cop challenged. "Sleeping rough? Stealing food to survive? Drinking and shooting up, killing your brain cells?"

"We're not!" Gabriel protested.

"Come nicely, so I don't have to put you under arrest," he ordered through gritted teeth, the patient veneer wearing.

Renata made another effort to pull out of his grasp. Gabriel gave her a look. If she fought him, she was going to end up too tired to function. They needed to conserve energy. Already, they were going to be in bad shape from being woken up and denied the sleep that they needed. Renata growled in her throat.

The cop wasn't taking any more attitude. He pulled a pair of handcuffs off of his belt.

"Oh, seriously!" Renata complained.

He locked them over her wrists, allowing her to keep them in front of her and not removing her backpack from her shoulders. "I'm trying to help you kids out. I've seen kids like you before. They get killed out here. It's not a safe place to be. If you can't go home, then at least start a new life by making use of the city's resources."

Renata shook her head. The cop looked warily at Gabriel as if expecting him to either run or fight. But Gabriel couldn't do either.

"We stay together," Gabriel said. "The shelters won't let us stay together. They all separate boys and girls."

"It's the only safe option," the cop agreed. "Young love or not, you're going to be sleeping apart until you can get a place of your own. Isn't that a good enough reason for trying to get on your feet, to leave the street behind?"

"It's a good reason for not going to a shelter," Renata said.

They looked at each other, not sure what to do with the cop's 'young love.' Neither of them had ever claimed their relationship was one of love. They were good friends. They kept each other company if they could. They had never taken the relationship further, to one of intimacy.

"You coming, or you want to be handcuffed too?" the cop asked Gabriel.

Gabriel didn't move. "Where exactly are we going?"

"Central Youth Services," the cop decided, looking them over. "You're both minors, right?"

Gabriel shrugged. He'd seen Central Youth before. Not somewhere he wanted to be. He didn't want to deal with the filthiness of the new admissions, equally unhygienic whether they came from the street or from foster care situations where they had been neglected. The drug dealing that went on right under the administration's noses. Having to be separated from Renata for the rest of the night. And, of course, the possibility that they would be recognized and arrested once the cop or the administrators saw them in full light.

"You really want to spend an hour of your time getting us admitted, when you know that in a couple more, we'll just be out again? We don't want to stay. They can't keep us there. It's not a prison."

"They can help you there. You'll see once you get there. They have lots of programs to help kids like you…"

"They don't know anything about kids like us," Renata argued. "Gabe's right, we're just going to walk right back out of there. We've both been there before, neither of us wants to be there. So why don't you just let us go? We'll find somewhere to sleep that's not on your beat. Okay?"

The cop wasn't easy to persuade. His lips pressed together in a thin line of frustration. If he'd been looking for gratitude for his kindness in funneling kids into the system, he wasn't going to be getting it from Gabriel and Renata.

He gave Renata's arm a jerk and escorted them away from their sleeping place to a squad car he had apparently called before waking the two of them up. Another cop was waiting there, younger, dark hair and eyes. The new cop looked over Renata and Gabriel.

"This one being uncooperative?" he asked, noting the handcuffs.

"They're both being uncooperative. That one a little more so."

"Take them to Central?"

"You don't have the right to take us anywhere against our will," Renata renewed her objections. "We were not breaking the law. You can't just relocate people because they're homeless. That's a violation of our rights."

"You'll like Central Youth," the new cop said brightly. "Lots of other kids there, good food and all the amenities. It's like living at the Ritz."

"We've been to Central before," Renata said with a withering glare. "It's no Ritz."

He looked away from her. "Anything to charge them with?" he asked the white-haired cop. He sat down in the passenger seat of the car and started to tap something out on the keyboard. Gabriel looked at Renata. If the cops were too curious, they were going to find out that Gabriel and Renata were wanted for questioning.

"I was molested last time I was at Central," Renata said. "You really going to send me back where I was raped? I'm not going back there!"

The cops both looked at her, startled. Gabriel held his breath. It was a good bluff. He couldn't think of a much better reason to avoid a place like Central. Other than wanting to avoid prison time.

"Central is a safe place," the younger cop said, frowning. "I can't believe that something like that would happen there. The boys and the girls are kept separate…"

"You think it was one of the other teens?" Renata demanded.

More uncomfortable looks from the cops.

"If there is someone at the shelter who is being inappropriate, you need to give us details so that we can charge them and get them out of there. Who was it that hurt you?"

Renata shook her head. She lifted her hands, cuffed in front of her, and covered her eyes and face. "I can't talk about it. I can't. The doctor said it's post-traumatic stress. I can't face it again. I can't go there. You can't force us to go there. Not where I was raped!"

She was bawling and Gabriel almost believed it himself. The cops were beside themselves. The older one leaned over and spoke quietly to the one in the car, discussing possibilities. Gabriel hoped that one of the options was just letting them go. The police didn't have the legal right to force them into a shelter, but that didn't mean they wouldn't.

"What about Mary's Door?" The older cop asked. "Have you been there before? It's just girls. And I've never heard any complaints about abuse there."

That was interesting. They hadn't said that they'd never heard of any abuse at Central Youth.

"No, I want to stay with John." Gabriel was startled until he realized from her gesture that John was Gabriel's new name. It was probably wise to avoid using their real names, with BOLOs out on them. "He takes care of me. He'll make sure nothing happens to me. Please, don't separate us."

The cops were gradually wearing down. Gabriel moved closer to Renata. "They won't separate us," he assured her. "They can see you can't manage on your own. We need each other. We take care of each other."

Finally, the older cop gave in. He moved toward Renata to unlock her handcuffs. Renata shied back. "It's okay. I'm just going to take those off."

"You'll let us go? We can stay together?" she sobbed.

"Yes, fine. I'll let you stay together. But you kids need to look at other options. There are lots of services. Even if you won't stay overnight at Central, they still run a lot of programs out of there that could help you. Or find a friend to stay with. Don't sleep on the streets; it's too dangerous."

"Safer than a shelter," Renata muttered, rubbing her wrists.

She grabbed Gabriel's hand. He pulled away from her grasp and instead put his arm around her shoulder, pulling her close. They walked away down the street, not looking back.

They were a block or two away before Renata let out a long sigh of relief. "That was a close one," she said. "Man, that do-gooder was determined, wasn't he? Heaven save me from helpful cops!"

"You did it, though. I didn't think we were going to be able to. That was a brilliant line. I don't think they would have broken otherwise."

"Is that what you think it was?" Renata demanded. "A line? With the number of foster homes, hospital wards, and institutions I've been passed through over the years, you think I somehow managed to avoid all the perverts?" She shook her head. "It sounds good because it comes from a place of truth. Always stay close to the truth when you tell your lies."

"Oh." Gabriel gave her shoulders a squeeze. "I'm sorry. You… never said anything about it before."

"Part of the foster kid experience."

Neither of them said anything for a long time. Gabriel watched for a good place to bed down and go back to sleep, but neither of them felt calm enough to lie down again. So they ended up wandering, occasionally sitting at a bus stop to rest, and taking a couple of early morning buses. Eventually, the sky started to brighten. Gabriel watched it, knowing Renata was doing the same.

Instead of the sunrise making him feel peaceful, like it usually did, relieved at having made it through another night, he felt anxious and unsettled. Leva was out there with Seth. Doing who-knew-what to him. She might be watching the same sunrise, eager to get started on another day. She needed to get her fix. To let everyone know what a wonderful, attentive mother she was to her poor, sick boy. And so far, they were no closer to finding her.

———

Their morning routine took time. Getting breakfast. Making their way to another library, avoiding the two they had already gone to. Which meant they had to leave the central core and go farther out into suburbia. A couple of hours on buses when they counted in the waiting time and the transfers required.

Gabriel washed up in the library restrooms before beginning. He was borderline obsessive about keeping himself and his clothes clean and neat so that he wouldn't be taken as a homeless person. As long as he wasn't sitting on the street panhandling. In the library, doing research at a computer, he could be a student. He was tall enough he could pass as a college student. No one would guess by the way he looked that he was homeless.

There was a big bruise on his arm where the cop had hit him to wake him up. What had been the reason for hitting him with a nightstick rather than shaking him awake, or nudging him with a toe? There was a lump under the bruise and Gabriel was a slow healer. It would be weeks before the mark disappeared. He dried off and pulled his sleeves down so that the bruise was hidden.

Then, settling in front of a computer, he logged into his mail and some of the forums he had sent messages on the previous day, hoping for some progress.

People still said that they didn't know where Leva was. There was one, though, who said that she would pass on his message if she ran into Leva. That was a good sign. Maybe she did know where Leva was but didn't want to give herself away until she knew how Leva felt about contact with Gabriel.

Then Gabriel spotted the duck avatar. Melanie Bruce had responded to his private message. Gabriel clicked on the duck and scanned the message window that opened.

I don't know what a teenager could do to help us, but thank you for the offer.

Gabriel felt cold. It was a pretty terse message. Was it Leva? He had expected her to fish for information. If she weren't Leva, then maybe a question about what exactly Gabriel could help her with. Or a message or question from her son about mito and how he handled it.

If the message were from Leva, it sounded like an accusation. The teens had helped her before and had completed the transfer successfully. Did she feel like they had failed her when she got arrested again? So why would she allow them to help now?

Gabriel pondered over what kind of message he should compile in return. How could he pursue further contact with her without frightening her away?

He could have used Renata's input on what to write, but she hadn't stuck around. Gabriel wrote and rewrote messages, trying to find one that felt right. He erased everything and sat staring at the blinking cursor.

We could help with paperwork. Do you need anything?

It was short. Maybe too short. But he couldn't afford to write anything long. If it were a cop on the other side of the duck avatar instead of Leva—and why not?—he didn't want to say anything that could be used against him. Keep it vague. Use double meanings. Be as cryptic as possible when forced to communicate in a medium that could be traced or recorded. If Gabriel could create a new profile and try to find Leva's new profile, there was nothing to stop the police from doing it too. Surely they had thought of the same thing.

He pressed 'send'. He stared at the screen. Too late to take it back now. Thinking about the police sent his mind back to the previous night's encounter. Gabriel and Renata were lucky to have been let go without being discovered or forced to stay somewhere under lock and key.

Renata had been quiet that morning. Maybe she had been tired. Or maybe she had been thinking about the close call, or about whatever experiences she had dealt with in foster care or the institutions she had spent time in. He'd never thought about it before. Renata was cheerful, tough, and plainspoken, and he had never seen her as a victim. She had always been strong. Even when her demons won out, she was still a strong, independent person. It scared him to think of her as vulnerable.

———

"Any luck?"

Gabriel startled. He hadn't been watching for Renata's return and had been deep in thought as he browsed through the various forums where he might find posts by Leva. The duck had posted a few comments, but not as many as the previous day, maybe spooked by his message to her. And he hadn't yet been able to identify her new profile on other platforms, though he had a few suspicions.

"Just wait a second," he told Renata. "I'll show you."

She pulled a chair up next to his. "Didn't mean to scare you," she apologized, but with a bit of mischief in her tone.

Gabriel shrugged. "Just startled me. I'm fine."

He pulled up the message from Melanie Bruce. Renata looked at the duck avatar for a moment; then her eyes moved over the brief message.

"Well, that's a bit harsh. Did you send her anything back?"

Gabriel navigated to his reply.

Renata nodded slowly. "Yeah, that works. We have to be careful. No idea who is going to be reading this stuff. Now or months from now."

"Yeah. That's what I figured."

"Well, chances are you're not going to hear anything back until tomorrow or the next day. She's not going to want to look too eager to get in contact with you."

"You in a hurry to leave?"

Renata glanced around the library. "I don't like to spend too long in one place. You've been here for hours already. We should be on our way."

"Okay…"

Gabriel didn't have anything else to do there. He'd only been wasting time after the first hour or so. There were some phone calls he should make. See if anyone had heard anything about Leva through their web of contacts. Make sure there were no other urgent cases that they needed to be on top of. Things had been busy before Seth's transfer, and Gabriel was anxious that no one fall through the cracks because he was distracted by Seth and Leva.

Renata waited until they were out of the building, walking down the street where they were less likely to be overheard.

"You'll never guess who I heard from."

Gabriel looked at her smile and dancing eyes. It wasn't bad news. Ray?

She didn't usually look that excited after talking to him. He couldn't think of who else she might be so happy about talking to.

"Who?"

"Skyler."

It took Gabriel an instant to remember who Skyler was. One of their very first transfers. He had been held in the same psych ward as Gabriel and Renata had been, back when they first met. He had mito and was autistic and transgender. Quite a unique package. He and his parents had been so grateful to get back together again. Gabriel felt a warm feeling wash over him, thinking back to that reunion.

"How is Skyler?" he asked, smiling.

"He's good. Getting along well at school. As healthy as could be expected. Most of his symptoms are under control right now. His parents say they've never seen him so happy."

"That's great."

Skyler was so smart. Gabriel wondered what kind of a program he was in at school. A fast track for genius kids? A special ed classroom for developmentally delayed kids, where he had to practice conversation and life skills? Or maybe he was mainstreamed and was able to fit in without any special programming.

He smiled at Renata, who was looking at him expectantly. "That's really good to hear."

CHAPTER FIFTEEN

Gabriel was eager to see whether Leva—or whoever was behind the duck profile—had answered his message. They couldn't do anything else until they got an answer. And he didn't want to wait a full day to get it. So they stopped at an internet cafe later in the afternoon to access his accounts again without having to rely on the library. Best not to be seen at the same place too often, especially if the police were actively looking for them on Judge Dee-Dee's instructions.

It was suppertime, and Gabriel ordered a hamburger with fries so that they wouldn't stand out from the rest of the internet cafe crowd. Though as Gabriel picked at the greasy fries, he wasn't sure why he had bothered. Renata's tube feeding wasn't exactly invisible. Even though she tried to be discreet about it, they still earned a few glances. But Gabriel refused to suggest she feed in the bathroom instead of out in the open. It was a matter of principle. They had had enough people in the past act as though Renata were doing something rude or disgusting, and he wouldn't do anything that might suggest they had been right. There were times when security had to take a back seat to acceptance. He would never chance hurting Renata's feelings by suggesting she should hide her tube feeding. If the cops were onto Gabriel's new online identity and traced his IP address to see where he was posting from, they would find the internet cafe, and if one of the servers recognized Gabriel and Renata because Renata had tube-fed there, then so be it. That was a risk Gabriel would take. That would confirm that they were trying to contact Leva, but it would also prove that they weren't part of her kidnapping Seth from the hospital. That they weren't complicit in it. Yet.

"You okay?" Renata asked mildly.

Gabriel realized that he'd been staring at her while he munched on his fries, lost in thought.

"Oh. Sorry." Gabriel looked at the computer. They were there to log in and check for messages, so he might as well do it instead of sitting there worrying about getting caught. He navigated to the support group and logged in.

"She's responded," he said eagerly.

Renata leaned closer so that she could read over his shoulder.

"I could use help with paperwork, but funds are low. I can't pay anyone."

Renata looked at Gabriel, wrinkling her nose.

"What's that about?"

"She hasn't had time to earn any money. And she probably can't use anything she had in savings. The police would freeze her accounts, right?"

"We told her before we moved Seth to empty out her account. She should have cash."

"Maybe she didn't have much to start with. With the medical bills and a trip to Disneyland, she wouldn't have much."

"You told me she raised thousands with that online fundraising," Renata made a motion toward the computer. "She used it all up? When they were only at Disney for a day instead of a week?"

Gabriel drummed a couple of fingers on the back of the mouse without clicking any buttons. "She would still have to pay for the whole trip. And she had to pay for a new identity once already. That's not cheap. And whatever other expenses she had with the first move. The new car, which she probably had to ditch now."

Renata shook her head. "I saw that car. She made money on the trade; she didn't lose anything. I'm telling you, Gabe; she's lying. She's not out of money."

Gabriel stared at the message on the screen. "Then it's a test," he said finally. "She wants to know how much we know about her finances and how much we're willing to do."

"Yes," Renata agreed, nodding. "That makes more sense."

Gabriel chewed on the inside of his cheek and considered their options. "If we want to track her down, we have to say yes. That we'll get her new identity papers at our own cost."

"That's a lot of money."

"Uh-huh. I don't know how we're going to do it."

Renata busied herself with disconnecting her tube and tossing her wrappers in the trash. Gabriel could see she was working it through as well. Where were they going to get the hundreds of dollars that would be required to provide Leva and Seth with new identities? Especially since word was now out that they were fugitives. Merrick and other identity brokers would charge a premium if they were going to involve themselves in such a public case.

"We could just tell her that we got it," Gabriel suggested. "She wouldn't know until she met us to pick them up that we didn't have her papers."

"She'd know if she didn't have to get her photograph taken."

"We could say that we used the same photograph as last time. We just went back to the same broker for a second set."

Renata just looked at Gabriel, and he backed up in his thinking.

"Then she would just have to call him to ask if we were telling the truth."

"Yeah. I don't think we can get out of actually paying for the work if we want to get her trust."

"I don't know how we're going to raise the money. Calling volunteers on the underground railway to see if they'll donate? I can't think of any big donors who are going to step forward. It will all be piecemeal and it will take time."

"And I suppose you're averse to holding up banks," Renata teased.

Gabriel grinned at her. "Yeah, sort of," he agreed.

He decided to check his email and the other discussion boards while working through the problem of funding. It was no bigger than the other logistical problems they ran into on transfers. But it was going to take some thought.

"We could take their pictures ourselves. Say that was the most secure way to do it. Then wait the appropriate length of time and say that we've got the paperwork. We set up a meet, and then rescue Seth."

"You're going to meet with her twice, once to take the pictures and once to rescue Seth? What if she doesn't bring Seth to the meeting to pick up the papers? Why not just rescue him when they come for pictures, he has to be with her then."

"Yeah. We could do that. That makes sense."

Renata was already shaking her head. "Then she has to trust us before we've proven ourselves, and she's not going to do that."

"What about Judge Dee-Dee?" Gabriel asked after a while. "What about the police? They put money into investigating and arresting people like Leva. What if we brought them in? They provide the capital; she trusts us because we're just kids, and the police swoop in and arrest her."

Renata shook her head, her dark eyes cold. "No way. I'm not working with the cops or with Judge Dee-Dee. Forget it."

"I thought you liked Judge Dee-Dee."

"Yeah. At a distance. But if we brought her in on this…" Renata gave it a few more seconds of consideration. "No."

"But we know she's sympathetic to the cause. She's the one who suggested Seth to us in the first place."

"And that makes us super dangerous to her," Renata pointed out. "If we said the wrong thing, we could ruin her career. She'd need to reduce or eliminate the risk. We'd end up in prison. Or worse."

Gabriel made an effort not to roll his eyes. "Renata… Judge Dee-Dee wouldn't do anything like that. She's a judge. One of the good ones, with a conscience. She'd never bend her moral standards—"

"Gabe," Renata interrupted him, her voice quiet, but arresting. Maybe it seemed all the more important because it was so quiet, instead of raised in anger or hysteria.

Gabriel stopped talking and looked at her.

"She already *has*. I always thought she was so moral because of the way she still put my mom in prison, even though she didn't think it was right. Because that's what the law said she had to do. I thought that proved that she couldn't be swayed by personal opinion."

"I still think that," Gabriel inserted.

"But she's proven that she can be swayed. She came to us about Seth. Did an end-run around the law because she didn't think Leva had Munchausen by Proxy."

"And because of that, she can't be trusted?"

"Not only will she bend her standards and risk breaking the law, but now that she's done it, she's in danger of losing everything. We could ruin her reputation and get her defrocked, or whatever they do to judges. Bam! Game over, Ex-Judge Dee-Dee."

Gabriel's head spun. He sat there looking at Renata, trying to reconcile her feelings to his own. His instinct told him that Judge Dee-Dee could be trusted. But Renata had understood the medical kidnap situation when nobody could. Renata had devised a plan to make the public aware of the corruption. Renata had laid out the bare bones of the underground railway, so that Gabriel could get it set up and functioning. He couldn't discount what Renata had to say about Judge Dee-Dee, no matter how much it went against what Gabriel felt in his heart. The heart could be wrong.

"We would never do that to her."

"Maybe you wouldn't," Renata agreed. "But she would have to trust that one hundred percent if she's going to help us, and she obviously doesn't. And… I can't say that I wouldn't expose her if it was in the best interests of the railway. We have that option now, if she ever does anything to threaten us."

"So…" Gabriel gave a long exhalation, trying to get his brain back on track. "Our only option is to do what Leva wants. Get her new identification and find a way to cover the costs for her. If we do that, we can make face-to-face contact with her so that we can get her away from Seth."

Renata looked around the internet cafe before looking back at Gabriel and nodding. "I don't see any other way. If we want to pass her test, the only way is to do what she says."

"It's going to take a while to get the money raised. I don't know how long, but we're not going to be able to get this done tomorrow."

"No," Renata agreed. "And she's gotta know that too."

Gabriel looked back at the message on his screen. He hit reply and closed his eyes. Renata didn't jump in with any suggestions. Gabriel typed.

We will help with the paperwork. But fundraising is going to take a while. Are you safe now?

He looked at Renata. "Does that work? Is that going to freak her out?"

"No, I think you're okay. You didn't ask her where she was or for proof of life. Just whether she was okay."

Gabriel swallowed. "Proof of life?"

"That's what you say in a hostage situation. Prove that the person you're bargaining for is still alive."

"But that's not what we're doing. We haven't said anything about Seth. And he's… well, we know he's alive."

Renata raised one eyebrow. "Do we?"

"He's alive," Gabriel insisted. "She wouldn't be asking for a new identity otherwise. She'd just run. But she knows she has to be able to get Seth medical care. He has to have an identity for her to get him treatment."

"I don't think he's dead," Renata admitted. "But that may be the only thing keeping him alive right now. She needs to take him to a doctor soon. Just communicating with her friends online, as a dummy account, that's not going to be enough for her for long."

Gabriel clicked 'send' and then stared at his inbox, waiting for a reply from Leva to appear like magic. Was Leva somewhere she had internet access? Sitting at her computer waiting for his response? Or was she doing as they were, just going to a public computer once or twice a day to check messages?

"Do you think the police are watching her internet activity? They've got to know that she's going to go back online, right? They can get an IP address, find where she is staying or stake out whatever public computers she's using. They'll probably catch her before we even finish raising the money for a new identity."

"I would. If I had the kind of money and resources the cops do, there isn't anything that I couldn't find out. I'd know where she is, what she's doing, and what she ate for breakfast."

"But they have to do it legally," Gabriel reminded her.

Renata chuckled. "Always handcuffed by the law. I don't know how they can stand it. I don't know why more cops don't go around it, like that cop who tried to pick us up. Just ignore the law and do what they think is right. Wouldn't you?"

Before Gabriel could open his mouth to answer, she laughed and shook her head. "Look who I'm asking. The guy running the underground railway. Of course you'd go around the law to do what was right. Your conscience wouldn't let you do anything else."

"Would yours?"

Gabriel was curious to hear her answer. He knew that in spite of her disregard of the law, Renata was a highly moral person. And she was offended by the social workers, doctors, and judges who twisted some laws to get what they wanted and ignored others as they pleased.

"My conscience is flexible," Renata said. "What's right changes depending on the case and the circumstances. What was right, like getting Seth out of the hospital and care, can change. And I'm not so rigid that I'm going to do something I know is wrong. No matter what the law or society's moral code says."

Gabriel nodded. Renata thought Judge Dee-Dee was dangerous because she had bent her previously unassailable standards. But Gabriel thought Renata was even more dangerous because she could flip her perspective in an instant. He always worried about what would happen if Renata's paranoia made her perceive Gabriel as a threat. He knew that the shift could happen in an instant. He could go from being her best friend and confidante to being her worst enemy, someone she would avoid at all costs, or even try to harm. Her instability made her far more dangerous than Judge Dee-Dee, who had only made one carefully considered deviation.

———

They started on fundraising for Leva's new identity, which was even harder than Gabriel had anticipated. Because Leva and Seth had been on TV, Gabriel couldn't tell people that the money was to go to them. They were fugitives, and while the underground railway was used to spiriting youth away to their families, they weren't used to the details being public and all over the news. Everybody had heard the accusations and the evidence against Leva. Few of them would take Leva's side. Even those who did would question Gabriel's decision to involve himself in such a public case. One that could land them all in jail in an instant. Even without knowing that the money was for Leva, people were still leery of helping while the underground railway was in the news.

Gabriel started making calls to some of their primary contacts. He couldn't ask for money directly because it was his face on the news. The request needed to come from someone who was a little more removed. So that people didn't just see prison bars and shy away from donating. Gabriel had been surprised to find Renata had put Ray's name on Gabriel's list. He thought that she would want to be the one to talk to him.

"I've been talking to him too much," Renata said. "I don't want him to have the new phone number, or for the cops to be able to connect the dots from him to me. It's your turn. You haven't talked to him for a while."

Gabriel was happy to do it.

"Gabe!" Ray's voice was enthusiastic when he realized who was calling. "Hey, man, how's it going? How are our two outlaws surviving?"

"We're fine," Gabriel said, smiling.

"How's Renny? Still on her meds?"

"Yeah, she is." Gabriel had seen her put her meds into her feeding tube before her formula, so he was sure of the answer. "She's doing well. Says 'hi.'"

"Tell her 'hi' back and give her a big hug for me."

"I will. So—"

"I was hoping to hear from you soon. I don't know if you've been hearing the chatter through the grapevine?"

"Uh… no, I haven't heard much of anything the last couple of days. What's up?"

"Oh…" Ray didn't answer right away. Gabriel took a deep breath to prepare himself. The chatter wasn't likely to be good. If it were good news, Ray would have launched right into it without hesitations. It was going to be bad news.

"You put the word out that you were trying to find Leva. That you figure she's probably staying with friends," Ray started out.

"Yeah. Right."

"I think she is too. But I haven't been able to find out where."

"But you've heard rumors," Gabriel suggested.

"I've heard… questions about whether Seth is okay."

Gabriel frowned and rubbed his forehead, thinking about that. "What does that mean? *We* are asking questions about whether Seth is okay…"

"Well, not really. We're asking about where he is. Or where Leva is. But all we're hearing back is… questions about whether he's okay, or whether he's sick or in danger."

"Of course he's in danger. That's the whole point."

"I think there's more to it than that," Ray said. "I don't think we're just hearing back a reflection of our own concern. I think what we're hearing is… that he's *not* okay."

Gabriel swore. "What happened? What have you heard?"

"I haven't heard what happened. It's just… the feeling that I get from my contacts. Someone somewhere knows something, and what they're saying is, Seth's not okay."

"Then they need to tell us where he is. Or call the police. Something. They can't just spread gossip and think that's going to help anything."

"Yeah. I know. But I can't get anything more specific than that. You can try calling some others, see if you can get anything out of them. Or maybe Renata could find something out. People are more likely to talk to a girl than to me."

"All you can tell me is that Seth might be worse. He might be sick or in danger. That's it."

"Sorry, Gabe. That's all I can give you."

"No area of town? Who he might be with? What kind of shape he is actually in? He could be dead by the time we've raised enough money."

"Raised enough money?" Ray repeated. "What are you talking about? Paying ransom?"

"That's what it amounts to," Gabriel's answer was a growl. He knew he couldn't blame Ray for what was happening. There was no point in shooting the messenger. But he didn't know where else to point his anger. "She says she needs us to set her up with new identities. But she can't pay for it. So we have to raise the cash for the broker."

"She says? You've talked to her?"

"Only messaged her, or someone we think is her, on a discussion board. It might not even be her. We might be having a discussion with someone who has no idea what's actually going on. Or a cop who thinks that we'll lead him to her. But I think it's her. I'm pretty sure."

"That's closer than anyone else has gotten. Maybe you'd better ask her if Seth is okay."

"I asked if they were safe… that's as close as I could get. I don't know if she'll answer me. But she's not going to tell me where they are."

"Not directly. Why don't you have her send you pictures? On TV, they can always narrow down where someone is by the landmarks in their pictures. We could do that."

"Or get GPS coordinates off of them," Gabriel agreed. "Only she's not going to send me any pictures. She's hiding behind an avatar. Pretending to be someone else. It would sort of give things away if she sent me pictures of her or Seth."

"Say that you won't give her the new ID without proof that he's okay."

"She'll just go back into hiding if I do that. She's too worried about getting caught. She's not going to take any risks."

"Other than posting on these bulletin boards."

"Yeah. Other than that."

"I hope you know what you're doing, Gabriel. 'Cause this kid's life is on the line."

"I hope I do too," Gabriel agreed.

———

Renata stared into space, considering the news from Ray. Like Gabriel, she had learned to trust the word that they got out of their network. But it had been frustrating not to be able to get a location on Leva. Not even a hint of where she might be. Hearing that Seth might be in trouble made it all the more frustrating. If he were sicker and Leva couldn't take him to the hospital without new identification papers, he could be in grave danger. It was like standing by, watching someone drown, unable to do anything.

"Maybe we'd better get a message to Judge Dee-Dee," she said finally.

"But I thought…" Gabriel shook his head in disbelief. "You went through that whole thing about not being able to trust her or get her involved. You said it's too dangerous."

"That's when it was just about raising the money. But if Seth's getting worse, we might not have time to do anything for them. And if we call in an anonymous tip, they're not going to give it any more weight than anyone else's. We need them to take action, knowing how important it is. The only way to do that is a direct communication between us and Judge Dee-Dee. She has to know it's coming from us and that it's everything we can give her."

"Directly from us?" Gabriel echoed, his stomach knotting.

"Directly. Face to face."

"We can't do that. We'll be arrested."

"We have to."

Gabriel stared at her in dismay. Renata shrugged widely.

———

Gabriel sat on the pavement with his back against the outer wall of the building, waiting. Word was that Judge Dee-Dee always went out for specialty coffee, disliking the stuff offered at the courthouse. Gabriel wouldn't mind a good coffee himself. He rarely spent the money for coffee, except on occasion when he couldn't warm up in the morning. And then it wasn't at a fancy coffee stand. It was the cheapest cup at the cheapest fast food restaurant he could find.

He watched the people approaching the coffee stand. There was a surprising amount of activity so early in the morning. Lawyers and judges apparently started their days early. A gray-haired, slight woman walked up to the coffee stand. She had a briefcase in one hand and a purse in the other. She walked ramrod straight, managing to look taller than she really was. Gabriel pushed himself to his feet and walked over to stand beside her.

"Judge Dee-Dee."

She turned and looked up at him. She didn't look startled or angry. She didn't look around for the nearest cop. She continued to place her order.

"Gabriel. We've been looking for you."

"So I've heard."

"Coffee?"

"Sure."

She didn't ask what kind he wanted, just ordered a plain cup for him. Gabriel took the coffee that was handed to him. Judge Dee-Dee moved away from the coffee stand, motioning for Gabriel to go with her. He kept an eye out for security guards, court bailiffs, or cops, and they walked along beside the big granite courthouse.

"Where are Leva and Seth?" Judge Dee-Dee asked, taking a sip of her drink.

"I don't know. We've been trying to find them too. We were not involved with this… abduction."

"It smells like one of yours. And we both know…" She trailed off and didn't voice what they both knew. That she had put them onto the case and they had been involved in the earlier escape from the hospital.

"It wasn't us," Gabriel repeated. "It was Leva by herself. She might have learned some of our techniques, but none of our people were involved."

She didn't answer, her face contemplative as she took another tentative sip of the hot coffee.

"I was the one who called it in before," Gabriel said. "*I* called the ambulance, not Leva. And I told the doctor I thought she might have given him something. I told him that she had Epsom salts at her house."

"What did you see?" She turned toward him so that she could read his face. "Before you called the ambulance. What made you sure enough to tell the doctor she was poisoning him?"

Gabriel realized that she hadn't been surprised by his assertion that he had called the ambulance and talked to the doctor. Whatever she had previously said to the TV reporters, she had apparently looked further into the details of the case. He should have known that she would.

"It's hard to explain," Gabriel said. "She was so… in her element taking care of him. Dressed as a nurse, smiling, loving every minute of it. Taking pictures of him even though he was so sick. I was worried he was going to die, and she was taking pictures. And Seth… he hadn't wanted to leave the hospital at first. He said that the food his mom made wasn't good and that he got sicker when he went home."

Judge Dee-Dee nodded her steel-gray head slowly. "It would appear… that the doctor in California was correct, and ours were blinded by how well they knew Leva. This whole debacle is my fault."

Gabriel's coffee was still too hot to drink, but he raised it to his lips and pretended to take a sip, not wanting to look at her and not sure how to answer Judge Dee-Dee's self-recrimination.

"None of us are perfect," he said. "You're human."

"I sit on the bench all day judging other people. I pride myself in my ability to discern what kind of people they are, and when the law gives me enough leeway, in being able to make the right choice and give the appropriate sentence. I do that all day long. I can't be human. I can't make a mistake in a case like this."

He didn't say anything.

"So you didn't have anything to do with his disappearance," Judge Dee-Dee said. She wasn't asking a question, just making an observation. "Do you know anything about where they are? Or are you only contacting me to say that you weren't involved?"

"There are rumors in the underground railway. I can't get anything specific. No details, no location. We've been trying to get information from anyone who might know her. But all that we've heard back… is that he might be sicker. That he's in danger."

"We already guessed that. It seems like she's escalating. Like she needs a bigger splash, more attention. And now she's away from medical care… It's very bad for Seth."

"We need to find them now."

Her narrow shoulders lifted in a shrug. "Anything you can provide. The police are already doing everything they can. My haranguing them isn't going to make them find her any faster."

Gabriel pulled the folded piece of paper out of his pocket. "I think she's online again. She would have to set up new profiles, and she can't post any pictures, so she's probably pretty frustrated. I think this is her."

Judge Dee-Dee took it from him.

"The police might be able to tell where she is posting from," Gabriel explained. "If they can get IP addresses, they can narrow it down. I don't know if that will help. Maybe they already know about this."

"I'll have someone look into it." She fixed her gaze on him. "Have you communicated with her?"

"I've tried. I haven't been able to get any information on where she is or how Seth is."

"But you think he's sicker."

"Yes. That's the rumor. But I don't know where it's coming from. I would hope that anyone who knew how sick he is would call it in… but they apparently haven't."

"We need to find him before it's too late. If I gave you my private cell number, would you keep me informed about any new developments?"

Gabriel hesitated. As soon as he sent her anything, he could be traced, so any phone that he used to contact her would have to be limited to one-time use. Pay phones were difficult to find and he didn't want the police showing up on the doorstep of some harried mom whose phone he borrowed, or at a shop where the owner had been kind enough to lend him the use of the phone.

"Give me the number," he agreed finally. "But I don't know… if I find something certain, I'll let you know… one way or another."

"Good. Hold this." Judge Dee-Dee thrust her coffee into Gabriel's hands and dug a business card out of her purse. She wrote a number on the back of it and handed it to Gabriel. She took back her cup. "Is there anything I can do?"

Gabriel sipped his coffee, which had cooled down enough to drink. Renata had said that it was too dangerous to involve Judge Dee-Dee. But that was before things had gotten desperate enough to contact her. Now that they were face to face, was there any more danger in involving her further?

"I need money," Gabriel said. Judge Dee-Dee raised her brows. "If this is Leva," he gestured to the paper Judge Dee-Dee held, "she needs new identification. But she can't or won't pay for it. She wants the underground railway to cover it, but I'm having trouble raising it. No one wants to risk being connected to a high-profile case. Not when you've already publicly connected me and Renata to it."

"Do you really think it's her?"

"Yes. But there's no way to be sure. She's not going to meet with me. Not until I prove that I'm on her side."

"By providing the identification *gratis.*"

Gabriel looked at her.

"Free," she said.

"Yeah."

She handed him her coffee cup again and put down her briefcase. Gabriel watched her dig around and pull out a checkbook with a rich leather cover.

"How much?"

Gabriel stared at her.

"How much do you need?" Judge Dee-Dee demanded. "If this is the only way to draw Leva Wilcox out and get her son medical treatment before it's too late, do you think I'm going to wait around while you go peddling door-to-door? We can't afford to wait, and I'm certainly not waiting for anyone's approval for an expenditure. How much are we talking?"

Gabriel, still not sure, named the expected cost. Judge Dee-Dee scowled at him.

"It's a high-profile case," Gabriel said. "Everybody has seen it on TV. They'll know she's desperate and double the rack rate. Two people, birth certificates, driver's license, credit cards, medical cards…"

Judge Dee-Dee filled in the amount. Gabriel stood there with his mouth open, unable to believe that she was going to provide the entire amount. How much did she have in her bank account?

"Just make it out to cash," he said faintly.

Judge Dee-Dee shook her head. "I will not. Then you can just hand it over to the person who is creating this ID, and he sees my name and personal information. I don't think so. You can cash a check made out in your name."

"Uh… I'll find a way," Gabriel agreed.

She finished filling out the check, and the register in the leather folder. She tore off the check and handed it to him.

"You have my number. You let me know as soon as you're able to make contact. Let me know when and where you are meeting her."

Gabriel didn't say anything. He didn't want to scare Leva away. Keeping Seth safe was paramount. He looked around as he folded the check and put it into his pocket, making sure that they were not being watched. A car with tinted windows was crawling by. Gabriel looked at Judge Dee-Dee and saw her watching it as well.

"Who is that?" Gabriel demanded. "Do you know whose car that is?"

"One of the judges. I'm not sure what everyone drives. Or it could be a lawyer. Some of them drive pretty fancy cars."

Gabriel's heart pounded hard in panic. Had Judge Dee-Dee been able to call or signal someone without his realizing it? Maybe she carried a panic button or had given a high-sign to one of the other court employees who was outside getting coffee. He took a couple of steps away from her. He kept his eyes on the car, expecting at any second that it would stop, and some goon would get out to take care of him. A couple of police officers? A court employee or private security guard? Hired help from one of the clinics that paid the judges to rule in their favor?

"Gabriel, it's just a car—"

Gabriel turned away from her and melted into the crowd, losing himself in the streets as quickly as he could manage.

CHAPTER SIXTEEN

The bells rang as Gabriel slipped in through the door. Merrick wasn't at the counter, but one of his employees stood there instead. A thin-faced woman with long, greasy brown hair. She looked at him, her brows drawn down in pronounced frown lines over her nose.

"I'm looking for Merrick."

She looked like this just confirmed her worst suspicions. "Is he expecting you?"

Gabriel nodded.

The woman let out an exasperated sigh and walked the length of the counter to the 'employees only' door. It was a couple of minutes before she returned.

"He'll be out in a minute."

"Thanks."

Gabriel pretended to be looking at the merchandise while he waited. Probably Merrick was watching him and checking to make sure there were no police around outside. He was a careful man. Eventually, Merrick put in an appearance, peeking around the only door and making a motion for Gabriel to join him.

Gabriel went through the door and followed Merrick through a stockroom to a small office to the side. There was a curtained area used as a photo booth, several filing cabinets, and a desk strewn with papers.

"You have the balance?" Merrick demanded, not bothering with small talk.

Gabriel took out the cash and handed it to Merrick. Merrick's thick fingers flew as he rapidly counted the money out and nodded, sliding it into a drawer. He had initially asked for more, but Gabriel had negotiated down to what he figured was a reasonable fee. Considering it was all that he had. He had given Merrick a substantial deposit at the beginning of the job.

Merrick took out an envelope and slid the contents out to show to Gabriel. The package, including passports. He picked them up and flipped them open. Passport pictures always looked horrible, but Seth's was particularly bad. He was pale, his eyes half-closed, hair mussed like he'd just gotten out of bed. Merrick looked down at it.

"The boy was in bad shape," he said. "We could barely get him to sit up for the picture."

Gabriel nodded, swallowing. The knot in his stomach tightened. But soon he would see Seth for himself. He'd be able to get the boy free of Leva. Somehow. They hadn't quite figured out what they were going to do yet. But too much planning could be just as much of a problem in a case like that as too little. Gabriel had to be flexible, to figure things out on the fly and be prepared for anything.

"Did they say anything to indicate where they were living?" Gabriel asked. "Whether they were close or had to take the freeway? Or a bus?"

"They did not say."

Gabriel indicated the address on the passport with his thumb. "Not here?"

"That I don't know. It is a legitimate address, but I don't know if they live there."

Gabriel took a quick look over the rest of the contents. "This all looks great. Thanks for pulling it all together so quickly."

"Now they can take him somewhere?" Merrick suggested, his eyes following the medical cards as Gabriel put them away. "Now he can see a doctor?"

"Yes. Soon. I hope."

Merrick said nothing further and escorted Gabriel back out to the store front, one hand on Gabriel's arm. Merrick let go when they came out from behind the counter and walked to the windowed front of the store, looking out at the street. Gabriel hung back where Merrick had left him, waiting for him to indicate that it was safe. Merrick stood there for a few minutes, then he turned and nodded to Gabriel.

"Off you go, then. Nice doing business with you."

Merrick and the sour-looking employee watched Gabriel leave the store.

———

Gabriel waited until he was a few blocks away, well clear of Merrick's store, before stopping and texting the number Leva had given him.

"I have the package."

He waited, watching the screen of the phone for a response. Nothing. Gabriel put it into his pocket and shrugged off his backpack. He busied himself putting the package into his backpack and making sure that everything else was in order, waiting for the vibration of the phone to indicate that Leva had texted him back.

Still nothing.

He zipped up his backpack and pulled out the phone, checking the screen to see if he had missed the return message. He didn't always feel the vibration. Some phones were really powerful, just about making him jump out of his skin when an alert came up. Other brands were weaker, with barely noticeable vibrations that were easily missed if the phone were in the wrong position or he weren't paying close enough attention.

Gabriel pulled his backpack on and continued to walk down the street. She would text him back before long. She was just busy taking care of Seth, or driving, or she was somewhere else that she couldn't text him back right away.

Gabriel circled the block and found Renata. "Hey."

"You got it?"

"Yes. Everything looks good. I texted her."

"Where does she want to meet?"

"Don't know yet. She hasn't answered back."

Renata rolled her eyes. "Power trip."

"What?"

"She's on a power trip. She's making you jump through hoops, showing you who's boss. You have to do everything her way and on her timetable."

"Well… yeah. I guess so."

"So just breathe," Renata told him. "Don't let her wind you up. You know she's going to keep yanking your chain, so don't get stressed out about it."

"I can't help it. Merrick commented about what bad shape Seth was in."

"Worrying isn't going to make it happen any faster."

Of course, Gabriel knew that was true, but that didn't make him feel any better. He could see that Renata was worried too. She had that tense, set look on her face. But she wasn't going to show any weakness. They couldn't do anything about Leva not answering. All they could do was wait.

"Where do you want to go?" Renata asked.

"Shouldn't we just stay around here? For the hand-off?"

"No. She's not going to pick anywhere around here. If she wants to avoid the cops, she'll need to set up the hand-off for somewhere farther away."

Gabriel wasn't so sure. Leva knew where Merrick's shop was. It would be easiest for her to station herself somewhere close by. Swoop in, get her ID, and leave the city. She had passports; maybe she even planned on leaving the country. Gabriel wasn't quite sure how they were going to stop her, but they would do their best.

"Let's stick close and conserve energy," he advised.

Renata nodded. "Yeah, sure. Maybe we should go sit down somewhere. You need a snack?"

"Probably wouldn't hurt." Gabriel took a glance up and down the street. "There's a little park with some cool sculptures in it just a couple of blocks away. Why don't we try there?"

She agreed. Gabriel led the way. Gabriel looked around as he dug some food out of his bag. Watching for Leva or for anyone who was paying them too much attention. Or for any suspicious cars driving by.

"I saw another car with tinted windows at the courthouse," he commented.

Renata sat down beside Gabriel, shrugging. "You're bound to see them around there. Plenty of judges and lawyers want to show off how much money they've got. Or people don't want to be targets or for people to see them there."

"So you don't think it was anything? You don't suspect Judge Dee-Dee?"

"Of course I suspect Judge Dee-Dee. That hasn't changed."

"Even though she gave us the money?"

"Especially since she gave us the money. She's got a lot to lose."

Gabriel munched on some crackers. He looked around again. "You don't think she has us under surveillance, do you? I haven't seen anyone suspicious…"

"We're getting around on foot; it wouldn't be that hard to keep an eye on us. I haven't spotted anyone, but…"

The park was quiet, which would make anyone who were keeping an eye on them more obvious. Gabriel itemized them. A homeless man picking bottles from the garbage cans. A young, tattooed mother pushing twins in a stroller. A couple of professional-looking people taking a shortcut through the park instead of going around.

On the street, Gabriel looked for anyone sitting in parked cars. The cars all appeared to be empty. Nothing that rang alarm bells.

The vibration of the phone in his pocket made him jolt. Renata laughed. Gabriel fumbled the phone out of his pocket and looked at the alert screen.

"Is it Leva?"

Gabriel nodded. "Yes." He blew his breath out, relieved. He read through the message quickly. "She wants us to meet her at the monument."

"Uh-huh."

Renata didn't point out that as she had suggested, Leva didn't want to meet them close by.

"It's going to take us a couple of hours to get there. Do you think we should get a cab or see if someone can drive us?"

"No. She won't be expecting us right away. She knows we don't drive."

Gabriel read through the text again. "She doesn't specify a time. Just the place."

"If we get there, and she's not there, we can call or text her."

"Does this feel weird to you? Off?"

Renata shrugged. "It's a test. It always was. She's afraid we're working with the cops."

"How does she know whether or not we are?"

"It's her test. Not mine. If it was me?" Renata stared into the distance, considering. "I'd have an inside source. I'd watch, too, but I'd have someone close to us, to keep me informed about what was going on."

"But we run a decentralized structure. No one knows all of what we're doing."

"You do. And I'm here. Maybe *I'm* the informant."

Gabriel's skin crawled. He studied her closely. "But you're not."

"Would I tell you if I was?"

"You're freaking me out." Gabriel got up and started walking toward the nearest bus stop. "If you were Leva's informant, then you'd tell her the cops weren't involved, that it was just me. The only reason I'd need to worry about it is if I had involved the police and was worried about Leva finding out."

"Yup," Renata agreed cheerfully, falling into step beside him. "Of course, if *you* were her informant, you'd be wondering what I've been doing while you're on the computer or chasing after the paperwork and whether *I've* involved the cops."

Gabriel stopped short and looked at her. "You didn't."

"Of course not. I don't want to be locked up. I want to see Leva behind bars, not me."

He gazed at her for another moment, searching her face for any sign that she were lying or keeping something back from him. Renata smiled guilelessly.

"Don't you trust me, Gabe?"

He didn't know what to say. Like Renata said, she didn't want to get locked up. But what if she had worked out some deal to ensure that she wouldn't be? She had been distrustful of Leva from the start. She wanted Leva locked up even worse than Gabriel did. All Gabriel cared about was Seth's safety.

"You never could tell if I was lying," Renata observed. "I don't have a tell. It's part of my psychosis. I can lie without conscience. No guilt: no tells."

Gabriel started walking again without answering her.

"But I don't need to lie to you," Renata said, keeping pace beside him. "Because neither of us called the cops. We both want the same thing."

———

Gabriel's estimate was correct. It took a couple of hours for them to arrive at the monument. Gabriel looked around, hoping to see her pushing Seth down the pathway in a wheelchair. Or to see her car. Even though he knew that she must have ditched the car by now and replaced it with something that wasn't on the police watch list. The place was nearly deserted. A good and bad place to meet someone. She would be able to see that they didn't have any police with them, but there was no crowd for her to disappear into, either. It would be easier to hide her approach and departure if there were a lot of people around.

Renata took a look around. "And now we wait."

"I'll text her. Tell her we're here."

Renata shrugged. They kept walking, skirting around the big sculpture, hoping that they would spot her. She was just hidden around a corner or behind a tree. Waiting for them.

But she wasn't. It was nearly deserted.

Gabriel looked down at his phone, willing it to buzz. She had to text him back. Let him know when she would be there. Or tell them to go on to some other location, careful to ensure that they hadn't been followed or sent surveillance up ahead.

"Don't let her wind you up," Renata warned again.

"I know," Gabriel snapped. All wound up. He would have laughed at himself if he hadn't been so uptight. Hands in her pockets, Renata wandered around. She looked like she was enjoying the scenery. Gabriel wished he were.

Still no text back. "Do you think she could have missed it? Wouldn't she be waiting?" Gabriel asked.

"Maybe she's helping Seth to the bathroom. Or feeding him."

They both shifted around. There was nothing to do. Nowhere to look without being reminded that she wasn't there. And maybe never planned to be.

Gabriel took a long breath and dialed the number he had been texting. There was no answer. It wasn't Leva's voice on the voicemail, just a prerecorded greeting. Gabriel tapped the end button without leaving a message.

"She needs the papers," Gabriel said. He spoke aloud and directed the comment at Renata, but he was really talking to himself. Trying to convince himself it was true. "She has to make contact at some point because this is what she wants. She needs the papers to get away free. For Seth to get medical aid or to get out of the country. She wouldn't just lead us on a wild goose chase and then abandon it."

"Could be that it was just a distraction, so we wouldn't be looking for her to leave town. Just a diversion."

"How could she go anywhere without ID?"

"Who says she doesn't have any? She could have gone to someone else. Just because we never tracked down who sold it to her, that doesn't mean that she didn't buy it somewhere else."

"But she didn't have any money. She couldn't."

"That was just a line."

"Renata!" Gabriel was so frustrated, her name just exploded out of him.

She stopped, blinking at him in surprise. "Gabriel?"

"I'm not looking for you to play devil's advocate! I don't want to hear that she's not going to come. I don't want to hear that she lied to me and skipped town. I want you to say that she's still coming."

Renata gazed at him steadily. She didn't say that Leva was still coming.

"I need you to tell me she's going to come."

"She's not coming, Gabe," Renata's voice was low, gentle.

"She is. She has to come."

"She set us up. She never intended to come here."

"You don't know that."

Renata made a wide gesture, turning around to indicate their surroundings. "She's not coming here. She never planned to. This is a terrible place to meet. She just wanted to get us out where we're exposed. It's all part of the test. Or else she just wanted us diverted while she skips town."

"If she wanted us out where she could see us, that would mean that she's here."

"She could be. She could be watching with a pair of binoculars. Or a wireless webcam. Or a friend could be keeping an eye out. They could be stationed on one of the roads in, where anyone would have to pass them. I don't know. All I know is, she's not coming."

"Why would she bother getting the photos done if she never planned to use the ID? Merrick said that Seth was in a bad way. He could barely sit up. Why would she put him at risk for pictures that she was never going to use?"

"Because that's what she does. She puts him in danger and then shows him off to people. I'm sure she got a big rush out of showing Merrick how sick Seth was." Renata shrugged. "Or maybe just to buy some more time. I don't know, Gabe. How do you expect me to know what's going on in her head?"

Because as much as he hated to admit it, Renata had been right every step of the way so far. Did she really have that much insight into Leva's brain, or did she know something? Was she talking to Leva on her own? Or talking to the person sheltering her? Gabriel studied Renata with suspicion for a long, tense period.

Then Gabriel turned away. He went over to the monument and sat down on a bench. "I'm going to wait for her."

Renata didn't argue the point. "Whatever. How's your sugar?"

He didn't want to be mothered and told when to eat. But he also knew that she was right, it was time for him to have a snack to keep his blood sugar stable. He pulled out a stick of jerky and unwrapped it without looking at her or acknowledging her.

———

He had to hand it to Renata. There was no 'I told you so.' She didn't tell him to give up, that it was time to move on. She didn't tell him again that Leva wasn't coming. She just waited.

They each took turns studying each other covertly and looking down the street at the entrance for any sign of life. Gabriel couldn't help wondering if the cops had followed him, or been informed of their meeting place by Renata while he wasn't watching her. Or whether Leva had people close by watching them to see if they had come alone.

Finally, Gabriel stood up. His joints ached. "She's not going to come," he admitted.

Renata didn't agree or disagree. But she did reach out and take Gabriel's arm, and they walked back down the long entrance road, retracing their steps. It would take another couple of hours to get back to a more central area and to find somewhere to sleep.

The wild goose chase felt like it had taken the entire day. Waking up and waiting for the shop to open. Traveling to Merrick's. Meeting with him. Waiting for Leva's response. Traveling a couple more hours to the meeting place. Waiting there. Traveling a couple more hours back.

Then it was evening, and they were getting supper and bedding down for the night. Gabriel was tired and sore and wished that for once they had a soft bed to look forward to.

"One day I'm going to get a hotel room," he told Renata.

She grinned. "You're always complaining about beds. I thought you'd be all toughened up by now."

"I am… but it would still be nice to have a nice soft bed now and then."

"It's your money. Do what you want."

Gabriel shook his head. "I can't bring myself to do it. Not knowing how much I have to work to get every cent. I did get a hotel for a few days over the winter. Had a cough that I couldn't kick and just had to hole up and stay warm and eat soup for a few days to get back on my feet."

Renata nodded. "Well… I'm glad you did. You gotta take care of yourself. And if things are quiet, and there's no one actively looking for you… what does it matter if you get a room now and then if you can afford it?"

"But right now I can't. And I don't have the excuse that I have pneumonia this time. So… I'll just have to find someone to cuddle up with to keep me warm."

Renata smiled and laced her fingers through his. "I think that can probably be arranged."

CHAPTER SEVENTEEN

S o what are we going to do?"

Gabriel had splurged on a cup of coffee and held it between both hands, warming his fingers. He had a chill in his bones that wasn't going away even though they were sitting indoors.

Renata pursed her lips. "We keep asking questions, I guess. Watch for her online. See if the cops can track her down by her postings. Sooner or later, she's going to let something slip. She's going to say something that gives away her location, or take a picture somewhere identifiable."

"As long as Seth is still alive."

"That's what I love about you, Gabe. You're always so positive."

"You were thinking it too."

She gave a slight nod.

"What if she goes to the hospital?" Gabe asked. "I know she can't go under her own name, but what if she did get ID from someone else? Or what if she shows up and doesn't give her name? They'll have to treat Seth anyway, even if she doesn't have any identification or way to pay them. Right?"

"Yeah. But they would call the police and Social Services."

"I suppose. And they'd know them from her warrant and his missing persons report."

"Unless they got really lucky. And I don't see that happening. The police would have to make some effort to identify her, and they'd have to know that she was trying to hide something. Run her fingerprints…"

Gabriel took out his phone and looked at it. No alerts on the screen. No one had the number but Leva. "I suppose I should ditch this. If she wants to reach me, she can message me on the discussion forum."

"Yeah. Don't want to give the cops the chance to track it."

"I thought it was going to work, and we were going to be able to get to Seth. I feel like an idiot."

"You did your best. Nothing wrong with that. She's the one to blame here, not you."

Gabriel sighed. "I hope so. I keep thinking maybe there was something else I could have done… Maybe I made some mistake. Made her think that I couldn't be trusted."

"She probably knew from the start that you were the one who pointed the cops at her again. They probably ratted you out while they questioned her."

"Yeah." Gabriel hadn't thought about that. "Maybe."

"You can't control what the cops do."

The phone vibrated in Gabriel's hand and he just about dropped it. He swore and laughed at himself. Then he looked down at the screen. The only person who had the number of the phone was Leva.

I need to meet with you. I need that paperwork.

Gabriel turned the phone so that Renata could read the screen.

She raised her eyebrows. Gabriel swiped the message to reply to it and Renata snatched the phone out of his hands. She tapped back a message herself and sent it. She handed it back to Gabriel so he could read it.

No more games.

Gabriel shook his head at her. He didn't know why neither of them was speaking. As if Leva might overhear them.

He figured they'd have to wait another hour before she sent a reply, but it came back quickly.

I see Renata has control of the phone now.

Renata let out a low chuckle. "Darn right I do," she murmured.

She took the phone back, and messages zipped back and forth as they worked out the arrangements. Renata stood up, passing it back to Gabriel. "All set. Let's go."

Gabriel was about to put the phone back in his pocket when it vibrated again. He looked at the screen.

No police. I'll know if you're followed.

Gabriel swallowed and stuffed it into his pocket. He followed Renata out of the coffee shop.

———

"Do you think she'll be there this time? It's not another test?"

"I told her we're not playing any more games. If she wants these papers, she's going to have to follow my instructions this time."

Gabriel nodded. He wished he'd used the bathroom before leaving the coffee shop. He was cramping up, shots of pain working their way all along his intestines. He didn't feel like going to another fruitless meeting. He wanted to curl up in a comfortable bed and forget all about Seth and Leva.

Renata had set up the meeting, so it was in a shopping mall with lots of escape routes and people. It was too early to be busy, but there were still store owners opening up their shops and calling out to one another, seniors with coffee and walking shoes, and a few mothers with kids in their shopping carts, hoping to get their errands done before the crowds arrived. Renata and Gabriel moved through the mall, eyes open and alert for Leva and Seth.

Seth's phone vibrated.

Second level. I can see you.

Gabriel looked up and scanned the second level railing for Leva. "There she is," Renata breathed, nodding toward two figures standing above them, looking down.

They had to circle around to get to the bottom of the slowly moving escalator. Gabriel wanted to sprint up it, but Renata held him back.

"Just take it slow. Don't rush into this."

Gabriel nodded, trying to hold back the rush of adrenaline that was forcing his heart to pump so fast. He was having trouble catching his breath.

They got to the top and surveyed the situation. Gabriel was glad to see that Seth was on his feet, and not confined to a wheelchair or on his deathbed, as Gabriel had feared. But the boy didn't look good. Leva was holding onto him, keeping him on his feet. He was pale, his hair matted, and his eyes mostly closed. Leva held him in a strange, awkward position. Not held against her body, but held away from herself.

"Stop right there," Leva ordered. "That's close enough."

Renata's hand on Gabriel's arm kept him moving forward instead of instinctively stopping, obeying Leva's command.

"Hey, Leva," Renata greeted. "How's it going?"

"Just stay where you are!" Leva told them again. She gave Seth a jerk. "Or he's going over the edge."

Gabriel and Renata stopped. Gabriel studied the two figures. Seth was frail and Leva was strong, accustomed to having to move him around when he was sick. Pushing him over the rail would not be a matter of a simple shove. She'd have to lift him at some point. But she was strong enough to do it.

Seth didn't struggle. He didn't try to pull away from her to get to safety. He was probably too weak. And he loved his mother, despite what she had done to him. He was used to obeying her.

"Are you okay, Seth?" Gabriel called.

"He's sick," Leva snapped. "He needs medical care. I need those papers."

"I have them," Gabriel assured her. He slid his backpack off of his shoulders. "They're right here in my bag."

Leva looked down at the first level, back at Gabriel and Renata, and then her eyes took a quick circuit around the second level. While there were a number of people walking around on the first level, where the food court was open, the second level was pretty deserted. They could hear snatches of conversation. There was a girl who looked like she should still be in high school pushing open the doors of a boutique, chatting on her Bluetooth headset while chewing gum and drinking coffee. Gabriel rubbed his side, trying to soothe away a cramp.

"Hurry up. Let's see it," Leva snapped.

Gabriel dug into his backpack and pulled out the envelope he had stashed there the previous day. He remembered Merrick talking about how weak Seth had been. Maybe he was better in the morning, after a good night's sleep. Or maybe they had just arrived at Merrick's during a bad spell, or Seth had felt worse because of the trip there. He wasn't as bad as Gabriel had feared. He was on his feet.

"Seth," Renata called out to him. "Aren't you going to say hi to your buddy? Tell Gabriel how you're doing."

Gabriel clutched the envelope and looked at Seth. Seth was so thin. But the skin over his face seemed like it was pulled tight instead of being loose from his weight loss. It looked dry and thin. At least he wasn't still on oxygen and intravenous. He must have improved some since leaving the hospital.

There was still no answer from Seth. Gabriel saw his eyes roll up so that all they could see under his half-closed lids were the whites. Leva shoved him up against the railing.

"You bring me the envelope," Leva commanded. "Renata, stay where you are."

She obviously knew that Renata was the bigger threat. She might be shorter than Gabriel, but she was strong, especially when she was mad. He could feel her anger as she stood beside him, like heat rolling off of her.

He took a couple of tentative steps toward Leva, closing the distance between them. When he was a few steps away, Leva halted him again. "Let's see. Take them out and show me."

Gabriel obeyed, sliding the various forms of ID out of the envelope and juggling them, holding them up for her one at a time so that she could see they were legitimate. She wouldn't be able to read the writing or see any important details from where she was, but she could see that they were at least passable forgeries, with her and Seth's pictures on them.

"Put them back in the envelope and slide them to me."

Gabriel couldn't help looking back at Renata, which was the wrong thing to do. Leva shoved Seth hard against the railing, turning him to face it, so his head and shoulders were over the edge, looking downward. Gabriel's stomach turned at the noise of Seth's body thudding against the rail and the little whimper that escaped him.

"Give them to me now!" Leva shrieked.

The sound of her voice carried and an unnatural silence fell over the busy murmur of the mall. Somebody down on the first level called out. People had obviously noticed what was happening, and that was bad for Leva, escalating her still further. Gabriel saw her shift her grip to Seth's belt. Closer to his center of gravity. One hand on his belt and one around his legs would shift his center mass enough to throw him over the edge.

"I'm sliding them to you," Gabriel told her, his voice hoarse. He crouched down, trying to keep his movements smooth and reassuring. He skidded the envelope toward her. After it had left his hands, he realized he had shoved it too hard, and his heart was in his throat as he anticipated it sliding right past Leva, under the bottom rail, and plummeting down to the first floor.

But Leva's reflexes were quick and she stepped on it to stop it. Gabriel saw then that there was a tiled lip that would have kept it from going straight off the edge anyway. Leva let go of Seth with one hand to pick up the envelope, her other hand remaining to keep him pushed up against the rail. Gabriel saw Renata begin to move toward her. Leva retrieved the package and straightened again.

"Stay back!"

There were other approaching feet. Gabriel and Renata were closest, but Gabriel could hear the heavy steps of the security guards approaching.

"Everybody stay back!" Leva screamed.

Gabriel glanced around, trying to anticipate what was going to happen next. He and Renata needed to stay one step ahead of Leva. Renata made a tiny motion with her hand in Leva's direction. Gabriel thought it meant 'you take her.' It wasn't much of a plan, but they weren't exactly a highly trained tactical unit, either.

Leva would need to turn, readjust her grip, and lift Seth up to throw him over. And she had to do something with the envelope in her hand. Drop it or put it in her shoulder bag. It was restricting her movements.

"Now!" Renata mouthed.

Gabriel jumped into action without any further thought, trying to rush and grab Leva before she could do anything to Seth. She moved faster than he ever could have imagined, grabbing Seth's belt and bending over to lift his legs up without ever letting go of the envelope. Seth was up on the rail, his body folded over it before Gabriel reached Leva. He grabbed her and jerked her back, away from Seth and the railing. She fought back like a wildcat, twisting and spitting and hitting and kicking Gabriel in a mad whirl of arms and legs. He tried to wrap his arms around her to pin her arms to her sides.

"Gabe," Renata gasped. "Help me!"

He shoved Leva toward the nearest security guard and grabbed for Renata and Seth. Renata was holding onto Seth's arm and shoulder, but his body was on the other side of the glass, gravity pulling him down. He was wild-eyed, eyes wide open now in panic as he grasped the railing, trying to keep from falling to the floor far beneath him. There were yells and screams, but no one else was close enough to help. Gabriel reached over the railing to grasp Seth's jacket, trying to lift him a few inches so that he could get a more secure hold. Get his arms up over the rail. Gabriel leaned as far over the side as he dared, ignoring the vertigo, pulling at Seth's clothes, trying to shift Seth's center of gravity a little higher, so that they didn't have to work so hard to pull him up. His fingers caught the hard edge of Seth's belt, and Gabriel did what Leva had, grabbing his belt like a handle and hauling on it. Seth's mass shifted, and he was crawling over the top of the rail back to safety, and there were other hands beside Renata's and Gabriel's, helping to pull him across, pulling him back over to safety.

Seth collapsed to the floor, and Gabriel and Renata with him. Gabriel and Renata untangled themselves and tried to evaluate Seth.

"Are you okay? Seth? Can you tell me if you're okay?" Gabriel demanded, looking into Seth's wide eyes and feeling for his pulse.

Seth gave a slight nod, apparently unable to speak.

"He's safe," Renata breathed. "We got him. He's safe, Gabe. He's okay."

They were both breathing hard, gulping in the air. Gabriel turned and looked around at the other helpers. The security guards. Other bystanders pressing close for a better look. But one person was missing who should have been there. Leva.

"Where is she? Where did she go? Didn't anybody get her?"

"She slipped by us."

"Nobody got her?" Gabriel demanded, his anxiety for Seth morphing into anger. "Nobody? She tried to kill her son!"

He stood up and went over to the rail to look down at the lower level. Surely someone had detained her. People milled about in excitement, pointing and discussing what they had just witnessed. No sign of Leva.

"Can you close the mall? If she's still inside, we need to catch her!"

The security guard shook his head. "There's no automatic lock-down, we'd have to lock each door individually. By the time we did that…"

Gabriel swore and smacked the rail with an open hand. He knelt back down to look at Seth. "Is he okay?" he asked Renata.

She looked at him with grave eyes and shook her head.

Gabriel looked over his shoulder at the bewildered guards and bystanders. "Did anyone call an ambulance?" No one nodded or volunteered. Gabriel pointed at the guard who had answered him previously. "You. Call nine-one-one."

The man hitched up his wide belt, not making any move toward his phone or walkie-talkie. "He's okay. He didn't get hurt."

"He's very sick. He needs to be in the hospital."

The guard pulled his phone out slowly, looking at Seth. "What's wrong with him? What do I tell them?"

Gabriel looked down at Seth, trying to formulate an answer.

"He has mitochondrial disease," Renata said. "And he's been poisoned. That should do it."

Gabriel nodded. A few minutes later, a couple of first aid workers employed by the mall hurried over. They knelt down by Seth, ordering the bystanders back. Renata caught Gabriel's eye. Rather than objecting about being pushed back from their friend, they allowed themselves to melt into the crowd.

"We'd better scram," Renata murmured. "Cops will be showing up before long."

Leaving Seth in the hands of the first aiders and the paramedics who were en route, Gabriel and Renata slipped out.

CHAPTER EIGHTEEN

Gabriel felt like he had been sleeping for a long time. He shifted and stretched restlessly, nestled in the cozy sheets. His body was telling him it was time to get up, but he couldn't remember the last time he had been so comfortable. He didn't want to move or open his eyes. He turned over, trying to ignore the urgent signals from his bladder and find sleep again. But all the while, his brain was trying to sort out where he was and how he'd gotten there. Finally, he opened his eyes and sat up abruptly. He looked around the room, expecting to find himself in a jail cell or a hospital bed. But it wasn't. It was a bedroom. Somebody's guest room, judging by the lack of clutter.

"Whoa, there. Take it easy." Renata spoke to him from a wicker chair in the corner, where she was curled up with a book.

Gabriel blinked at her. "Where am I? What happened? Seth…?"

"Seth is okay."

Gabriel breathed out a sigh of relief. "He's okay? Did they get him to hospital? What about Leva?"

"She's in the wind. Haven't been able to track her down again. They've got the new ID on a watch list… but she's not going to use it." Renata's insights into Leva's mind had been right up until then; Gabriel had no doubt she was right.

"Is Seth being guarded? For real this time?"

"For now."

Gabriel looked around the room again, trying to identify it. It wasn't Heather Voegel's house. That was the first place he had thought of. He thought he should know whose house it was, but he didn't.

"Where is this?"

"Is he awake?" A head poked in the door. Blond. Young.

"Carmel!"

She laughed. "You don't need to sound so surprised. I do live here."

"I didn't know where 'here' was. This is your house?"

"Yeah. When you ran into trouble, Renata called for help. And we picked you up and brought you here."

Gabriel licked his lips. His mouth was dry. There was a cup with a straw on the nightstand. He reached over and sipped the lukewarm water.

"What trouble? What happened? I remember saving Seth, but that's all…"

"Well, apparently wrestling desperate criminals and saving kids from making thirty-foot swan dives isn't something your body is accustomed to," Renata informed him. "You should maybe work that into your exercise routine. You bonked. Big time. You didn't pass out right away, but you were talking crazy and slurring and staggering like you were drunk. So I sent out the bat signal and Carmel's mom picked us up and brought us here."

Gabriel shifted uncomfortably. "I have more questions, but… I need the bathroom."

Carmel gave him a smile. "Two doors down. You need help?"

Gabriel pushed off the blankets and looked down at the unfamiliar pajamas he was wearing. "No… I don't need any help."

His legs were weak and vibrated when he walked, but he did make it to the bathroom under his own power and was back in the bedroom a few minutes later. He sat on the edge of the bed. Carmel sat down beside him.

"How long have we been here?" Gabriel wiped his mouth with the back of his hand and ran his fingers through his matted hair.

"Couple days," Renata advised.

"A couple days?" It was no wonder Gabriel felt so disoriented. "I slept for two days?"

"You weren't asleep the whole time," Renata said. "You've been up a few times. But not really… coherent."

Gabriel smoothed the pajamas against his skin. "Did I, uh… change by myself…?"

"Mostly," Renata said. Both girls laughed.

Gabriel looked back and forth between them. "Oh, boy. So I've just been here? No hospital?"

"I figured all you needed was sugar and fluids. And rest," Renata said.

"If there had been anything worrisome, we would have taken you in," Carmel advised quickly. "But your vitals were all stable. You were tired, but you would wake up when we checked on you. We figured you just needed time."

Gabriel's face burned. "I can't believe I did that. I've been trying to be careful, but I don't know how I could have prepared any better for what happened. The adrenaline and trying to hold onto Leva, and then pulling Seth up… it was just hard on my body."

Renata shook her head, her eyes dancing.

"You didn't crash?" Gabriel asked her. "You had to do just as much as I did. I know I have a harder time controlling my blood sugar than you do, but when you… have to do something so physical… you usually crash too."

"Don't let her make you feel bad," Carmel said. "She was asleep almost as long as you were. She's only been awake and alert for a couple of hours."

"Oh." Gabriel narrowed his eyes at Renata, who was still laughing. "Is *that* the whole story? You bonked too."

"You bonked first."

"At least Renata was easier to get some nourishment into," Carmel laughed. "I can see the attraction of a feeding tube. With you, I had to fight to keep you awake every bite."

Gabriel was embarrassed again at the thought of her trying to spoon feed him. What a great way to make an impression on a girl. Be as helpless as a baby for two days just because he'd had a little excitement.

"Well… thanks for everything. Your mom too. I really appreciate it."

"Mom's always picking up strays. Why do you think I got involved with the underground railway in the first place? I come by it naturally."

"Still," Gabriel stared at his hands. "I do appreciate it. Without you, I probably would have ended up in hospital and back behind bars."

"You're welcome. Happy to help."

"So what's the word on Seth? He's okay?"

"He's good," Renata said. "The hospital says he's stable and can be released in a few days. He was dehydrated and malnourished. She must have stopped feeding him."

"Maybe he wouldn't let her anymore. After she was arrested. They must have told him that she was poisoning him."

"He already knew she was poisoning him," Renata disagreed.

"I don't know if he did. I don't know if he really understood what she was doing."

"I don't know if any of us can understand what she was doing."

"They don't have any clue where she is?"

"They're looking." It was Carmel who answered. "But word is they're not getting anywhere with it. There have been lots of bulletins on TV, and of course, Seth was all over the news. A couple of people got video on their phones of him going over the side, and you and Renata pulling him back up. You're heroes."

Gabriel smiled at Renata.

"Of course, the mall security is a little embarrassed about the fact that they lost you," Carmel went on. "That they just let you walk out of there, without any explanation or having to talk to the cops."

"Yeah, that could be sort of embarrassing. I suppose there are a bunch of bulletins out on us too. Wanted for questioning."

"There's been a few. But not so much. They're keeping that part of it pretty quiet. And if you did want to talk to the police, I don't think they'd put you in jail. It would be too much bad press for them."

"I don't think so." Gabriel shook his head. "I don't have any desire to turn myself in." He looked at Renata. "You? Any hankering to confess to the police?"

"Not me."

"Judge Dee-Dee is pretty ticked at the two of you for not keeping her in the loop. She said you had her private cell number and were supposed to keep her informed if you talked to Leva."

"Uh-huh."

"But she's happy that you got Seth away from Leva. I think she was really worried he was going to die, and it would be partially her fault for having us return Seth to her in the first place. She's frustrated about Leva getting clean away, but she'll live with it."

"Do I still have that phone?" Gabriel asked Renata, not remembering whether they had destroyed it or not. "I could text her from it once before I fry it."

"Yeah. All charged up and everything."

"It's not turned on, is it?" Gabriel demanded, worried.

"No," Carmel gave him that tolerant smile that most people reserved for Renata when her paranoia was obvious. "We charged it for you, but we kept it off."

Gabriel blew out a whistle of air. "Good. Thanks."

Carmel stood up. "Well, I'll leave the two of you alone to discuss… things."

She nodded a goodbye and left the room. Gabriel looked at Renata. "So what do we do next?"

"Make sure you're rested up. Then… what do you want to do?"

"I mean about Seth. I guess we shouldn't… interfere."

"No." Renata laughed. "No, no, no. I think we've had enough involvement in this case. It's time to just back off and let the authorities figure this one out."

"She could still come back looking for him. She hasn't necessarily left town. Or the country. She could be sitting, waiting for another opening."

"They're going to have to figure that out."

"They can't guard him forever. Sooner or later, they're going to decide there is no further danger, and drop all of the security."

"We can't do it, Gabe. We can't guard him any better than they can. We couldn't do it forever either."

"But we could hide him. Change his identity. And teach him… what to do if she showed up again."

"Suggest it to Judge Dee-Dee. But I'm not getting involved in this one anymore." She gave him a stern look. "*We* are not getting involved in this one anymore."

———

Carmel looked up when Renata entered the living room. "Oh, hi."

"Hey. He's still pretty tired and weak. He's conked out again for a while."

"He's improving. That's the important part."

Renata nodded.

"And so are you. Your recovery has been a lot faster than his."

"Yeah, well, I haven't been living on the streets for a year like he has. I've spent most of my time pampered in the hospital. My reserves are stronger."

"But not having real food must make you slower to heal—"

"What's real food? My nutritional intake is very carefully balanced. More than yours or Gabriel's."

"But whole foods offer better nutrition."

Renata shrugged. "For you, maybe. Whole foods would kill me. And like you said, I'm recovering faster than he is."

Carmel shrugged and nodded, obviously thinking better of arguing the point. "I guess."

Renata sat down on the couch, and for a few minutes, she just sat with her eyes closed, breathing and thinking things through.

"So… what's your relationship with Gabriel?" she asked eventually.

Carmel didn't say anything. Renata opened her eyes and looked at the petite blond.

"Well?"

"No relationship. Friends. Trainer. Mentor." Carmel considered Renata seriously. "What about you? I haven't been able to figure out if you two are… friends or a couple."

"If you two are just friends, then why do you care?"

Carmel's eyebrows went up. "It's best to know these things from the start. If he's in a relationship, I'm going to be a lot more careful about where things go than if he's free. We're just friends now. Barely. But if we spend more time together… I don't know…"

Renata folded her arms across her chest, thinking about how to respond. "We're friends," she said finally. "Best friends. I don't want to lose him."

"I'm not going to interfere with who he's friends with."

"We could be more. He's… we have a lot in common. And a history."

"And you both could have died, jumping in to help Seth and using up all your energy. Don't you think Gabriel should have someone stronger to help him?"

Renata's anger flared. She kept her face expressionless, not showing the rage she felt at the suggestion. "Who, you? You spend most of your life outside this house in a wheelchair. I can at least get around on my own."

They both stared at each other, challenging, waiting for the other to back down.

"He's mine," Renata said, steel in her voice.

"Yes. Your best friend. It sounds like the position of girlfriend is still open. And you can't dictate who fills it. That's up to Gabriel."

EPILOGUE

Gabriel set up a new profile and logged onto the discussion board, browsing through the newest posts. Seeing if anyone had posted anything new about Seth and Leva. Or if there were newbies with questions about mito or any new cases claiming medical kidnap.

Things seemed to be pretty quiet. The chatter about Seth's near-death encounter and Leva's escape had died down as nothing more was heard from her. No one seemed to have any intel on where she had run away to. If she was staying with someone who was active on the boards, it wasn't obvious.

Gabriel's eye was drawn to a recent discussion on self-care and parents making sure that they were getting enough sleep and nutrition to stay healthy, practicing meditation techniques, and getting outside help. All of those things that parents of chronically ill children had to pay attention to if they were going to survive the long haul and not get completely burned out.

There was a post at the end of the thread by a user Gabriel wasn't familiar with. A Toni Hall. She had a cartoon avatar and had just registered for the forum a couple of days before.

If anyone is looking for part-time nursing care or respite services, I cared for my son with mito for fourteen years and am very familiar with the disorder and with treatment options. I've spent a lot of time on research and figuring out what worked for my little boy. I recently lost him and am trying to work through the grief by helping others in the community. Message me if I could help with your child. Am willing to travel.

Did you enjoy this book? Reviews and recommendations are vital to making a book successful.

Please leave a review at your favorite book store or review site and share it with your friends.

Don't miss the following bonus material:
Sign up for mailing list to get a free ebook
Read a sneak preview chapter
Other books by P.D. Workman
Learn more about the author

Sign up for my mailing list at pdworkman.com and get Gluten-Free Murder for free!

PREVIEW OF TOXO

CHAPTER ONE

Mrs. Bradshaw touched Caleb on the shoulder. He looked up at her through the fringe of brown hair that hung in his face. Mrs. Bradshaw spoke, but Caleb's sound processor clicked and buzzed. He tapped it, frowning and focusing on her face to try to understand what she was saying. She wore very red lipstick and made a weird fish-face when she was trying to make it easier for him to read her. It didn't help.

She asked him something. Caleb tapped on his sound processor, trying to make it work properly. The battery shouldn't have been dying already. His school day was not even over. Mrs. Bradshaw touched Caleb's hand lightly to make him be still and spoke again. He thought she was talking to him about catching the bus.

"Bus?" Caleb repeated. "Catch the bus after school?"

She nodded, making a motion toward the bus loading zone and repeating her instructions to catch the bus.

Caleb nodded impatiently. He tapped his sound processor again, trying to make sense of the bursts of noise. Mrs. Bradshaw nodded and moved on, walking down the aisle between the desks, toward the back of the room. Caleb put his head back down to puzzle through his math questions.

He heard the buzzing in his ear when the school bell rang, felt it through his fingers on the desk, and saw the other students moving to put away their books and pack up to go. Caleb closed his book, stacked everything up, and headed for the door. Mrs. Bradshaw made a motion to get his attention. He waved his acknowledgment and went to his locker to pack his backpack.

———

When he got out to the bus loading zone, the crowds of students were already thinning, the earlier buses having already loaded up and left. Caleb looked for his bus, scanning the window placards for bus D. He couldn't see it in the line. Had it already left without him? He'd taken longer than he'd intended to at his locker, the noise of the students around him buzzing angrily in his head, making it impossible to concentrate on sorting out his books. He'd eventually turned the sound processor off to silence it, but then Jenny C had tapped him on the shoulder and tried to talk to him about the English essay they had been assigned. Caleb had turned it back on, tried to listen to her, turned it off again, and had done his best to read her speech and answer her questions. Eventually, Jenny C had shaken her head, thrown up her hands in disgust, and walked away from him without even saying goodbye.

But Caleb didn't think the bus would have left without him. Usually, even if he were late, Mrs. Mills still waited. There were not that many kids on his bus, and she knew to wait. Caleb paced up and down the street, looking for bus D, until most of the buses had pulled out.

It was obvious that Bus D wasn't there. Maybe there was a substitute driver and she didn't know to stay and wait for Caleb if he took too long like Mrs. Mills did. Caleb headed back to the school to go to the office and tell them that he'd missed the bus, but when he reached the doors, they were all locked.

Caleb bit the side of his hand, trying to decide what to do. His bus wasn't there and he couldn't get back into the school. He would have to walk home. It would take longer, but he knew the way. He'd walked that far before. Not by himself, usually. But he knew the way. He would just walk.

He swung his backpack up over both shoulders and snugged the straps so that it was properly balanced on his back. If he'd known he was going to be walking, he would not have taken so many books. The backpack was heavy, weighing on him even after the few minutes he'd been looking for the bus. Mom said sometimes his backpack weighed as much as he did, but that's because he was skinny.

Caleb started walking down the street.

His brain was whirling with thoughts and worries. Mom would be worried when he didn't get off the bus. She always said to go back in the school and call her, but he couldn't. She would be mad.

He snapped his fingers beside his head. Even though he couldn't hear the sound with his processor turned off, it was still calming. He rubbed his eyebrow with the other hand and shaded his eye from the direct sun. Some of the anxiety eased, but he was still worried. Mom would call Dad. Dad would be mad. They would both want to know where he was and why he'd missed the bus and why he hadn't called. If he hurried, maybe he wouldn't be too late. He picked up his pace, but in doing so, tripped over a crack in the sidewalk, and the heavy backpack prevented him from regaining his balance. He fell down, smashing his chin on the pavement and getting the wind knocked out of him by thirty pounds of books landing in the middle of his back.

Caleb groaned. He rolled over and picked himself up slowly, his whole body vibrating with the impact. He swiped at his chin to see if it was bleeding, but his fingers were dry. He readjusted the backpack and started to walk again, his regular pace, not trying to hurry. Caleb knew he was going to take longer getting home, and anxiety flooded through his whole body, making his stomach hurt and his muscles move jerkily like he was a robot that hadn't been programmed properly.

He snapped his fingers rapidly. He pulled his hood up over his head so that it blocked some of the sun from his eyes. He smoothed his eyebrow. He started to count. He snapped his fingers as fast as he could beside his face.

He covered one block at a time, focused on his goal of getting home. He tried to structure a script in his head to explain to Mom what had happened and why he was late getting home.

Someone grabbed Caleb's shoulder and he tried to jerk away, startled by the contact. With his hood up and his hands by his face, his peripheral vision was cut off and he hadn't seen anyone approaching. He tried to jerk away a second time, dropping his left hand to widen his field of vision.

It was a big, blue-uniformed policeman. Caleb knew he could go to a policeman if he needed help. But he didn't need help. He was just walking home and he knew the way.

"No," he told the man. "Go home."

The policeman's grip on Caleb's shoulder tightened and he gave Caleb a hard shake. Caleb watched his face and read, "Where are you going?"

"Go home," he insisted. "Caleb go home."

He tried to pull away and the officer pushed him hard into a big tree with deep, craggy, rough bark. Caleb was walking on the pathway through the park. That was the way home. That was the way Mom always took him home if they were walking. Caleb stopped snapping his fingers and flapped his hand beside his face.

"Let go!" He struggled to pull away. He didn't need help. He knew the way home.

———

Purnell took the tweaker to the ground, tripping himself in the process and landing hard on top of the boy. The boy struggled to get away, shouting incoherently in his cracking adolescent voice.

"Hold still!" Purnell shouted, trying to get control of him. "Give me your hands! Stop fighting!"

But the boy kept thrashing wildly, too far gone to understand a word Purnell was saying. The heavy backpack was in the way, and Purnell fought to jerk it off of him. He had his billy out and smacked the addict several times in the arms and shoulders to subdue him.

"Just hold still. Stay down and quit fighting me! You want to get tased?"

The boy kept shouting. Purnell was aware that they were attracting the attention of the park users. The kid could have friends and Purnell was there alone. He succeeded in getting the backpack off the boy and pinned him down. He fumbled with his radio, calling for backup while the boy bucked and screamed incoherent curses, completely off his head. Purnell grabbed one of the wildly flapping hands and twisted it up behind the boy's back. He shoved his baton back into his belt and managed to grab the other hand.

Like other tweakers Purnell had dealt with, the boy was surprisingly strong for his slight frame, immune to any pain while high. On amphetamines, a skinny man could fight off several cops with seeming inhuman strength, breaking his own bones in the process without even noticing. Purnell twisted the boy's second arm hard, hoping that he wouldn't break anything, but knowing that he had to get the boy under control before he could hurt Purnell and before any of his friends decided to help out. Purnell finally managed to get both hands close enough together to ratchet the handcuffs into place.

The boy howled and bucked, still trying to escape. Purnell did his best to pat down the thrashing junkie and search his pockets for more drugs. He didn't have anything on him. He must have taken his whole buy at once.

Two more units rolled up and, with the help of the other officers, Purnell managed to get the kid locked up in the back of his car for transport. He wiped his forehead with the back of his hand, sweating in spite of the chilly temperature. Officer Jacobs, in one of the backup units, laughed. "Quite a workout, hey?"

"Stupid tweakers. It doesn't seem like it matters how many times we tell them to stay out of the park, they just gotta come here to shoot up."

"This one's pretty young." Jacobs peered through the window at the boy, howling and crying in the back seat, trying to tell the whole world his woes. "Probably not shooting yet."

"Well, whether he's popping or shooting, he's high as a kite. Gonna take some time before he comes down."

* * *

Toxo, Book #4 of the *Medical Kidnap Files* series by P.D. Workman can be purchased at pdworkman.com

CHAPTER TWO

After having a coffee to decompress, Purnell returned to the cool-down room to see how his arrestee was doing. Kristen Oakes, supervising in his absence, looked up from the monitors when he entered the control room.

"How's my guy?" Purnell asked. "Coming down yet?"

"I don't think your tweaker is a tweaker," Kristen advised.

"You wouldn't say that if you'd seen him in action. Classic signs."

He looked at the two monitors showing his subject in the cool-down room. The boy was sitting in the corner, back against the wall, knees drawn up to his chest, rocking back and forth. Kristen touched the audio dial to turn up the volume and he could hear the boy humming or moaning to himself. He shrugged.

"Still looks like a tweaker to me."

"Well, he's calmed down, so why don't we see if we can get anything coherent from him?"

Purnell agreed and they went together to the cell, barely bigger than a caretaker's closet, the wall and floors rubberized to cushion against injury. There was not much space for socializing.

"Hey," Purnell said, when the boy didn't look at him. "Time to talk. You want to tell me your name and what you were doing in the park today?"

The boy continued to hum and rock. Purnell could see they were going to have to clean him up. He had a number of scrapes and smudges on his face and his bare knees and shins. His hoodie covered his arms and most of his head and face.

"Are you going to behave yourself?" Purnell demanded. "If I take the handcuffs off of you, will you behave?"

The boy continued to rock and paid him no attention.

Purnell raised an eyebrow at Kristen, wondering if she still thought that he was just a regular kid, not high at all.

"Let's give it a try," she agreed. She moved toward the boy.

"You'd better let me do it," Purnell warned. "He was pretty violent at the park. He's crazy strong on whatever he took."

"Do you think I can't handle myself?" Kristen challenged.

She was medium height and compact, but he knew she was no marshmallow. He'd seen her boxing at the gym and she had a reputation as someone who didn't put up with any nonsense. Soft when she was dealing with a victim or a remorseful perp, but hard as nails when confronted by a disrespectful or violent detainee.

"Sorry. Go ahead, if you want."

She nodded and went over to the boy. She crouched in front of him, directly in his line of sight, and murmured something comforting. His eyes rolled up and away from her, avoiding eye contact. She reached up to pull back his hoodie, and he jerked away from her, his hum going shrill. She pulled her hand back.

"I'm going to take the cuffs off," Kristen told him in an even, reassuring voice. She squished herself up against the wall to try to get them unlocked without moving him. It required some contortion, but she managed to get the handcuffs off.

The boy immediately had both hands up beside his face, flapping one hand back and forth beside his eye, and smoothing his eyebrow with the other, folding in on himself, blocking out the rest of the world.

"You see?" Purnell pointed out. "He's tweaking bad."

Kristen nodded. "I see," she agreed. She reached again for his hood, and though he flinched away from her, the boy didn't block her from pulling it back.

At first, Purnell didn't see anything out of the ordinary. The boy had longish, shaggy, light brown hair, wavy, disordered from having had his hood over it, a fringe falling over his eyes. Then Purnell saw the odd plastic circle and the wire running down to a bulky hearing aid wrapped around the boy's ear.

"He's hearing impaired?"

Kristen tapped the boy's shoulder. "Can you hear me?"

He stopped tweaking for long enough to motion her away. He tapped the hearing aid and made a noise that might have been speech, but was too slurred to understand.

"Not hearing impaired," Kristen said. "Deaf. This part," she pointed to the plastic disk but didn't touch it, "is a cochlear implant. It feeds electronic impulses directly into his cochlear nerve, which the brain interprets as sound."

The boy tapped his ear and grunted again, then went back to tweaking.

"I don't think it's working properly," Kristen said. "I think that's what he's saying."

"He can talk. When I first stopped him, he told me to go home."

"Some of his speech may be clear and some of it may not be. He might need to be able to hear his own voice to be comprehensible."

"Being deaf doesn't mean he isn't tweaking."

Kristen caught the bottom of the boy's hoodie and lifted it slightly. He didn't move at first, but as she tugged it up, he moved automatically to withdraw his arms through the sleeves and allowed Kristen to pull it up over his head. Kristen handed it behind her to Purnell, and he double-checked the pockets to make sure they were empty. With his face fully visible and the bulk of his hoodie not hiding his skinny frame, Purnell could see that the boy was even younger than he had originally estimated. He couldn't have been even fifteen.

Kristen again tried to talk to the boy, making gestures as she spoke. "Do you sign? Can you read my lips?"

He remained remote, rocking, flapping his hand, shielding his eyes from her.

"He didn't have any kind of identification on him?" Kristen asked.

"Nothing on his person. I'm ready to inventory his backpack now. Might be something in it."

"Okay." Kristen looked at the boy for a minute. "I guess leaving him in here is the easiest for now. I'll continue to monitor. You want to bring his backpack into the control room so I can see what he's got too?"

Purnell felt a stab of resentment at her taking such an interest in his collar, but there was no reason for him to feel possessive about it. Not like he'd broken open an organized crime ring. All he'd done was pick up a kid tweaking in the park. Trying to keep the streets clean. The kid would be in jail for a few days, they'd release him until his trial date, and he'd be back at the park shooting up again. At his age, it was likely his first offense, and he'd get nothing more than a slap on the wrists.

"Sure," he agreed. "I'll be right back."

The backpack was heavy, full of textbooks and binders. That was the first dissonance. If the kid was a tweaker, why was he taking so many books home? He planned on getting high and then doing his homework? Or were the books a cover, something to convince his parents that everything was normal and he was still doing fine at school? *Leave me alone, Mom, I'll be in my room doing my homework.*

He stacked the schoolbooks neatly in a pile. Opening the cover of the first textbook, he found a name neatly printed on the inside.

"Caleb Hibbert," he told Kristen. "Unless it's a second-hand textbook and that's the previous owner's name." He opened each textbook. They all had the same name in the same neat printing. "Yep, looks like that's our tweaker's name."

She frowned, but didn't correct him.

Purnell dug back into the backpack, pulling out odds and ends; pens and pencils, mashed up permission forms, snack wrappers. He checked the front and side pockets and found a thin wallet, stiff, obviously used little. He opened it to find Caleb's student ID card and a business card printed on a home inkjet printer, streaky and a worn. He read the first few lines on the business card and swore, his gut clenching.

Kristen looked away from the monitor to see what was wrong. "What is it?" she asked, looking at the information card he held in his hands.

"He's autistic."

———

Riley Hibbert looked up from her computer and out the window, pushing her straight brown hair back behind her ear. Something was wrong. Her ears, well-attuned to the sound, caught the noise of the engine of the school bus. It didn't stop in front of the house, but continued to trundle on down the street. She rushed to the door and stepped out, hurrying down to the city sidewalk. She expected the bus to stop a little farther down the street when the driver realized she had missed her stop. Probably a substitute bus driver. The kids would shout at her that she had missed his stop and she would be sure to pull over and let Caleb disembark. Even if Caleb was lost in thought and didn't notice he'd missed his stop, there were enough other students on the bus who would notice as soon as there was a change in the usual routine.

But the bus didn't stop. Riley hurried after it, waving both arms, trying to get the driver's attention. But it was moving too fast, and in a few seconds, was making a turn at the corner and disappearing from sight. Riley hurried after it, pulling her phone out of her pocket.

She wasn't the most well-coordinated person, and chasing the bus while trying to operate her phone was more than she could manage. She stopped where she was and searched for the school's phone number. The office number rang through to voicemail. She tried again, with the same results. She tried a third time, not giving up. There was bound to still be someone in the office. It was just a matter of persistence. Someone would pick up the phone.

Riley looked at the time on the phone, startled to see how late it was. Had something happened? If something had disrupted Caleb's routine, he would be frantic. Even if someone had taken the time to explain it to him, he was likely to be upset.

She dialed the office again, growling at the office staff under her breath to pick up the phone. As if they had heard her, the phone was picked up, and there was a pause before she heard Mrs. Beauvais's calm, even voice.

"Central Middle School. How may I help you?"

"It's Riley Hibbert. Caleb's bus didn't stop to drop him off. Can you get ahold of the driver?"

"Oh, we were informed she was running late today, Mrs. Hibbert. The bus should be there shortly."

"It was here. It just went by the house. But it didn't stop. Caleb must still be on the bus and he'll be upset when he realizes he missed his stop."

"Oh…" Mrs. Beauvais considered this. "I see. I'll have to call the bus company and get their dispatcher. They'll give the driver instructions to keep Caleb on the bus until she can return and drop him at your house."

"They'd better not just let him out…" It seemed like at least once a year, some driver let a kindergartner or special needs student off at the wrong stop, leaving them to wander aimlessly until someone stopped to help them or they reached home in tears, hysterical over having to walk five miles home.

"I'll get right on it. Can I reach you back at this number, Mrs. Hibbert?"

"Yes. Please call me back as soon as you know what's going on. I'm really worried."

"I'll call back as soon as I can."

Mrs. Beauvais disconnected. Riley went back to the house. She packed everything she needed in her purse, put on a jacket, and went to the door, watching for any sign of Caleb and waiting for the return phone call. Every minute that passed was excruciating. Finally, the phone rang.

"Hello?"

What she wanted to hear from Mrs. Beauvais in her calm, reassuring voice was that Caleb was still on the bus, which would loop around back to her house once it had finished the rest of the drop-offs. Instead, Mrs. Beauvais's voice was higher than usual, anxious and staccato.

"Mrs. Hibbert… I've talked to the bus driver… Caleb was not on the bus today."

"What do you mean, he wasn't on the bus? Where else would he be?"

"We're trying to find out now if anyone saw him or talked to him. I'm so sorry."

"Sorry?" Riley tried to stem the flow of words before she said something she would regret later. She knew this was going to happen. She'd always worried about Caleb being able to ride the bus on his own, but the school had assured her that Caleb was capable of managing it. He didn't need someone to walk him to the bus and see him on, as he had in the younger grades. He was used to the routine. There was no danger whatsoever. "Did you talk to the bus driver directly? Or was this relayed through the dispatcher? Did they even talk to the right bus driver?"

"I talked to her directly. It was Maria Mills, his usual driver. She said that Caleb didn't get on. She asked the other kids, and they said they hadn't seen him. So she assumed he wasn't riding today."

"You said the bus was delayed. What happened?"

"Maria called to say she was going to be late. There was a traffic delay on the freeway. All of the kids were told that the bus would be late and to wait in the resource room."

"Caleb was told to wait in the resource room?"

"Yes. All of the children were told."

"Did you talk to Mrs. Bradshaw? She confirmed she told him?"

"No… I'm still trying to get her. She's left for the day and I haven't been able to reach her yet. But I will. I'll confirm that she told him."

"Well, it doesn't matter whether she told him or not," Riley said impatiently. "Because he didn't go to the resource room to wait there, did he? Or he would have been waiting there with the other children."

"Yes… I'm afraid that's true," Mrs. Beauvais admitted. "For some reason, he didn't go to Resource and he wasn't there to catch the bus."

"So he walked home?"

"I… suppose so. Unless he might have gotten on one of the other buses."

Riley rubbed the middle of her forehead, where pain was burrowing in like a maggot. "I don't think he would have, but you're going to have to call the bus dispatcher back and tell them to check with each driver to see if they ended up with an extra kid. And you need to have someone search the school. I'll have to get someone to watch the house in case he shows up here, and drive our usual route to the school looking for him. Hopefully, he just decided to walk, and I'll find him along the way. If not…"

"I'll talk to the dispatcher and we'll make a search," Mrs. Beauvais agreed immediately. "I'm so sorry, Mrs. Hibbert. We've never had something like this happen before…"

Riley hung up. She didn't believe for a minute that they'd never had a bus mishap before. Not when she saw them in the news every year. She'd told them that Caleb wasn't ready to take the bus himself. She'd told Wes, but he'd said that she needed to give Caleb a chance to develop some independence. Caleb needed to learn to do things on his own without his mother or a teacher or mentor hanging over him all the time. He needed to develop his own confidence.

Well, that had worked out well, hadn't it?

She hurried across the street to Mrs. Fields's house. She had known Caleb ever since he was a toddler and she was always home. Mrs. Fields came to the door. She made a show of rubbing her arms to demonstrate to Riley how cold it was, inviting her to come inside and shut the door. Riley stepped into the overly warm house.

"Mrs. Fields, could I ask you a favor? I need someone to watch the house in case Caleb gets home. He wasn't on the bus and I'm going to drive back to the school and hopefully find him somewhere along the way. But if I miss him and he comes home, would you look after things until I get back?"

"Of course!" the old woman patted Riley's arm. "I'd be happy to. You must be scared to death! Just leave the door unlocked, and I'll watch and go over if Caleb shows up."

She knew better than to suggest she bring Caleb back to her own house while they waited for Riley to return. Caleb would go ballistic if she tried to drag him away from home, where he was supposed to be after school, especially when Riley hadn't arranged it with him ahead of time.

"Thanks so much. I appreciate it."

Back across to her own side of the street, Riley jumped in the car and pulled out. She made a U-turn and headed over to the school, watching the sidewalk like a hawk for any sign of Caleb. She was sure she would see him two-thirds to three-quarters of the way home, trudging along in his shorts, hoodie, and overloaded backpack. If she had known he was going to end up walking home, she would have insisted on long pants; it was too cold for shorts. But she hadn't known and Caleb would have had a meltdown over it.

When she reached the halfway point, she was starting to panic. She should have seen him before that. Unless he left the school very late or was walking very slow, she should already have intersected with him. A red Taurus cut in front of her and she came within an inch of hitting it. She slowed down even more and ground her teeth. Getting in another car accident would not help matters. She needed to stay alert and she needed to find Caleb.

———

Caleb had settled down enough in the cool-down room that they were able to move him to an interview room, where he sat in one of the plastic chairs and they gave him a can of pop to help make him comfortable. He was still flapping his hands around, but not as frantically, and he stopped occasionally to take a drink.

Stimming is what Kristen called the hand movements that Purnell had taken for tweaking. She had a nephew who had autism and she told Purnell she'd had suspicions about Caleb when she saw him rocking and stimming in the cool-down room. When she suggested that she should be the one to keep him company while they waited for DFS, he was happy to pass the duty off to her.

He could already see the headlines. He'd made a righteous arrest, taken down a tweaker in the park, with all kinds of people watching, only to find that the boy wasn't high, but had autism. How many of those people had taken pictures or video on their phones? How long before they were online, proclaiming him an abusive cop trampling all over the civil rights of a defenseless, disabled child? He knew he had to get his reports written up immediately and talk to his superiors to explain what had happened before it was all over the internet. Give them a chance to mitigate the damage.

"Why get DFS involved?" Pete McMillan asked, as Purnell relayed the required information to him. "Why not just call the mother to come pick him up?"

"There are some concerns. He's out wandering by himself, apparently without any supervision. There's no missing report on him. He has a lot of cuts and bruises. His hearing thing isn't working. He's thin. Maybe it's nothing. But maybe it's neglect and abuse."

"Probably just wandered off from wherever he was supposed to be. These kids are like that, you know. Prone to wandering."

"Then maybe he should have better supervision. Or an ankle tracker. If he can't communicate his own needs, he shouldn't be alone."

McMillan nodded his agreement and logged the request for DFS.

———

Toxo, Book #4 of the *Medical Kidnap Files* series by P.D. Workman can be purchased at pdworkman.com

ABOUT THE AUTHOR

Award-winning and USA Today bestselling author P.D. (Pamela) Workman writes riveting mystery/suspense and young adult books dealing with mental illness, addiction, abuse, and other real-life issues. For as long as she can remember, the blank page has held an incredible allure and from a very young age she was trying to write her own books.

Workman wrote her first complete novel at the age of twelve and continued to write as a hobby for many years. She started publishing in 2013. She has won several literary awards from Library Services for Youth in Custody for her young adult fiction. She currently has over 50 published titles and can be found at pdworkman.com.

Born and raised in Alberta, Workman has been married for over 25 years and has one son.

———

Please visit P.D. Workman at pdworkman.com to see what else she is working on, to join her mailing list, and to link to her social networks.

———

If you enjoyed this book, please take the time to recommend it to other purchasers with a review or star rating and share it with your friends!

facebook.com/pdworkmanauthor

twitter.com/pdworkmanauthor

instagram.com/pdworkmanauthor

amazon.com/author/pdworkman

bookbub.com/authors/p-d-workman

goodreads.com/pdworkman

linkedin.com/in/pdworkman

pinterest.com/pdworkmanauthor

youtube.com/pdworkman

9 781988 390437